KING OF
THE CORNER

Also by Loren D. Estleman

BLOODY SEASON
PEEPER
WHISKEY RIVER
MOTOWN

KING OF
THE CORNER

◆◇◆◇◆◇◆◇◆◇◆◇◆◇◆◇◆

Loren D. Estleman

BANTAM BOOKS
NEW YORK · TORONTO · LONDON · SYDNEY · AUCKLAND

KING OF THE CORNER
A Bantam Book/June 1992

Library of Congress Cataloging-in-Publication Data

Estleman, Loren D.
 King of the corner / by Loren D. Estleman.
  p.   cm.
  ISBN 0-553-08926-9
  I. Title.
 PS3555.S84K54   1992
 813'.54—dc20   *92-742*
                                                          CIP

Published simultaneously in the United States and Canada

Bantam Books are published by Bantam Books, a division of Bantam Double-
day Dell Publishing Group, Inc. Its trademark, consisting of the words
"Bantam Books" and the portrayal of a rooster, is Registered in U.S. Patent
and Trademark Office and in other countries. Marca Registrada. Bantam
Books, 666 Fifth Avenue, New York, New York 10103.

PRINTED IN THE UNITED STATES OF AMERICA

RRH 0 9 8 7 6 5 4 3 2 1

For Linda and Jeff Marl
the heart of the order
and
in memory
For Ray Puechner
the coach

To the Reader

Approximately ninety-nine and nine-tenths percent of the characters who inhabit *King of the Corner* are fictional creations intended to represent a tiny cross section of the population of the city of Detroit in our time. The remaining one-tenth of one percent are factual. Although their personalities and backgrounds are presented accurately, they have not been faced with the specific circumstances that occur in this story, and their reaction and behavior are pure speculation. This is what makes *King of the Corner* a work of fiction.

During what should be rush hour, reporters from the Free Press play a macabre game, called King of the Corner. The object is to stand at a downtown intersection and look all four ways. If you can't see a single human being in any direction, you are King of the Corner. Every morning anoints its own royalty. Detroit, America's sixth largest city, is the only metropolis in the country where you can walk a downtown block during business hours without passing a living soul.

—Ze'ev Chafets,
Devil's Night:
And Other True Tales of Detroit

When I came up to Detroit I was just a mild-mannered Sunday-school boy.

—Ty Cobb

Detroit Free Press Magazine, Sunday, April 8, 1990:

GRANNY AT THE BAT:
LONGTIME BENGALS ROOTER REMEMBERS
By Leon "Bud" Arsenault

Loyola MacGryff hasn't missed an opening day at Tiger Stadium since her father took her to her first game in 1908.

Mrs. MacGryff, who has lived at her present address on Trumbull near the stadium for most of her 87 years, remembers that day as clearly as if it were last Saturday.

"The colors—I never saw so many in one place at one time," she recalls. "The men all wore straw boaters and the women were dressed like Easter Sunday. And, oh, it was noisy! People were much more vocal then. Papa asked me if I was scared. I said, 'Oh, no, I want to see Ty Cobb.'"

And did she?

"Not that time. He was out with a groin pull, only they didn't say that then, they just said he hurt his leg. But I saw him lots of other times.

"He wasn't a kind man, that Mr. Cobb. Once this boy in the row in front of me leaned over the rail and touched a fly ball Mr. Cobb was running to catch and put it out of play. The Orioles scored a run on it. Well, he just jerked that boy clean out of his seat and went to beating on him till the rest of the team ran out and pulled him off.

"I never saw it in the paper, so I guess Mr. Jennings—Mr. Hughie Jennings, he managed the Tigers then—I guess Mr. Jennings made it right with the boy's parents.

"But, my, that man Cobb could run."

Tragically, young Loyola's fateful first trip to Navin Field (as it was known then) had been intended for her older brother Paul, but he was in the hospital recuperating after a trolley car accident claimed both his legs.

"We wanted to bring him a souvenir ball, but we were out of luck that day so Papa bought him a pennant at the stand. He kept it on his wall till the day he died."

Eighty-one opening days later, Mrs. MacGryff's record remains pristine, although there have been close calls along the way.

In 1924, when it seemed that her first child would make his appearance close to that all-important date, she had the baby delivered by cesarean section two weeks early.

A flat tire and a night in jail for husband Horace when he declined to pull over for a motorcycle patrolman were the cost of a timely arrival in 1930.

"But 1935 was the closest I ever came to missing," says this blue-eyed, apple-cheeked grandmother of eight. "Horace got beat up on the picket line at Ford's and died of a brain hemorrhage, but I postponed the funeral a day.

"That was the year we beat the Cubs in the Series and it was grand to see Charlie Gehringer come to bat for the first time in one of his best seasons. I got my picture taken with him outside the door where the team came out after the game."

(to be continued)

PART ONE

Breaking Ball

◆◆◆◆◆◆◆◆◆

Chapter 1

◆◇◆◇◆◇◆◇◆

The day before Doc Miller was released, a hammer murderer named Ed Friend blew his one-hitter to hell with a two-out double in the bottom of the eighth.

Blaize Depardieu, the team manager and a 1982 second-round draft choice for St. Louis currently doing eleven to twenty for rape, came out to the mound and turned on his thousand-candlepower grin. "Man got a hell of a swing, that's why he's in here," he said. "Don't sweat it."

"I'm not," Doc said. He struck out the last man and retired the side in the ninth with a strikeout, a pop fly to center field, and a grounder to first. Afterward Depardieu gave him the ground ball signed by everyone on the team, a roster of killers, rapists, drug-runners, and state congressmen that would have kept a city block in terror for a month. "Gonna miss you in the Milan game," he told Doc. "Talk is they's transferring a embezzler from Marion that bats three-eighty."

"Earl can handle him if you can get him to lay off that knuckleball. Every time he tries it his control goes to hell." Doc turned the ball around in his hand, unconsciously lining up his fingers with the seams. Standing there in the shower room with its stench of sweat and mildew, he suddenly realized he had pitched his last game.

The grin illuminated Depardieu's blue-black face. "Getting sprang tomorrow, Stretch. You look like they's fixing to feed you the gas."

"You know a team that's scouting ex-cons?"

"All of 'em. Lookit Gates Brown and Ron LeFlore."

"Denny McLain. Pete Rose."

"They was over the hill when they went in. You're what, thirty?"

"Thirty-three."

"Thirty-three-year-old with a ninety-mile-an-hour fastball and a split-finger that Henry Aaron couldn't hit on his best day."

"Nobody ever heard of Brown and LeFlore until they got out and joined the majors. I took my headlines going in. Nobody wants a southpaw with a sheet." He smacked Depardieu's naked muscular shoulder with his open palm. "You're a great manager, Blaize. You'd be in the Show now if you'd kept it in your pants."

"What I should of did was send flowers."

They shook hands.

The next morning, Doc put on a gray suit of clothes and tried the necktie that had come with it, but too much time had passed since he'd had a knot at his throat and he rolled it up and put it in the side pocket of his jacket. The suit was one of his old ones and the lapels were out of fashion, but it still fit, which was why he had asked his brother to send it to him instead of putting on one of the ready-mades the state provided. Doc stood six-five in his socks and weighed less than two hundred. Suits that weren't made especially for him tended to fall way short of his wrists and ankles when they didn't wrap twice around his waist.

As a matter of fact the trousers were a little snug, but that was penitentiary food. They fed you well in Jackson, lots of mashed potatoes and fatty pork chops and buttered vegetables, on the theory that an overweight prisoner was less likely to hoist himself over the wall. Doc, who was indifferent to food, would start dropping pounds without even thinking about it as soon as he was outside.

Kevin Miller had become Doc back in double-A ball when it got around that he had studied pharmacology for a year. The gold-rimmed glasses he wore to correct astigmatism, with a clip behind his head to keep them from sliding off during his follow-through, had made the nickname stick when he joined the Tigers. That year he had fourteen saves and was on his way to a Cy Young Award when the Detroit Criminal Investigation Division got to him first.

As a starter for the Southern Michigan Penitentiary at Jackson he had won 116 games in seven years. The team played fewer than a hundred games a season.

He evaluated his buzz cut in the mirror over his sink and decided he wouldn't grow it out much. Styles had changed since he'd left his collar-length mane on the floor of the prison barbershop, and the look took a couple of years off him. The black hair and his cheekbones came courtesy of some Cherokee blood way back on his mother's side; for the rest he was German-Irish and a third-generation native of Kentucky. In high school it had seemed strange to be swinging an aluminum bat with the company that made the Louisville Slugger operating just forty miles away. When he'd mentioned this to his coach, the coach had slapped him on the butt and said, "Play. Don't think."

That was one piece of advice Doc wished he'd forgotten.

Earl Hardaway, the other starter and a trusty with six months to go on a one-to-three for reckless endangerment, unlocked Doc's cell. He was a chunky redhead with freckles the size of dimes, one blue eye and one brown, and an appointment to check in with the Tigers' front office the first Monday after his release. His fastball had been clocked at ninety-nine miles per hour. That was six less than he had been doing the night he wrapped his father's Porsche around a dead elm, fracturing his left ankle and turning his girlfriend into a paraplegic.

"Where's Howard?" Doc asked.

"Mopping C Block. We traded. I didn't get a chance to say good-bye after the game." He turned his blue eye on Doc. Earl thought he saw better out of it, although the ophthalmologist who visited Jackson had told him he had twenty-twenty vision in both. "I got the knuck down now."

"Give it up. It isn't your pitch."

"I wish I could show it to you."

They were walking down the corridor. Doc shook several of the hands dangling between the white-painted bars of the cells. He felt like Jimmy Cagney walking the Last Mile. He had to remind himself he was being freed. "You've got the heat and a good sinker. All you need's a curve you can count on and Blaize will show you how to throw that."

"I'll need more than three pitches if I'm going to be in the Show."

"That's one more than Koufax had. Your knuckleball can't find the plate."

"It don't have to if they can't hit it."

"You can fan them out and still give up first while the catcher's chasing the ball all the way to the backstop. You'll never see the Show if you make your catchers look bad. They're mean sons of bitches. They'd pass up a shot at the pennant to send down a cocky pitcher." He stopped before the door at the end of the block.

The face that came to the gridded window when Earl banged

on the door didn't have a name. The turnover among guards was high; there would be no warm handshake at the gate or snarled "You'll be back." This one unlocked the door, swung it open, and made an impatient noise when Doc grasped Earl's hand. "When Grant Hoover gets to first in the Milan game, keep him there if you have to go over there a hundred times. If he steals second you might as well hand him third. I don't know what he's in for, but it must've been purse-snatching."

"He won't get to first."

A second guard, equally anonymous but one Doc had seen before, took him to Admissions, where a young harried clerk with an acne condition spent twenty minutes looking for Doc's paperwork before stamping it and giving him a copy. It contained the name of his parole officer and the date and time of his first appointment. The clerk broke the seal on a manila envelope with dog-eared corners and tipped out items Doc hadn't seen in seven years: gold Hamilton wristwatch, class ring, black enamel money clip with no money in it, and a Franklin half-dollar struck the year Doc was born, his lucky piece. He'd carried it in his pocket during all his saves. On the other hand, he'd had it with him the night he was arrested and the day he was convicted. He considered giving it to the stressed-out clerk, but minutes away from freedom he worried that it might be considered bribery and break his parole. He signed a receipt, put on the watch and ring, and pocketed the other items.

His brother Neal was standing in the waiting room with his hands in his pockets looking at the framed prints on the wall when Doc entered with the guard. (No halfway measures here. He was a prisoner until he was not.) Fair and balding, two inches shorter than his brother and running to fat, Neal had gotten most of the Irish blood in his family, down to the leprechaun jowls and a twinkle in his gray eyes that was entirely illusory; the elder of the two Miller boys had no humor. For the reunion he had put on a plaid sport coat over a clean work shirt and gray woolen trousers gone fuzzy in the knees. Doc was pretty sure the sport coat was the only one Neal had ever owned.

"Put on some," was the first thing he said to Doc.

"Not since your last visit."

"You was sitting down then."

Under the guard's eye they shook hands briefly. Although Neal had washed—outside the shop he always smelled of the brown grainy Fels Napthe soap he used—there was a cross-hatching of old black grime in the creases of his palm. He had been a mechanic at a John Deere dealership on Middlebelt since his teens, and the grease was ground in as deeply as the central Kentucky drawl that he had hung on to years after Doc's had slipped away. "I was starting to think you got yourself in trouble again and they wasn't going to let you out."

"Paper chase." Doc thought about something else to say. Communication had always been difficult with this brother who left high school the year Doc entered first grade. "How's Dad?"

"The same. He's coming over for dinner next week."

The female security guard at the desk, pulled-back hair and burnished cosmetics in a pale blue starched uniform blouse, buzzed open the door. At the gate the guard who had escorted Doc from the cellblock turned a key in the mechanism. It clonked, and the gate shunted open. "Have a nice day." They were the first words the guard had spoken.

In the parking lot Neal unlocked the driver's door of a new GMC three-quarter-ton pickup, heaved himself up and under the wheel, and reached across to open the door on the passenger's side. Suddenly locks were opening everywhere. Doc stepped up into the plastic-smelling interior. It was a great square silver tank of a vehicle that had cost as much as a

Cadillac, and which his brother would probably still be paying for in five years. By which time he'd have traded it in on something bigger with an even higher testosterone level.

It was a typical nippy Michigan early-April day. The sky was the color of iron, and crusted snow clung to the shady side of the berms on both sides of the road. Neal drove with the seat pushed forward almost as far as it would go—a painful sight when it involved a man his size—his shoulders hunched over the wheel and his big heavy face screwed into a strained expression as if power steering had never been invented.

They took Michigan Avenue through Jackson, four flat, faded lanes cleaving between new-looking glass and steel buildings that soon gave way to horizontal structures of crumbling block with signs rusting through their paint; a prison town whose personality matched the gray bland decaying interior of the penitentiary itself. An electric sign ringed with yellow bulbs flashing in a spastic pattern advertised the Island Health Spa. A number of cars and a van with its fenders eaten away were parked outside the building.

"You start Saturday."

"Saturday?" Doc shifted on the seat. The sight of the massage parlor had given him an erection.

"Sure Saturday. Farmers can't afford to farm full-time, they all got jobs. Saturday's the only day they got to shop."

"What am I selling?"

"Well, not tractors. That's commission work. You sell parts and accessories. Anyone comes in wants to look at the heavy equipment you steer him to a salesman."

"What's it pay?"

"Three hundred a week. I'm sorry it ain't a million a season and your own car." Neal sounded testy.

"It's better than I've been making."

"You wouldn't of got parole if the board didn't think you had a job waiting."

"Thanks, Neal. I know you went out on a limb."

"Not so much." He relaxed a little. "Warren's a baseball fan. That's the manager. Probably ask you a million questions."

They entered I-94 then and didn't exchange another word until they reached the suburbs of Detroit.

Chapter 2

❖❖❖❖❖❖❖❖

Willie Hernandez, back when he was still Willie and not Guillermo, before he lost home plate and his sense of humor, had told Doc after the last Minnesota game he was the greatest reliever Detroit had had since John Hiller. That was the best night of Doc's life. Hiller was his hero when everyone else in school was talking about the starters McLain and Lolich; and when it was really going well, when the plate looked as big as a manhole cover and Doc couldn't miss, he borrowed an old Hiller trick and threw three balls in a row just for the hell of it before striking them out. Those days the third strike was like ejaculating, and the look of surprise and rage on the batters' faces when the umpire's thumb went up was better than a cigarette afterward.

That particular night he had come on in the seventh at three-two with two men on base and sent down eight men in order for the save. On his way to the dugout everyone had come over to shake his hand and pat his butt, Lance Parrish, Kirk Gibson, Sweet Lou, Tram, Darrell Evans, Roger Craig, and Sparky. DOC DIAGNOSES TIGER WIN, read the headline in the *Free Press* the next morning.

The headline in a different section of the *News* the next evening read MILLER CHARGED IN COCAINE DEATH.

Asked by the police and later by reporters if he'd known there were drugs at the party he threw at the Westin, he said no; but there were always drugs, joints and little glittering capsules and square white paper packets like the ones that used to contain the prizes in boxes of cereal. He was the host, and the girl who died, some little high school ride brought by a batboy Doc didn't remember inviting, was underage. The EMS crew was still working on her when the detectives, one black and neatly dressed, the other white and smelling of cherry cough drops, took Doc into the bedroom to talk. They called on his house the next day with a warrant.

The lawyer sent down by the front office gave advice, then bowed out, saying something about conflict of interest. The lawyer Doc retained on the recommendation of a friend on the TV 2 sports desk got the charge reduced from negligent homicide to third-degree manslaughter and told Doc he'd get probation and community service. Doc pleaded guilty. The judge, facing re-election the next year, made a speech about sports figures having a responsibility to behave as role models and sentenced him to ten to fifteen years.

Doc's appeal was denied. He fired his attorney and hired another with a national reputation, who went to work on getting the guilty plea set aside and securing a trial based on the first attorney's incompetence. Meanwhile his client began his incarceration. Penitentiary life, Doc told himself in the beginning, wasn't so different from life on the road; the cells weren't that much smaller than some of the hotel rooms he'd stayed in, and you could even get room service once you learned which trusties would share their bribes with the right guards. At least you didn't have to put up with roommates. His size protected him from homosexual rape, and although there was resentment on the part of some of the other prisoners toward a young man who would throw away a bigger break than they would ever see on the same sort of mistake they had made, he wasn't unpopular enough to be made a victim of the gang variety, and besides, the Jackson team needed pitchers.

But prison was not the road. On the road you could always bust curfew and the worst you'd get would be the bench or a fine or both. In prison they locked you in. He had thought the fact obvious, but the reality was worse than the most hair-raising movies he had seen. The lights went out at 9:30 and you lay in the gray twilight shed by the recessed bulbs in the corridor, reliving all your best plays while the rest of the world was forgetting your name. The warden was a frustrated George Steinbrenner, and so you stamped books in the library to avoid ruining your arm on the punch presses in the shop, and you spoke across the table in the Stranger's Room with your brother and your attorney, and you lost your edge pitching to batters who wouldn't make the first cut in double-A, and time passed in lockstep. He'd had a girlfriend, a live-in blonde who slept in one of his old jerseys and talked his roommate in Cincinnati into bunking somewhere else one night so she could greet Doc at the door of his hotel room naked. She wasn't in court the day he was sentenced. Two years later, during a game he was watching in the TV Room, the camera cut to the wife of the Philadelphia catcher applauding her husband in the stands, and she had put on weight, but not enough to erase the memory of that evening. In his cell after the game he had tried masturbating to the memory and failed for the first time. And time hung like cobwebs, and his lawyer told him to be patient until the Republicans were out of office.

In the end it was his own mild demeanor that got him out,

that and a warden's gratitude for his first Midwestern Penal System Championship trophy in the glass case outside his office. Meanwhile the attorney had attached Doc's house, car, and bank account and written a best-selling memoir in which Doc's name did not appear.

Neal Miller lived in a tract of aluminum-cased ranch-styles, constructed on a block formerly occupied by saltbox homes built by Ford for employees of the Dearborn plant. Neal wedged the big GMC into the garage between a plastic tricycle and a stack of pop bottles, and they went into the kitchen through the side door. In the big room paved with brick-colored linoleum and lined with new appliances—bought, like the truck and the house, on time—Doc embraced his sister-in-law stiffly. She was a small thin woman a few years younger than her husband and an odd match for Doc's beefy brother. He could feel her ribs and shoulder blades clearly through the thin cotton of her dress. Her dark wavy hair was her best feature, but it threw into relief the lines of strain in her skeletal face.

They parted quickly and she said, pushing back a lock of her hair, "I hope you're hungry. I made enough to feed the city."

The kitchen smelled of roasting meat and boiling vegetables. Just then Doc realized he was famished. In Jackson they were sitting down to lunch.

"Billie overfeeds everybody but herself," Neal said. "She don't eat enough to keep a roach alive."

"No roaches in this house. You try eating after you've been cooking all day." Doc noticed that she had picked up some of her husband's twang. She was born in Detroit.

The conversation lagged. After a moment Doc said, "Where's Sean?"

"In school. He can't wait to meet you." Billie turned to stir a pot on the stove. Creamed spinach and garlic thickened the air.

16

It was comforting to learn that the national hysteria over healthy food hadn't spread to the Miller home.

"It's hard to believe he's in school. Last time I saw him he was just learning to walk."

"Wait'll you see him," Neal said. "Kid's built like a truck. I bet he's your size by the time he's sixteen. Billie feeds him too much, too."

"He needs it if he's going to get that football scholarship." She replaced the lid on the pot.

"He don't stand a chance if we don't get him away from that fucking TV set and out in the backyard. She thinks Nintendo's a day-care center," he told Doc.

"We had some video games in Jackson. I didn't take to them."

A look passed between Billie and Neal. Neal said, "Kev, we'd take it a favor if you didn't talk about Jackson when Sean's around. We've been telling him you were in California."

"Who with, Oakland or San Francisco?"

"We told him you're a salesman. He don't know his Uncle Kevin is Doc Miller. When they talked about you on the news we didn't let on."

"We thought it was best," Billie said, pushing back the lock of hair. "If it got around school—well, you know kids. Thank God Miller's a common name."

He knew a chill of mortality.

The room Neal took him to on the second floor looked out on the driveway they shared with the house next door. It had a single bed, a nightstand, a chest of drawers, and toy soldiers on the wallpaper. "Sean's room," said Neal. "We moved him into the basement. We didn't think you wanted to be down there."

When his brother left, Doc opened the small case he'd carried from the prison and laid away his change of trousers and two shirts in the drawers. He took off his jacket and hung it in the closet. In the bathroom down the hall he washed his hands and face. He wondered if the daily routine would just fade away on its own or if he would have to change it himself. He hooked on his glasses, and his face came into focus in the mirror. In that light he looked older, creased under the eyes, the line of his chin blurred. Silver glinted at his temples like steel shavings. He looked down and saw that he had crumpled the wet washcloth into a tight sphere roughly the size of a baseball. He shook it loose and hung it up.

Lunch was odd. His tastebuds had accustomed themselves to bland institutional fare, and the pungent flavor of the beef and the vegetables floating in butter made him slightly ill. He attempted to disguise it with conversation. "Is there a neighborhood team?" he asked Neal.

"Team? We got the Watch, fat lot of good it does us. The Robinettes was broken into last week. They got a VCR and some silver."

"No, a baseball team. Or softball. When we were kids every place had one."

"Nothing like that around here." Neal bent his head over his potatoes.

"I thought maybe they could use a coach. As long as I could pitch, too."

"Didn't playing ball get you in enough trouble?" Billie was looking at him.

"I did that all by myself. I didn't need any help from baseball."

Neal said, "You won't have time for it anyway. The dealership'll keep you busy. We're shorthanded."

At the end of the meal, Doc offered to help with the dishes, but Billie said that day he was a guest and why didn't he take a nap, he must be exhausted. He said he wasn't and asked if he could take a walk. She set down the dishes she was clearing from the table and reached over and touched the back of his wrist. "This is your home, not your cell. You don't have to ask anyone for permission to do anything." He smiled then, it felt funny on his face, and said he guessed that would take some getting used to. Neal said he was going to take advantage of having a day off in the middle of the week and find out what was on television while he was at work. When the set warmed up he said, "Who's this little fucker with the patch on his eye?" Doc went out.

Dearborn was a working town, and in the middle of a working day the streets were empty. Doc had finished growing up five blocks over after his father moved the family north when he went to work at the River Rouge plant, but the names on the mailboxes were unfamiliar and mostly Arab. Chilled in his thin suit coat, he walked briskly to get his blood circulating. A front door opened and a gray-haired man in a plaid bathrobe let a tabby cat out onto the porch. The cat bowed its back, haunches in the air, then sat down and began licking its genitals. The man in the bathrobe stood watching Doc while he passed the house. Behind the man a radio or television was tuned to a baseball game. Doc couldn't tell who was playing. A color expert who clearly didn't know much about the sport was explaining why the manager had brought the infield in on the last play. The door closed with a bang, separating Doc from the game forever.

Around the corner was a string of vacant lots overgrown with weeds and littered with Styrofoam food containers and plastic rings from six-packs. City trucks had been using the space to heap the snow they plowed off the street, and there were deposits of salt and orange rust where the heaps had melted. Doc realized with a start that the lots had belonged to a row of empty HUD houses. He had brought a girl to one of them the autumn he turned seventeen. The city had knocked them down to keep children out or to deny shelter to crack operations, and nothing had come along to replace them.

Standing there all alone on the broad sidewalk, he wept silently, fogging his glasses in the damp cold. Not for the houses, and not even for himself or the lost years, but for a neighborhood with so much open space and no baseball team.

Chapter 3

◆◇◆◇◆◇◆◇◆

Baline's John Deere Sales & Service on Middlebelt had been owned and operated by the same family for more than forty years. Mickey Baline, the father of the two brothers who now ran the dealership, wandered in every afternoon to sit on a stool behind the parts counter where Doc worked and converse with the older customers who came in, pausing between phrases to spit into a box of sawdust at his feet. He was a bantamweight at sixty-six, bowed in the knees, with a small hard pot rolling over his brass Winchester belt buckle and a big red face that crumpled up like a fist when he chewed whatever it was he chewed; Doc never saw him put anything into his largely toothless mouth, but his jaws were always working. He wore stiff new jeans, a fresh pair every day, a succession of corduroy shirts in solid colors buttoned to the neck, and a baseball cap square over his eyes with the dealership's full name stitched on the front. On the third day of Doc's employment, Mickey hoisted himself onto his stool, spat into the box of sawdust, drew the back of a freckled hand across his lips, and said, "So didja fuck any cons when you was in stir?"

Doc was looking through the big catalogue on the shelf under the counter for an item for a telephone customer. "Just myself."

"Big fella like you, bet you had your pick of all them nice firm assholes."

"Do we carry intake manifolds for the 1980 diesel tractor?"

"Ask Neal. So which do you like best, getting a blow job or giving one?"

He closed the catalogue. "Thinking of changing sides?"

Mickey cackled—Doc had never actually heard anyone cackle before, outside of Walter Brennan in the movies—spat again, missed the box, and stretched out a leg to rub the spittle into the linoleum with the sole of his shoe. "Just ragging you some, young fella. Everybody gots to stand still for a rag, he wants to work here. I was inside my own self for a year, down in Ohio. The boys don't know about it. My first wife turned me in for burning down the barn for the insurance. The boys don't know about her neither. Don't you tell them."

"So did you like getting them or giving them?"

"Hell, getting 'em. But I held out longer'n a year plenty of times."

Doc excused himself and went off to find Neal to ask about intake manifolds. He considered that colorful old men were overrated as company.

His brother was in the large cluttered back room, testing a tire for leaks in a galvanized tub filled with water. He had on gray coveralls stained brown with grease and high-topped shoes with the leather scuffed down to bare steel on the toe of one. When he found where the tire was bubbling, he lifted it out and had it plugged in two seconds. "That's a back order," he said, leaning the tire against the wall. "Just add it to the weekly list for the manufacturer."

When Doc didn't leave, Neal took a battered Thermos off a shelf supporting a row of John Deere mechanics' manuals bound in streaked green vinyl, poured coffee into the steel cup, and held it out. Doc took it. His brother emptied a chipped mug of screws and washers, blew dust out of it, and filled it for himself. "Mickey giving you shit?"

"I can live with it. I'm just wondering if he's my boss."

"He's been senile a long time. Jack and Fred made him retire after he traded this old fart buddy of his a brand new combine even up for a 1966 Rambler. Pretend he ain't there."

"It's not just him. I'm not sure I'm cut out for this work. Today I sold my first clevis. I still don't know what it is."

"You'll get the hang of it. Beats stamping license plates, don't it?"

"Pays better, anyway." The coffee tasted like crankcase oil. Neal always made his own when Billie, a substitute cook at Fordson High School, was working in the cafeteria. "I'm not bitching about the job. It's the first one I've ever had if you don't count ball."

"I don't. A man can't play his whole life, ain't that what Dad said?"

"It'll be good to see him. What time's he coming over?"

"We're picking him up after work. We don't have to sign him out if we can get him back before ten."

It sounded like Jackson. "I didn't know they were that strict."

"Goddamn home changes hands every six months, and the rules with it. I'd move him someplace better if I could afford it. At least they don't tie him to his bed like the last place."

"Jesus, Neal."

"Yeah, I know."

The outside door opened and a man came in wearing coveralls

like Neal's over a dirty quilted coat, carrying a long bent shaft of metal. He had brown hair curling over his collar and wore dark glasses. "Going ice fishing, Spence?" Neal was looking at the twisted shaft.

"We can straighten it and sharpen it. I don't give a shit if it lasts a week." Spence grinned at Doc. "Son of a bitch runs his riding mower over his wife's rock garden and wants us to give him a new blade."

Doc indicated the dark glasses. "Is it that bright out?" He and Neal had driven to work that morning in a snow squall.

"Is from this side. I had the cab out all night."

"All that money we get from the Balines ain't enough for Spence," Neal said. "He's got his own business."

"Taxi company?"

Spence said, "Fleet of one, and the heater don't work for shit. But she's got a hundred and twelve thousand miles on her and she's good for another hundred. You drive?"

Doc said he did. He was going into the Secretary of State's office that week to renew his license.

"I'm gone all next week; my brother's getting married in California. The cab'll just be sitting there. Like to take her out? On a good night you can pull in a couple of hundred. I'll split fifty-fifty."

"I don't have a chauffeur's license."

"Use mine. We don't look that much different, and the picture stinks anyway. Neal won't do it. He's got a family."

"Forget it," Neal said. "All he needs is to get stopped and they'll yank his parole."

"Sorry," Doc said.

Spence shrugged and carried the bent mower blade over to the vise on the workbench. Doc finished his coffee and handed back the cup. On his way back to the parts counter he multiplied a hundred times seven in his head and wondered what the security deposit was on the average Detroit apartment.

The nursing home in Warren was smaller than expected, a one-story brick building with two long wings lined with windows like a school in a not too prosperous village. Neal and Doc went through the main doors into a narrow carpeted lobby and around a corner without stopping at the door marked OFFICE. A black man nearly Doc's height in green work pants and a white shirt with the sleeves rolled up was buffing the linoleum in the corridor, the purring of the machine a familiar and oddly comforting sound that reminded Doc of the trusties at work early in the morning. Steel rails lined the corridor on both sides. The doors to some of the rooms stood open. He saw a pair of bare legs in a bed, an old woman in a wheelchair staring at a television screen full of static, a man his own age seated in an odd chair with casters and a fold-down table like a high chair, pulling himself down the corridor with two feet turned at odd angles and talking to himself. Neal paid no attention to any of this.

"Each door's a different color," Doc said. "I guess that's to help them find the way back to their own rooms."

"Don't work, though. These people don't notice nothing."

Neal stopped so suddenly his brother almost bumped into him. A woman built exactly like Neal in a nurse's uniform bustled out an open door without slowing and passed both of them carrying a curved plastic pan. The sour urine scent reached Doc's nostrils as an afterthought.

They entered the room. It was large and airy, painted in pastels and patched with sunlight coming through the glass the length of the opposite wall. Dollops of snow clung to juniper hedges outside. A male cardinal flicked in and out of a feeder on a stand and was gone, a lick of bright red flame in the monochromatic landscape. Neither of the two occupants of the room looked at it.

"Good, we don't have to help him into the chair," said Neal.

A huge old man sat slumped in a wheelchair beside the nearer of the room's two beds. He wore a stiff new shirt buttoned all the way up, tweed pants with a sharp crease, and gray suede shoes without a wrinkle across the insteps to show they'd ever been walked in. His head was round and jowly and hairless, and he had on thick bifocals. The left side of his face looked collapsed, like a fallen-in barn, and he was leaning left in the chair. When he saw Neal he stirred and said something that Doc didn't catch.

"I brought somebody with me." Neal grasped Doc's arm and pushed him forward.

"Hello, Dad," Doc said.

The old man looked at him a long time. A gray tongue came out, slid along his lips, and withdrew. Doc thought of the cardinal. "Ke'in?"

Kevin put out his hand. After another long time the old man laid his in it. It felt warm and soft like a baby's. On Doc's sixteenth birthday his father had arm-wrestled with him to test his manhood; he still remembered the corded muscles, the callus like a leather sole. They broke contact.

Neal stepped behind the chair and grasped the handles. "Time to go, Dad. Billie's waiting supper."

They had been watched the whole time by the man in the other bed, lean and white-haired in a striped shirt and dark trousers and slipper-socks, with bright dark eyes and a tolerant smile on his closed lips. Doc raised a hand in farewell. The white-haired man nodded.

"Who's your roommate?" Doc asked when they were in the hall.

"So'bitch," his father said.

Neal said, "Old Man Warner. He spits on the other patients."

Neal had removed a heavy sweater from the sheet-metal wardrobe closet in the room. In the lobby he and Doc helped their father into it and Doc held open one of the wide doors while his brother pushed the old man out into the crisp air. Straining, they lifted him out of the chair into the cab of the pickup, Doc propping him in place with a hand while he climbed in beside him. Neal folded the wheelchair, laid it in the pickup bed, and climbed under the wheel. They rode wedged together all the way to Dearborn. Their father, coming alive now, read aloud the legend on every sign they passed.

At the house Neal parked in the driveway and they pushed the man in the wheelchair up the snow-covered walk to the front door. Billie was ready and held open the door from inside while Neal backed in, jumping the wheels over the threshold while Doc steadied it from the front.

"Sean!" Neal called when they were all inside. "I told you to shovel the walk when you got home from school."

"I forgot, Papa. I'm sorry."

The boy, short for his age and pudgy in khaki pants and a Teenage Mutant Ninja Turtle sweatshirt, was standing with his back to a television screen gridded with green and blue lines. The video game control box was in his hands.

"I should have reminded him," Billie said.

"He's got a brain. Turn that goddamn thing off and come say hello to your grandpa."

Suppertimes were hardest on Doc. He couldn't get used to the food, and Sean, a quiet boy who avoided his parents' eyes and mostly ignored his uncle, ate as much as any adult, which seemed unnatural and faintly repulsive. Neal didn't believe much in table conversation, and so the meals generally took place in silence but for the clinking of flatware on crockery and the odd request to pass a dish. Tonight was worse for the old man's presence, which added an element of forced hospitality, and for his disconcerting habit of removing pieces of meat he couldn't chew from his mouth and lining them up on the edge of his plate. He gave no indication that he realized he wasn't still in the home. Doc, who had always been closer to his late mother, was nonetheless shocked by the old man's deterioration. He seemed to be spreading and blurring into the background.

Later, after they had wheeled him into the living room and while Neal was calling Dan Rather an arrogant commie asshole more or less to his face, Doc went out. Billie, clearing the table, made no comment. His after-dinner walk was an accepted routine.

Damp dusk was settling in. This time he didn't stop to look at the real estate going to waste, although it still saddened him. He kept walking to the Perry drugstore on the next corner and used the public telephone inside the entrance to call Information. There was an embarrassed moment while he struggled to recall Spence's full name before he was able to ask for his number at home.

Chapter 4

❖❖❖❖❖❖❖❖

Fate, Doc Miller knew, never came dressed in a suit of lightning. He was a master of disguise. One time he might be a tall man in a striped double-breasted who intercepted you on your way to the showers after college baseball practice to give you his business card; another time he might camouflage himself as a spacey adolescent girl hanging around the neck of a pimple-faced batboy who came to your party without an invitation. Even if you did recognize him as Fate you never knew what he had for you.

On this night, one week after the telephone conversation in the Perry drugstore, he was a rumpled-looking fat man who stepped out between parked cars with an overcoat over one arm and a hand in the air in a desperate hailing motion. He had on a gray suit selected more for durability than style and black thick-soled Oxfords with exposed stitching. Fat men were often light on their feet, but this one, hurrying, landed flat on heel and toe with each step, the impact jarring him visibly to his scalp.

It had been raining heavily all night, the first night since Doc had been driving that came close to Spence's rich predictions. On a normal evening in a city like Detroit where everyone owned a car and used it for any journey longer than a block, Doc was lucky to take in seventy-five dollars, half of which belonged to Spence. Tonight, with the rain and a new show opening at the Fisher Theater, he was attracting passengers like mud.

As he braked for the fat man, another man, half the fat man's weight and thirty years younger, wearing a glistening leather sport coat and a cashmere scarf knotted sloppily around his throat—the uneven ends an unmistakable sign of wealth—made a dash for the cab all the way from the corner. He got his hand on the door handle ahead of the fat man. Doc waited for the altercation with professional detachment. He almost missed what happened next.

The fat man's weight shifted so fast Doc thought he'd slipped on the greasy pavement, and then the younger man in the leather coat was backpedaling away from the cab, swinging his arms for balance. He almost caught it, then tripped on the curb and dropped out of Doc's vision. The fat man swung open the door without looking back, threw his overcoat into the backseat, and followed it. The cab heaved on its springs.

"The Independence Motel on Jefferson," he said. "Know it?"

Doc nodded and cranked over the meter. "Nice body check."

"What? Oh, yeah. These Grosse Pointe scroats think they own the fucking town."

Light from streetlamps and shop windows stuttered into the backseat as they picked up speed, illuminating the passenger's face in freeze-frames in the rearview mirror. In youth it would have had strength, but now the flesh hung away from the prominent bone and eddied over his collar, obliterating the knot of his necktie. His hair, black and gleaming like a new tire, lay flat against his scalp. Even in that light Doc could tell he dyed it.

"You a policeman?"

The fat man glanced up at the mirror. The bags under his eyes were like bunting. "Me? Shit, no."

Doc thought that was the end of the conversation.

"I used to be a lawyer," the fat man said then. "Guess I still am, but I don't practice."

"Writing a book?" The one Doc's attorney had written was still in the stores.

"Boy, if I ever did." He sat back. Then he leaned forward. "I advertised on TV. Maybe you caught one of my commercials. Maynard Ance, Your Friend in Court."

"I guess I missed them."

"They ran twenty times a day during *I Love Lucy* and *The Beverly Hillbillies*. The flu would be easier to miss."

"I've been away."

"I did one in front of these shelves of law books, like I ever used them. You want to know the secret to winning a personal injury suit? Stall. Sooner or later the other side gets tired of showing up for depositions that don't come off and settles. My record was seven years on a five-mile-an-hour rear-ender."

"How'd it come out?"

"Search me. I retired while it was still on and handed it over to my partners. We don't keep in touch. For all I know it hasn't got to court yet. That'd make it eleven years. Christ, I hope the poor son of a bitch isn't still wearing the neck brace."

They traveled ten blocks in silence. The radio was tuned low to an oldies station. Doc liked to keep it low and try to guess what song was playing. He'd heard them all a thousand times.

"This is twice this month that asshole Taber has left me standing around holding my dick," Maynard Ance said. "He swore he'd pick me up in front of Carl's Chop House at nine-thirty. What time you got?"

Doc checked the dashboard clock. "Nine twenty-three."

"No shit? Jesus, I'm a half-hour fast. Fucking Rolex." Something rattled. "Well, let the cocksucker find out what it's like to

31

get stood up. You as tall as you sit, Joe?" He paused. "Reason I ask, some people sit six feet, when they stand up they're more like five-four. Honest to Christ, they're sitting on a half-foot of lard. Joe?" He paused again. "Shit, maybe that's not your name. Where'd I leave my fucking glasses this time?"

It was the third time that week Doc had been slow to answer to the name on the chauffeur's license clipped to the dash. He covered. "Most people call me Spence."

"Right, like I'd know. So how tall are you?"

"I'm six-five."

"Yeah? Hey, I lucked out. You in the market for a hundred bucks?"

"I'm on parole." It slipped out.

"Who cares? It's legal. Probably just come to standing around looking tough as old cabbage. I'm picking up a client."

"I thought you were retired."

"Just from the bar. I'm a bail bondsman. Here's the buzzer." He tipped open a leather folder over the back of Doc's seat. It contained a plastic-coated ID bearing Ance's picture and a gold-plated Wayne County deputy sheriff's star. "The client skipped. It's a routine pickup, but if I show up alone he might get ideas. He's not bright or I wouldn't know where to find him."

"What's the charge?"

"Simple assault. I'm armed if it comes to that. Believe me, it won't." He withdrew the folder. "This is kosher. I'm an officer of the court requesting assistance from a citizen."

"Hiring it, you mean."

"Nothing in the statutes says you have to do it for free."

Doc turned onto Jefferson. The lights of Windsor looked like a string of beads on the opposite bank of the river.

"I'd be like, what, some kind of bounty hunter?"

"Don't pin any glitter on it. Lothar the Human Orangutan could do the job, only the circus isn't in town."

"Make it two hundred," Doc said. "I'm not sure how it'll look to my parole officer."

"I'll write him a note. I'll even notarize it. I'm a notary public."

Doc said nothing, the same thing he had said during his first and only contract negotiation. A Roadway van passed them going the other way. The concussion of air smacked the side of the cab twice.

Ance said, "Shit. Okay, two hundred. You sure you were never in the legal profession?"

"I've been around it."

The Independence Motel came up on their left, a square horseshoe striped with four tiers of narrow balconies overlooking a small parking lot in need of resurfacing. Doc had delivered several male passengers there that week in the company of long-legged black girls with short skirts and big hair. He parked beside a dumpster and accompanied Ance into a shallow lobby smelling of cigarette butts and d-Con. A black shaven-headed clerk of indeterminate age in a raveled sweater and glasses with white plastic rims slouched beyond a square opening in the wall, watching the Tigers on a thirteen-inch TV screen. Ance slapped the bell on the counter.

"Keep your pants on," the clerk said without turning. "Petry gonna strike out George Brett."

"What inning?" Doc asked.

"Bottom of the fourth."

"Buck says he gets on base."

"You *on,* man."

Two pitches later Brett walked. The clerk said shit, pulled a tattered wallet from his hip pocket, and slapped a bill on the counter. He looked up at Doc, doing a take when he saw how far up it was. "How'd you know?"

"Petry fades after the third. That's how he flushed the only game Detroit lost in the '84 Series." Doc pocketed the dollar.

"Sparky won't take him out, neither. Old fart been chawing so long his brain done turned to spit."

"I got a bet, too." Ance spread the leather folder on the counter. "I bet you your next visit from the fire marshal you're going to give me the key to sixteen."

The clerk peered at the card over the top of his glasses. "That ain't no detective's ID."

"I don't need one to call the City-County Building. If anybody's inspected the wiring in this dump since the riots I'll get you a box at Tiger Stadium."

"Tell that to the A-rab owns the place. I just watch the desk."

Ance put the folder in his pocket. "Spence, explain to the man his situation."

Doc wasn't sure what to do. He leaned into the counter, filling the opening. He made his face a blank sheet. On TV a gaggle of aging athletes debated the properties of a low-calorie beer. After a moment the clerk snorted, said, "Shiiit," and handed Doc a brass key from the pegboard. Doc gave it to Ance.

"He in?" Ance asked.

"How the hell should I know? The A-rab don't pay me to take them to the shitter."

Ance led the way around the corner and down a hallway paved with printed linoleum and lit greasily by three twenty-five-watt bulbs in the ceiling. Brass mailbox numerals were screwed to the hollow wooden doors. Ance unlocked number sixteen, turning the key slowly to avoid a click. Winking at Doc, he reached under his left arm inside his suit coat and brought out a blue automatic. Then he opened the door. Immediately Doc smelled something harsh and squalid and, smelled once, identified itself instantly every time it occurred thereafter: Burnt hair. Ance went inside. A minute later he came back to the door and motioned Doc in. The pistol was gone now.

The room jinked around a small bathroom with its door ajar, the mildew ensnared with the other odor that grew stronger with each step. Drapes made of some stiff-looking material covered the far wall, where sliding glass doors would open on to a small enclosed patio corresponding to the balconies on the upper floors. There was an industrial carpet, a dresser with a glass top, a nightstand and lamp, a double bed. The upper half of the man who lay atop the covers was drenched in darkness. He had on mottled jeans and dark socks.

Ance switched on the lamp with a hand wrapped in a handkerchief. The man on the bed was black, in his middle forties, balding in front, with graying chin whiskers and one of those moustaches that start at the corners of the mouth and straggle down until they lose interest. The beard hadn't been trimmed in days and the splintery new growth on his cheeks and neck were white. He was bare to the waist. His chest was sunken and hairless, his ribs showed. The whole front of his jeans were wet through, and Doc noticed a second stink, fully as organic, under the first. The hole in the man's head, bluish and puckered, was a little forward of his right temple, the singed hairs curled back from the edge. His right arm hung off the side of the mattress. A black, short-barreled revolver with plastic side grips like the handle of a Boy Scout knife lay on the carpet almost under the bed.

"Had to fuck somebody even at the end, didn't you, cocksucker?" Ance said. "Don't look like he'd come to better than four hundred bucks a pound, does he? Fifty large, that's what I'm out."

"That's stiff bail for simple assault." Doc felt his own stomach crowding the back of his tongue.

"He's got a history of not being in when the law comes to call. He was on the FBI's Ten Most Wanted list for fifteen years."

"Who was he?"

"Most recently, Ambrose X. Dryce. Before that he was Wilson McCoy."

The name thudded in Doc's memory like a wooden gong. "Black Panther?"

"Not for twenty-five years. You're looking at what's left of the grand exalted poobah of the loyal and malevolent Marshals of Mahomet."

That meant nothing to Doc.

"I wouldn't've taken him on at all except I thought he was too pooped to run any more. I sure as hell hit that one square on the head. No offense, Wilson." Ance turned toward the dresser, where a wallet and a straight razor lay in what looked like a scattering of plaster dust from the ceiling.

"How long do you think he's been dead?"

"Somebody saw him check in this morning. I'll let the cops take his temperature." He drew a silver pencil from his breast pocket and poked through the wallet. "Asshole spent his last nickel on the room. My luck." He licked a knuckle, touched it to the white dust, licked it again. "Well, we know where he found the balls to jerk the trigger. None of that cheap Michigan Avenue crack for the leader of the M-and-M's. Too bad he couldn't afford enough to just glide on out."

That name—M-and-M's—struck a chord. "Somebody should call the police, I guess."

"I'll do it. No sense you hanging around." Ance handed him a business card. "Call me and I'll get your money to you. Not two hundred, though. It'd be different if you had to earn it."

"The clerk saw me."

"Shit, I forgot. You better stick." He misread Doc's expression. "Sorry about this, Spence. I'll put in a word with your parole cop."

"My name's Miller," Doc said.

36

Chapter 5

❖❖❖❖❖❖❖❖

"Second suicide this year," muttered the clerk while Ance used his telephone. "They going to stop their clock anyway, why don't they check into the Westin, order room service?"

"If they could afford the Westin, they wouldn't be committing suicide, schmuck." Ance waited for someone at the police department to pick up.

Doc was watching the game on the clerk's set. "What's the score?"

The police started arriving in pairs, some in uniform, others in sport coats and slacks that didn't quite match, like high school basketball coaches. Some were white, most were black. One of the first two officers on the scene was a black woman with her hair pinned up under her uniform cap. She asked most of the questions, scratching the answers in a pocket notebook. Doc noticed she used shorthand. While he and Ance were answering the same questions for the plainclothesmen, the medical examiner arrived with his black metal case and went into the room. He was a small neat Vietnamese wearing a Hawaiian shirt and khaki pants under an overcoat with the sleeves turned back, who looked as if he had come there directly from the boat. Doc overheard jokes told in low voices and chuckling. There was an air of lightness about the proceedings, like relatives getting together for the first time in years at the funeral of a despised aunt.

After an hour or so a man came alone who looked nothing like any of the others. He was black, nearly as tall as Doc but more substantial and a few years older, in tailored charcoal worsted and a blue silk tie on a shirt with a small check. His hair was trimmed close to his skull and frosted with gray, and he had coarse features that reminded Doc of a *National Geographic* special he had seen on the Ashanti. He stopped to speak with several of the officers and detectives crowded in the hallway, then went into the room. When he came out he caught Maynard Ance's eye and motioned him over. Doc drifted that way.

"When you take home a cockroach, you can't expect him to make honey," the black man told Ance, then turned to shake Doc's hand. "Charlie Battle. I'm a sergeant with Major Crimes."

His grip was surprisingly gentle. Doc had met his share of bone-crushers in baseball and again in prison and could tell when strength was being held back. "I'm Kevin Miller."

"I know. You signed my son's scorecard the day you shut out Cleveland. I didn't know you were sprung."

"It's been almost two weeks." He was conscious of the bail bondsman's curious gaze. It was the first time anyone had recognized him. He felt suddenly naked, as if he'd been performing in a porno film under a pseudonym and someone had called out his name.

"I was just telling your boss he ought to choose his clients more carefully. Someone else would have capped McCoy if he hadn't done it himself. This isn't the kind of case where you ask if the victim had any enemies."

It had been Ance's idea to claim that Doc was working for

him. At his suggestion Doc had parked the cab around the corner before the first squad car squealed in. "I thought he was dead a long time ago," Doc said. "I haven't heard about him in years."

"He jumped bail on that Orr killing in '66 and went underground for fifteen years. Should've been held without bond, but nobody much cares when a mafioso gets himself gunned. When he finally turned himself in—feds had him down for unlawful flight to avoid prosecution—he had to remind them who he was and why they wanted him. The jury hung, and they decided not to try him again. Then he got involved in this Marshals of Mahomet thing."

"What is it?"

Battle grinned incredulously. It made him look a little less like a warrior. "Don't they have TV in Jackson?"

"Mostly I watched sports."

"Who's your parole officer?" The sergeant patted his pockets. Doc couldn't tell if he was looking for cigarettes or a notebook.

"Peter Kubitski."

"He's a horse's ass, but that's the job description." The patting stopped. "He know you're working with Ance?"

"I just started. I haven't had a chance to tell him."

"Better call him before he sees it on the news. The press is going to like this one. Wilson McCoy's been the maggots' meat since Cavanagh was mayor. I bet they make a hero out of the bloodthirsty son of a bitch just like they did the first time." He looked at Ance. "Got any more M-and-M's in your drawer?"

"That's privileged."

"Bullshit, it's court record. Personally I don't give a rip, but if I were you and any of them are jumpers, I'd call 911 before I went haring after them. Department policy's to tag them Armed and Dangerous as soon as we find out they're Marshals. They see you coming up the walk to any safe house in this city, they're not looking at the man bailed them out. All they see is your color and a big fat bull's-eye on your chest."

"So I call you and you make the arrest and I'm out whatever I dropped on them," Ance said. "My way I get back at least a percentage. I've been shot at before, Charlie, remember?"

"Good thing it wasn't in the wallet or you'd've bled to death."

"Yeah, well, fuck you, too."

But Battle was looking at Doc. "My boy still has that score-card. His mother and I opened up a safety deposit box for him so he wouldn't lose it. You had Hall-of-Famer written all over you that year."

"I thought so, too."

"My uncle who raised me wanted me to be the first black State Supreme Court justice. He was a pro wrestler." The sergeant moved his shoulders. "I'll need a statement from both of you by tomorrow. Ance knows where my office is at Thirteen Hundred. Take the stairs. The elevator's just big enough to hold the fat tub of shit." He shook Doc's hand again and went over to talk to the desk clerk, who was leaning dejectedly against the wall next to the office.

"He doesn't think much of you," Doc told Ance.

"He's just about the best friend I've got in this town."

Doc was too tired to laugh. It was past midnight. He'd been up since 6:00 A.M., and he was due at the John Deere dealership in less than seven hours. He stirred to leave, but the bail bondsman kept his hands in his pockets. "Pro ball, huh? What was it, gambling?"

"Drugs."

Ance turned half-around, disgusted. "Kids, Jesus Christ. What the fuck's the matter with bourbon? It's legal and you don't have to mug old ladies to pay for it."

"I only did drugs once. It loused up my control."

"Sure, you got a bum rap. All my clients are innocent too. Take me home, kid."

The address Ance gave him was in Taylor. The bail bondsman, Doc had figured out, fueled himself on talk, but not in the aimless, redundant, can't-get-a-word-in-edgewise way of Mickey Baline and others of that generation; even in his exhaustion Doc found himself paying attention. And as Ance talked, his speech grew more relaxed and less profane. Doc sensed that a guard was being lowered.

"This wasn't anything," Ance said. "One time Taber and me traced this good old boy rapist all the way down to Tennessee, this little jerk-off place called Frog's Creek or Toad's Dick or something stuck way up on the side of this fucking mountain. Honest to Christ, we're hanging on by our foreskins in the front yard. Well, Pa Kettle opens the door and there's the whole family sitting in the parlor like you see in those oval pictures in antique stores, even Grandma in her hickory rocker with an autoharp in her lap and little Charlotte Rose on the floor with her Raggedy Ann. Pa says it's been six months since he saw Veal—swear to God, that's his name, Veal—but the place is built out of packing crates and I can hear someone walking around upstairs and it's August so it can't be Santa Claus. But we got out. I don't start trouble in people's homes. There was a saloon in town and we staked that out for a couple of nights, listened to "Okie From Muskogee" about a thousand times on the juke, until the good old boy comes in. Well, everybody in the place was his friend that night except us and they kicked the living shit right out of Taber and me, I mean my ears are still ringing. Next day we went back to his house with the sheriff, and he came away with us gentle as you please, on account of he was hung over bad with a fractured wrist to boot. Only little Charlotte Rose smashes Taber on the big toe with a hammer on our way out. They thought for a while he was going to lose the toe, but now it just gives him hell when it rains."

"Why didn't you bring the sheriff with you the first time?"

"Local law charges too much. They don't care for bail men on principle, and bail men from out of town are lower than a snake's asshole in places like that. They're still waiting for Rhett to come back to Scarlett down there." He lit a cigarette—Doc thought he had to see the NO SMOKING sign on the back of the front seat when he struck the match—and coughed. "Okay, so this time I'm out five grand plus your two bills. Beats hell out of getting stomped in a Tennessee saloon. I piss my pants every time I hear Waylon Jennings."

"I thought I was just getting a hundred."

"That was before I found out who you were."

"You never heard of me."

"Hockey's my game. But a baseball player with a record has got to be some kind of celebrity, and a celebrity ex-con takes twice the risk getting tied up in shit like this. You're lucky Battle got the squeal and not some squirt looking to get up in the department through the Six O'Clock News. You'd be on your way to County right now, booked as a material witness."

"I'm not that well known."

"Save it." Ance coughed again and lowered his window two inches. Doc saw the shower of sparks the discarded cigarette made in the side mirror. The window went back up. "Trying to quit. You handled yourself okay with the cops. I was afraid you might freak."

"When I get in a jam like that I imagine I'm coming to the mound with the bases loaded and only one out."

"Why one out?"

"I need it to keep from freaking."

The bail bondsman didn't laugh. "How'd you like to go to work for me?"

"As a driver?"

"That too. I never had a lesson. Taber's getting unreliable. You're an athlete, so I'm guessing you can take care of yourself when it gets heavy. The job pays five bills a week."

Almost twice what he was getting at the dealership. "I'd better not."

"Why not?"

"It pays too much to be on the square."

"Hey, if that's all that's bothering you I'll make it two-fifty." Ance sat back on the springs. "Seriously, I'm licensed. As long as these scroats are in my custody, the law says I can bring 'em back in a shoebox if they'll fit and I punch a few holes in the lid. I don't even have to do *that* more than a dozen times a year; if I weren't any better judge of character than that I'd be broke. My tax bill last year was forty thousand. Most of the time you'll just be driving me around."

"For five hundred a week."

"I said most of the time."

They were entering Taylor. "I don't think so. But thanks."

"You're too wasted to decide. Hell, maybe I'm too wasted to make any offers. Let's sleep on it. Maybe we'll both change our minds."

The bail bondsman's house was a deep white frame saltbox on Empire with a small front yard and one of those novelty lawn ornaments where a little wooden man sawed furiously at a log whenever the wind blew. The windows were dark. Doc stopped the car and looked back at his passenger. "You paid forty thousand in taxes last year?"

"I've got four ex-wives. You figure it out." He slid four crisp fifties out of his wallet and passed them over the back of the seat. "You've got my card. Call me." He got out.

43

The electric clock in Neal's kitchen read 1:28 when Doc came in and threw his keys on the kitchen table. His brother was seated there in his bathrobe smoking a cigarette. "Anybody hurt?" he asked.

"Hurt?" Doc leaned against the counter.

"In the accident."

"I had an involved fare. I thought you gave that up."

Neal looked down at the cigarette as if someone had just put it there and punched it out in a bronze ashtray Doc recognized as one that had belonged to their father. "When's Spence getting back from California?"

"Day after tomorrow."

"Good."

The clock was clogged with cooking grime. It buzzed and moved ahead in jerks.

"Better sleep fast," Neal said. "You got about four hours."

Doc said, "I quit."

By Leon "Bud" Arsenault
(continued)

The Great Depression was especially hard on Detroiters. People who owned cars were making repairs and making do, and those who did not rode the trolley. Horace MacGryff was just one of thousands of workers laid off indefinitely from the stagnant auto industry.

Bad times were a double blow to his wife, who although she cheerfully offered her services as cook and housekeeper to residents in the more well-to-do neighborhoods to help keep her young family solvent, dearly missed her frequent trips to what was now called Briggs Stadium. Listening to a distracted announcer on the Philco trying to simulate Hank Greenburg's virile connecting swing by clapping two sticks together hardly compared to an afternoon in the sun with a cold beer and a hot dog.

But a paltry ticket to one game would not do for Mrs. MacGryff. Such a day could only prickle her pallate and render the unavoidable return to her mop-and-bucket existence unbearable.

Loyola MacGryff wanted season tickets.

Not just for her, but for her whole family, which now numbered five with the latest still in diapers. Just knowing that the entire brood could on a moment's notice pile into the

Model A, rumble seat and all, and tool down to that green place where men in baggy uniforms played a boys' game under the sky would be the beacon that lit their way through the dark days yet to come.

Obsessed with obtaining capital, Mrs. MacGryff cleared garage and attic of bric-a-brac, stuck price tags on the lot, and set her oldest son to work painting and posting signs for blocks around advertising a yard sale.

At Horace's pleading, she made certain to drape a sheet over his priceless collection of salt and pepper shakers stored in the garage, the passion of a lifetime, lest any of the pieces be damaged or stolen in the confusion of commerce.

The sale was an enormous success by Depression standards. The MacGryffs cleared thirty-seven dollars, enough to purchase season tickets for the neighborhood, with enough left over for souvenirs and refreshments.

It was scarcely the fault of the family in those less cautious times that a victim of hard luck, mistaken for a straggling browser, showed Mrs. MacGryff an old black revolver while she was counting the profits and made off with them.

The police were sympathetic, but explained that the bandit had as like as not already departed Detroit on the same freight train he had come in on. The money was irretrievable.

This is one MacGryff story with a happy ending, however.

On the following Saturday they held another sale; and while the proceeds from Horace's cherished shaker collection fell somewhat short of the previous weekend's total, they were more than adequate to treat parents and children all to a season in the bleachers.

"You should have seen the look on Horace's face when he found out," reminisces the widow. "I don't mind telling you I was so happy I cried right along with him."

(to be continued)

PART TWO

Change-Up

◆◆◆◆◆◆◆◆◆

Chapter 6

◆◆◆◆◆◆◆◆

Peter Y. Kubitski, Doc's parole officer, was one of these comfortable avuncular types in a mohair jacket that had worn to fit his angular construction and a nubby knitted tie on a blue button-down shirt. His hair, receding on either side of the widow's peak, was salt-and-pepper and fluffed out at the temples and he had a long pale face and one of those noses that looked as if he had slept on it wrong; when he put on his reading glasses he had to come around a corner. A pair of tiny blue-black eyes like gooseberries glittered under the moss cliff of his brows. Doc disliked him on sight.

His office, on the third floor of Detroit Police Headquarters at 1300 Beaubien, was small and overheated and smelled of the rotting bindings of social science books in glass cases and apple-scented pipe tobacco, Doc's least favorite kind. Kubitski had all the irritating habits of a pipe smoker: the constant fussing with the charred blob of brier, charging and recharging and tamping and lighting and relighting, the browsing in the dilapidated leather pouch, the business of pointing the stem at his visitor when he was making an observation and then biting down on it

as if stamping the whole thing in granite. Sparky Anderson
smoked a pipe too, and Doc had never gotten on with the aging
Tigers manager.

Kubitski seated him in an uncomfortable chair facing the
desk and kept him waiting while he read Doc's file spread out on
the blotter. At length he sat back, communed for a full minute
with his pipe, and said, "You're changing your employment?"

"Yes." Doc didn't elaborate. If his time in prison had taught
him anything it had taught him never to volunteer information.

"Are you unhappy at the farm dealership?"

"No, it's okay."

"Maynard Ance is well-known around here. He skates the
edge of the law. Working for him wouldn't be in your best
interest."

"Is it a violation?" Before coming in that morning, Doc had
called the office to report last night's adventure and his decision
to accept Ance's offer. He hadn't mentioned he was driving a cab.

Kubitski sucked on his pipe. The gurgling made Doc think of
a rain gutter. "How are things at home?"

"Okay."

"But?"

"Everything's fine."

"Oh, come on. A grown man, forced to live with his brother
and his brother's family? I'd have gone berserk with a chainsaw
before this."

Doc saw he was going to have to give Kubitski what he
wanted. He sat back as far as the straight chair allowed. "I had
friends in Jackson I knew better than Neal. I was just a kid the
last time we lived under the same roof. He's still got the first job
he ever had. We don't exactly speak the same language."

"What about the others"—the parole officer glanced down at
the file—"Wilhelmina and little Sean?"

50

"Billie's great. I don't remember my mother that well but she was a lot like my sister-in-law, warm but tough."

"But?"

"She think's baseball's what got me in trouble. Maybe she's right, but not in the way she thinks. I think that has something to do with why she's turning her boy into a carrot. All the kid does is watch TV and play video games. He's getting to look like eighty pounds of pork."

"And you've argued with her about this."

"No. He's not my son."

"But?"

Kubitski's *but* was getting on his nerves. "I take a lot of walks."

"Going to work for Maynard Ance at all hours must seem like a nice change."

"I'm going to work for him because he offered me more than I've been getting."

"Enough to move?"

Doc hadn't expected him to catch on so quickly. "I'll just be driving him around. Is it illegal?"

"No more than operating a taxi cab under someone else's license." Kubitski unhooked his glasses to catch the other's reaction. "I work at this job, Doc. I don't play at it. A certain kind of parole officer would send you back to serve out your sentence on a complaint like that. He would think you hadn't learned your lesson."

"The only lesson I learned is who to throw out of my parties."

He wished immediately he hadn't said it. Roger Craig had once told him the only thing that would keep him out of the Thirty Game Club was his tendency to rattle when a batter anticipated one of his pitches. The gooseberry eyes glittered dangerously, but after a moment the man behind the desk struck three matches in a clump and relit his tobacco. His pale cheeks billowed and caved in rapidly. He deposited the matches in an ironwood ashtray. "How much did Ance tell you about himself?"

"Just that he was a lawyer. And something about a job he did down in Tennessee."

"Did he mention he was disbarred?"

"What for?"

Kubitski puffed. Doc was beginning to realize he didn't give answers. "He's a grandstander, a cowboy. Either he doesn't know how to turn down work or he likes going on these midnight raids to bring back jumpers, because he averages five to the ordinary bail bondsman's one. If I were you I'd keep on selling manure spreaders. You stand a lot better chance of finishing out your time on the outside."

"Does that mean I can take the job?"

"Just stay behind the wheel."

Doc thanked him and left. Heading toward the elevators he thought he might have been less belligerent with Kubitski and to hell with his habits. But he wouldn't have known how to explain to the parole officer that during his time in the Independence Motel with Ance, from the moment he had leaned menacingly on the clerk's counter until they got away from Sergeant Battle, when a wrong word could have revoked his parole, he had felt more alive than at any time since the two-hitter he had thrown his last day in Jackson.

A uniformed officer carrying a large manila envelope down the hall directed Doc to Major Crimes, where he almost collided with Battle coming out of the squad room. The sergeant, in striped shirtsleeves and a burgundy leather shoulder clip that actually matched his tie, caught himself with a hand on the doorjamb, thanked Doc for coming in, and asked him to wait in the lieutenant's office.

The lieutenant's office was the only enclosed cubicle in a room full of desks and detectives talking on telephones. It had glass walls that stopped short of the ceiling and was just big enough for a desk half the size of Kubitski's, two chairs, and a row of gray steel file cabinets stacked with folders that had overflowed the drawers. In spite of that the room was neatly kept, the telephone, calendar pad, and portable scanner on the desk squared in line with the corners and a fistful of yellow pencils standing at attention in a rubber cup with their razor points directed at the ceiling. Doc felt certain that Sergeant Battle used the office more than anyone. He wondered idly if the sergeant owned a matching gun rig for every tie in his wardrobe.

Atop one of the cabinets a portable TV set was tuned to CNN with the sound off. When a still photograph of Wilson McCoy appeared on the screen, Doc went over and turned up the volume. The report of the discovery of McCoy's body was sketchy and, like every other news event Doc had ever witnessed firsthand, bore little resemblance to what he remembered. Biographical footage followed: McCoy at twenty in jungle fatigues with the sleeves cut off, haranguing an all-black crowd with a banner behind him bearing the initials B.L.A.C.; McCoy in handcuffs and streaked coveralls being escorted to a squad car by white Detroit Police officers in uniform; McCoy standing on the steps of the City-County Building wearing the same coveralls but without manacles, raising a fist in the Black Power salute to a mob hooting and pumping placards reading FREE WILSON; McCoy, many years older and almost unrecognizable in a blue county jumpsuit with his hair cut short and no goatee, being arraigned before a judge on three counts of first-degree murder and one count of interstate flight; McCoy looking much as Doc had seen him last night, graying and emaciated, entering the auditorium of the Detroit Light Guard Armory with the crowd, turning to look at the camera with an expression that reminded Doc of the uncomprehending faces of the old people he had seen in the nursing home in Warren. The last shot dissolved to the still photograph he'd seen before, over the dates of Wilson McCoy's birth and death. In the late footage he had looked much older than forty-four.

The program turned from there to a second Detroit story, wherein a group of journalists were asking Mayor Coleman Young for his reaction to a number of allegations made against him by yet another of his aides currently standing trial for misuse of public money. His reply was mostly bleeped out and after thirty seconds he shoved his way through the pack and out of the frame. Sergeant Charlie Battle entered the office then and turned off the set. "Nothing wrong with this city couldn't be cured with an asshole transplant, you old fart," he said, stepping behind his desk. He opened the top drawer, took out a typewritten sheet, looked at it, and laid it on Doc's side of the desk. "I typed up what you told me last night from my notes. Anything else you remember, tell me now."

Doc read the statement. It was almost word-for-word what he had given the detectives. "I didn't see you taking any notes."

"I did all that later."

"Can't see someone's eyes when you're writing down their words, huh?"

The sergeant laughed shortly. "Eyes aren't the part that talks."

Doc borrowed a pen and signed his name on the bottom, adding the date. Battle took the sheet over to the file cabinets and put it in the folder on top of the pile. "Where's Ance?"

"I haven't seen him since last night."

"He's a pistol, your boss. When I'm his age I plan to be sitting in one of those condos they're building in the warehouse district, flipping my wang-doodle across the river at Canada. That's if I can still get it up."

"I thought you were married."

"Oh, I expect to outlive her." He was still holding the file. He removed a stiff rectangle of yellowed paper sealed in clear laminate and handed it to Doc. "I brought it in this morning. I wasn't sure you believed me last night."

It was a Detroit Tigers scorecard. He'd forgotten how elaborate his signature was then, full of loops and flourishes. Jackson had cramped it up. He gave back the card. "I believed you. How old is your son?"

"Fourteen. I almost called him down here last month to help me dope out the new computer. I guess *his* boy'll fly a rocket to Mars for his first science project."

"He play any ball?"

"Shoots the hoops better than his old man ever did, for what that's worth." He switched off the scanner. "Your boss been in touch with Starkweather Hall lately?"

The change-up caught him looking. "Who's he?"

"You really did watch nothing but sports," Battle said. "Wilson McCoy was just window dressing on account of he knew Mahomet personally. Hall *is* the Marshals. Without him they're just a bunch of throwbacks spitting up black revolutionary slogans from the sixties. Ance put up his bail last time we popped him. It didn't take, but he's wanted again on a case we can make stick."

"What are the Marshals of Mahomet?"

"Jesus. Well, you remember Mahomet."

"Some kind of double-A Malcolm X. Somebody shot him."

"Kercheval Street, 1966. Looked like the riots were going to start that night, but it rained. The real riots the next year and then King's assassination in '68 shoved him into the backseat—

he was just starting to make a name for himself locally with his white suits and Lou Rawls pipes when some nutso Mafia hitter took him out—but it looked for a while like the whole white establishment in this town was going to come apart that week. Then McCoy cut down Patsy Orr and a couple of his *paisani* in the Penobscot Building, and nobody knew if it was racial or just another gangland blowout and the whole thing just lost momentum."

He sat on a corner of the desk. "McCoy jumped bail on the Orr killing and just disappeared. These revolutionary types aren't your average lamster, they don't keep in touch with their friends and families. The FBI staked out his mother's house until she died. They even went to her funeral, like if he didn't break cover to see the old lady when she was alive he'd come out for the planting. Finally they gave up on him. By the time he turned himself in down in Atlanta or someplace a new generation had taken over the Bureau and they didn't know him from Dillinger. But his trial got a lot of publicity—Remember Jimi Hendrix, *Gilligan's Island,* and Watts?, that kind of thing—and when the jury couldn't decide and the prosecutors didn't retry and cut him loose, he did the lecture tour for a while; then Starkweather Hall came to him with this crackpot Marshals of Mahomet idea and he just lapped it up.

"The organization's all black, founded on the notion that Mahomet was God and McCoy was his prophet on earth. Mahomet used to speak at meetings of McCoy's Black Afro-American Congress, so it made sense in a lunatic kind of way. They started meeting in the basement of a crummy house on Erskine, and in six months they were pulling in crowds of thirteen and fourteen hundred in the National Guard Armory downtown. That new African-American thing, you know, second generation. Like Lester Maddox never died, and George Wallace isn't just filling a shitbag in his wheelchair in Alabama."

"Sounds legitimate." Doc leaned against the door.

"That was the idea. The M-and-M's make a lot of noise about lobbying for new laws to protect minorities, but they're the chief source of crack cocaine in this town. Those beat-up buses they take to Washington to march on the capital are so loaded down with dope their bumpers practically touch the ground. And they're branching out. Starkweather Hall thinks he's some kind of Lucky Luciano, trying to tie together all the black drug operations in the country under one governing body with him as chairman of the board. Had a shot at it, too, if he didn't get careless three months ago and sign his name to the lease on an apartment on Vernor. We frisked the place on a warrant and recovered enough rock candy to light up Pittsburgh. Then Hall powdered. McCoy bellying up last night was our first break in—yeah?"

Someone had rapped at the door. Doc stepped away as a big white detective in an orange shirt and a wide necktie opened it and leaned in. "Autopsy report, Charlie."

Battle sprang off the desk and snatched the sheaf of paper from the detective's hand. He skimmed it. "Shit!"

"McCoy?"

He looked at Doc without focusing, as if he'd forgotten he was there. "For a while there I hoped Hall fell out with him and capped him, give us a handle." He sailed the report at the desk. It skidded across the top and off the other side. "Blood workup HIV positive. Son of a bitch killed himself because he had AIDS."

"I thought he didn't look well," Doc said.

Chapter 7

◆◆◆◆◆◆◆◆◆

Look who's here: Give 'Em Another Chance Ance. Hey, Maynard, is it true you offered to put up a million to spring Chuck Manson?"

"Now, Phil, you know I never bet on anybody crazier than myself."

Doc had been almost out the door of police headquarters when he overheard Ance's name behind him and the bail bondsman's reply. He turned around and saw his new employer leaning on the watch sergeant's desk in the same blue suit and overcoat he'd had on the night before. By daylight his hair definitely looked dyed, blue-black under the fluorescents and showing the marks of the comb. Doc went over there. The uniformed sergeant, a beefy fifty with big red hands and the face of a Greek fisherman, was showing his teeth at Ance in a smile of uncut malice. "I hear your boy Wilson took fifty G's of your money with him."

"Yeah. I'll have to work through next weekend to make it back. Phil, I've been meaning to ask, what's that chipped beef the government hands out taste like? I'm thinking of picking up a can for my cat, but I don't want him to get sick."

"Fuck off, lardass." The sergeant transferred his attention to the duty roster clipped to the wall over the desk.

Ance turned and shook Doc's hand. "Thought you'd be at work now. Just coming in?"

"Going out. I signed my statement. I don't think Battle's in any hurry to get you to sign yours. His murder theory blew up in his face." He told the bail bondsman about the autopsy report.

"Wilson looked like shit for a long time. I thought he was just doping too much. Well, hell." He looked at his watch. "Had lunch?"

"A little early, isn't it?"

"Only if you ate breakfast. You know the Acropolis?"

Doc said he did. They left the building and walked down Beaubien. It was the first warm day of spring. Last night's puddles were drying and the few people they encountered wore their overcoats open. As usual the downtown sidewalks were almost empty. Far from revitalizing the city, the People Mover electric train had merely plucked its remaining pedestrians off the pavement.

"You're not popular with the police," Doc said.

"Who, Phil? He's a shithead or he'd be a lieutenant by now."

"It looked like more than that."

"Somebody else'd put up the money if I didn't. Their gripe is with the judges that set the bail in the first place. But the judges don't come down to thirteen hundred. You get canned?"

"I quit. I decided to take the job."

"Yeah, well, I slept on it." Ance struck out across Monroe against the light, holding out a palm as he stepped in front of a Buick with mismatched fenders. Brakes squeaked, the driver cranked down his window and shouted something that was lost under the rap beat that thumped out with it. Doc hung back while the car squirted past, its slipstream lifting the tails of Ance's coat, then loped across.

"Change your mind?"

"Taber's been with me four years. He fucks up plenty, but he's taken a lot of stitches for me. I can't just fire him. You should've called me before you gave up your job. I said last night I was wasted."

"Who says you have to fire him?"

"They're making drivers' seats smaller and smaller. You won't both fit." They were in Greektown. The block was lined with restaurants and markets with five-syllable names on their signs. Ance grasped the brass handle of a wooden door with beveled glass panels.

"I get it he's always late picking you up," Doc said. "Let me do that. He can go on taking stitches for you and I'll do the driving."

The restaurant was a dimly lit rectangle with a bar and tall booths lining the wall opposite. Murals of the Parthenon and various other ruins Doc couldn't identify covered all four walls and a fishnet hung in hammocks from the ceiling. A tiny waitress with blonde hair and blue eyes, not a Greek, showed them to a booth and left menus. At the only other table that was occupied at that hour, a waiter set fire to a dish of cheese soaked in retsina with a halfhearted cry of *Opah!* and smothered the flame quickly.

"For five bills a week I'll hire A. J. Foyt to drive me around. I need muscle. Taber's not good for much else, but he's good enough for that." Ance studied his menu.

"Who is Taber, anyway?"

"Up till Old Numb-Nuts became mayor he was a Detroit police officer, a twenty-year man. Something about misuse of deadly force." He summoned the waitress and ordered moussaka and a glass of cold milk.

61

Doc asked for water and a dish of inflammable cheese. When the waitress left with their menus: "I'm in good shape. A third man would've come in handy in that bar in Tennessee."

"That's old history. These days I don't accept clients with out-of-state addresses. Except Toledo. Half my business comes from there."

"Beside the point."

Ance put away the glasses he had put on to read the menu. His eyes were that shade of gray that looked like coins in shallow water. "Your P.O. know you're having this conversation?"

"He said I could take the job." Doc had decided not to mention the part about staying behind the wheel.

"What'd he say about me?"

"He said you're a cowboy and that you must like running down jumpers or you wouldn't get so many."

"Yeah, I can see why he gave you the green light." He lit a cigarette.

"You can call him if you don't believe me. His name's Kubitski."

"I know. I was there when you told Charlie. Just a second." The waiter who had ignited the cheese at the other table arrived with Doc's order. He looked more Arab than Greek. Before he could touch off the retsina, Ance tossed his burning match into the dish. The liquor went up in a sheet of orange and blue flame and the bail bondsman shouted *Opah* loud enough to make glasses ring behind the bar. "That's how it's done, Farouk," he said as the flustered waiter fumbled the cover in place, extinguishing the blaze. "Tell your boss to hire the real thing if he wants to compete with Colonel Sanders."

The waiter served Doc and withdrew without a word. The cheese was charred at the edges. "How many restaurants have you been thrown out of?"

"They can't throw me out of this one. I own half of it." Ance put out his cigarette. The little blonde waitress had brought his eggplant and milk. "Kubitski doesn't know me. He's just repeating what he's heard around headquarters. I'm sixty-two next month. Three doctors told me two years ago if I didn't quit smoking and lose weight I'd never see sixty-five. I buried one, but three of a kind's a hand I'd bet on any day of the week. Does that sound like I look forward to climbing mountains and getting the shit kicked out of me in saloons?"

Doc shrugged. The cheese tasted fine.

"Kubitski say anything else?"

"He said you were disbarred."

"He say why?"

"No."

"I was standing up for this little scroat on a charge of first-degree criminal sexual conduct." The bail bondsman spoke between forkfuls of moussaka. "It was outside my specialty, but the scroat's old man was a friend. First day of testimony the prosecutor asked the victim to identify her rapist, and she pointed right at the punk sitting next to me at the defense table. Only it wasn't my client, it was a kid we had doing errands at the office who looked a little like him. Well, the judge got all bent out of shape over it. It was his evidence tipped the board of review against me. Some of my colleagues had been trying to do that for years."

"I think Perry Mason pulled that trick once."

"Perry's judge wasn't an asshole. He was lucky that way."

"It doesn't seem like enough to get you thrown out of the profession."

"Well, a lot of old shit got dragged out at the hearing. Point is, you measure your success by how many enemies you've made. I play dirty, son. Life ain't baseball."

"I found that out."

"Fuck that." Ance chewed and swallowed. "You keep looking behind you, you bump into what's in front of you. Think I'm bitter? Hell, disbarment was the best thing ever happened to me. All the money in this town that isn't in the mayor's personal investment company is in dope, and I represent more drug dealers than Parke-Davis. They pay their bills. In their business it's a good habit to get into if you don't want your creditors cutting off your dick and shoving it down your tonsils. The clients that come through outnumber the jumpers twenty to one. Everything else is a tax loss. When I was a lawyer I'd've killed for odds like that." He drank his milk and whisked away the moustache with a knuckle. "So you don't get your picture on a bubble-gum card. Life don't serve all the courses."

"Does that mean I'm hired?"

"On approval. You handle cops okay, but handling cops is the smallest part of the job. Show me how you do in heavy shit and maybe we'll talk about making it permanent."

"What do I do first?"

"Get the tip." Ance stood and took his overcoat off the hook.

Chapter 8

◆◆◆◆◆◆◆◆

Doc had returned Spence's cab and ridden a bus into town. He and Ance took a taxi to Inkster. On Michigan Avenue they got out in front of a block of two-story yellow brick buildings sheltering a Kid Koin Laundry, a used furniture store, and a health spa with a rear entrance under a blue awning and a sign reading WE EMPLOY ONLY AMERICAN MASSEUSES.

"Need a back rub?" Doc asked.

"That's about the only thing they don't rub here. We're home." Ance led the way around the side of the building.

That side bore a ten-foot cartoon of a coin wearing a cowboy hat and drawing a pair of six-guns. One of its booted feet decorated a steel fire door. Stopping there, Ance glanced around the unpaved parking lot and sorted through a dozen keys on a ring the size of a softball. "No sign of the crate. Taber's sleeping one off again."

He unlocked the door, and they entered a narrow hallway paved with broken linoleum that ran the length of the building. It smelled like a bus station.

Near the end was another steel door painted to look like wood with a gridded-glass window lettered in black:

M. W. ANCE
KNOCK BEFORE ENTERING

"What's your advertising budget?"

Ance used another key and opened the door. "Strictly Yellow Pages and the county grapevine. You don't get much off-the-street trade in this business."

The office was square, well-furnished, and surprisingly neat. It contained a large pearwood desk with a leather top, a telephone and fax machine, a copier, and a complicated-looking coffee maker with a checkerboard of flashing colored lights atop a nine-drawer file cabinet. The rug looked expensive and too ornate for the room, and the desk was bunted up against the wall under a window overlooking the parking lot. Outside, a pickup truck bearing the name of a well-known construction firm on the door of the cab pulled up and a driver in dusty coveralls got out and went into the massage parlor.

"Dumb putz." Ance was watching, too. "He owns the company. The feds have had that skin shop under surveillance for a couple of months. They think it's one of the places where city contracts go to get fixed. Rumor is the company that owns the place is a subsidiary of our right and honorable mayor's holding corporation. You'd think a construction boss would know better than to drive up in one of his own trucks." He hung up his coat. "Terrible what's happened to corruption in this town. Under Cavanagh it had style."

"How come you know so much about it?"

"Secrets are only secret from the people who want to know them. When you don't give a shit, you hear things. That's your first lesson." He sat down at the desk and lifted the receiver off the telephone.

His was the only chair in the office. "Where do the customers sit?"

"At home. I work here. I don't entertain visitors." He dialed, took out a cigarette while he was waiting, then crumpled it and tossed it into the metal wastebasket next to the desk. "Maynard Ance. Any messages? Yeah. Yeah. Okay." He hung up and wrote something on his calendar pad. "We got an appointment in Redford at two. You know the Kingswood Manor Apartments on Livernois? They're down the street from Baker's Keyboard Lounge."

"I know Baker's. Is that where the appointment is?"

"That's where the transportation is. Apartment 612. If Taber doesn't answer, tack a note to his door and bring back the bus. Here's the extra set." He opened a drawer and handed Doc a pair of keys attached to a miniature license plate.

"What do I do, compare numbers?"

"You'll know it when you see it. Believe me."

Doc opened the door. "A guy doesn't get to do much sitting around this place."

"One thing you won't get working for me is hemorrhoids." Ance put on his glasses.

Kingswood Manor was a quiet complex set back from the road with potted trees on the balconies and patios and a taxi stand in front. Doc paid the driver and went in through the main entrance. Finding the inner door locked, he studied the rows of mailboxes built into the wall and pushed the button next to R. TABER. When there was no answering buzz after his second attempt, he pressed another button at random. A buzzer sounded and he went through the door.

Sunlight slanted through a tall window at the end of the

corridor on the sixth floor. When he knocked on 612, the door moved. He knocked again, then pushed it open.

The living room was large and took up most of the apartment, with a kitchenette to the left and a door at the back that he assumed led into a bedroom. Parts of a newspaper, or of several newspapers, lay in tents on a blonde pile carpet and a smell of stale tobacco hung in the air like shabby laundry. On a green vinyl Stratolounger a man lay as if in state, with his stockinged feet on the swing-out footrest and his head on the cushioned back. He was a blocky, fortyish six feet and two hundred pounds in a white shirt and dark trousers with gray in his short rumpled brown hair and looked like a truck driver, or what a truck driver used to look like before power steering. Between the first two fingers of his right hand resting on the chair arm a cigarette had burned down to the flesh and gone out.

For a second Doc thought he'd found his second dead body in twelve hours. Then something broke loose and a fierce racking snore made him jump. After that the noise became rhythmic. It remained loud.

A pony glass and a fifth of Ten High two-thirds empty stood on an end table next to the chair. Doc thought he knew something about Taber then, if this was Taber. It was a special kind of drunk that didn't wake up when a cigarette scorched the tender flesh between his fingers.

Doc didn't try to wake him. In a desk with a pullout leaf he found paper and pencils, wrote a note explaining that he was from Maynard Ance and that he was taking the car, signed it, and left it on the leaf, weighting it down with a dirty ashtray. Taber was still snoring when he went out.

A small paved parking lot for the tenants elled behind the building. Four cars were parked there early on a working afternoon and none of the plates matched the number on the key ring Ance had given him. Walking around the outside of the complex to see if there was more to the lot, he spotted a Coach-men motor home as long as a city block, parked next to the building with two wheels up on the berm that flanked the driveway. The numbers checked out. He hadn't paid much attention when Ance had referred to it as a bus.

The inside was a higher climb than Neal's pickup. Both front seats were mounted on swivels. Behind them was a dining nook, a stove and refrigerator, a couple of fold-down beds, plenty of drawers and cabinets, a closet of a bathroom with a stainless steel basin and a chemical toilet, and something next to it that had a drain in the floor and so might have been a tiny shower before someone had installed bars around it that opened on one side, turning it into a cell.

The tallest of the cabinets was locked. He unlocked it with a small brass key that didn't match the others on the ring. Two shotguns, one with a cut-down barrel, a .30-30 Winchester car-bine, assorted handguns, and a Thompson submachine gun glistened under a sheen of oil inside foam-lined compartments. Doc had never seen a Thompson outside of old-time gangster movies. The guards on the catwalks at Jackson had carried rifles. He removed the full-length shotgun, a twin of the Ithaca his father had given him on his fourteenth birthday to hunt rabbits, and inspected the breech. It was loaded. He wondered if that was legal in a motor vehicle in Michigan. He wondered if that mattered with the bail bondsman. Feeling suddenly that someone was watching him, Doc put back the weapon and closed and locked the cabinet. Just holding the gun was a viola-tion of parole.

The motor home's controls were the same as a car's. He started the motor and, proceeding slowly—he had never tried to ma-neuver anything so large—pulled forward into the parking lot and backed and turned the wheel and went forward again and backed again, angling the vehicle's nose out toward the road. He was straightening it for the last time, using both big side mirrors to avoid hitting parked cars, when a face came to the window on the driver's side eight feet above the ground. Startled, he stamped on the brake.

The face's mouth was moving, distorting it, but he recognized the man he had left snoring in apartment 612. He rolled down the window.

"—going, you son of a bitch?" The cab filled with the stench of half-digested whiskey.

Doc said, "Maynard Ance's office. I left you a note. Want to come along?"

"Give me them keys." An arm in a white sleeve flashed past Doc's face. Instinctively he slapped it up with his left hand. Taber almost fell off the step but caught hold of the mirror post and hauled himself back up. "Fucking prick cocksucking car thief bastard." Doc rolled up the window quickly.

An open palm struck the glass, flattening out like a ham and shooting hairline cracks in four directions. Doc's foot slipped off the brake pedal, and the Coachmen lurched forward. Taber, still off-balance from his own blow, lost his grip on the mirror post and dropped below the window.

Doc braked again a few feet ahead and opened the door to look back. Taber was sitting on the pavement. He hadn't put on shoes before leaving the apartment and the soles of his socks were filthy. After a few seconds he pushed himself to his knees, rested, and started to get up, cursing loudly the whole time. For a moment Doc was indecisive. Then he yanked the door shut and accelerated. His last view of Taber as he pulled out into Livernois was a flash in the right side mirror of a man running after him, mouth working silently.

Driving along, one hour into his new job, Doc wondered if five hundred a week was going to be enough.

Chapter 9

◆◇◆◇◆◇◆◇◆

Standing in the dirt lot behind the office, Maynard Ance scowled at the cracked window, crushed another half-smoked cigarette under his toe, and spat after it as if to make sure it was out. "Lucky I got glass insurance. What'd he use?"

"His hand." Doc played with the keys.

"Hope he didn't bust it like last time."

"He's done this before?"

"No. Tried to punch a hole in a block wall. Taber's one mean drunk. He isn't anybody's Mother Theresa sober, but when he gets a snootful he's worse'n the bleeding shits. You're lucky it was just the window." He brightened; or at least became less dour. "So how do you like the bus? I had it customized."

"I didn't think it came with the cell."

"Oh, that. That came later. I used handcuffs until this Robbery Armed we were bringing back from Chicago snapped the chain and brained Taber with a jack handle. Taber was driving and we ran up a bank and turned over. I busted my collarbone. The scroat was a pro wrestler, the Mad Sheik or the Hindu Warrior, some crap like that. About a thousand cops tied him

down in Evanston ten days later and I was out eighty grand plus
the hospital bill and five hundred bucks deductible on the bus.
That's when I ordered the bars. They're made of the same kind
of steel they use on the space shuttle. The torch hasn't been
made that can cut through them."

"Ever use them?"

"Wilson McCoy was going to be the first one, but Taber and
me missed connections. Well, that's why you're here. Let's go to
Redford." He walked around to the passenger's side.

Doc got in and started the engine. "Quite an arsenal back
there."

"Checked it out, did you?" The bail bondsman cut him a
quick glance from the other seat. "The tommy gun's just for
looks. You'd be surprised how fast they come around when you
slam one into the breech. One thing these scroats know is their
Eddie Robinson flicks."

They had been on the road several minutes when Ance spoke
again, his eyes on the scenery. "Don't worry, it's legal. A motor
home isn't a vehicle behind the front seats. We could be hauling
around a loaded howitzer."

"Which we're not."

"Too hard to get shells."

They arrived at the address in Redford a few minutes ahead of
the appointed time. There was just room enough to park the
Coachmen in the driveway of a red brick house with an attached
garage and a picture window in front. A small white-haired
woman in a gray wool dress and orange beads answered the door.

"Mrs. Wizotsky? I'm Maynard Ance. This is my associate
Kevin Miller." It was a manner Doc had not previously seen in
the bail bondsman.

She grasped her beads. The creases from her nose to the
corners of her mouth were as deep as gashes and there were

pink swellings like welts under her eyes. Doc noted with a start that she was at least ten years younger than his first estimate; fifty at most. She said something welcoming and got out of their way. The living room was small, neat, the furniture fairly new but unremarkable. It looked like a display in a discount furniture store. Family pictures crowded the mantel of the gas fireplace, the only personal items in the room.

"Thanks for coming. I'm Howard Wizotsky."

Ance and Doc shook hands in turn with the man who got up from the sofa when they came in. He looked younger than his wife but was probably about the same age, a solid man starting to go soft around the middle in a blue work shirt and slacks with shards of gray in his black crew cut. His hands were heavily calloused, with square, thick nails, and his face was burned reddish brown and grainy as if from long exposure to the sun or some other source of dry heat.

The men sat down. Mrs. Wizotsky turned off the TV set in the middle of a commercial for a trade school and went to the kitchen for coffee. "I hear you work at McClouth," Ance told her husband. "I poured steel a couple of summers when I was going to Wayne State."

"They laid me off last week. Business went all to hell when GM took the Saturn to Tennessee."

"Bastards. They'll have to do a lot more than dump Roger Smith to turn that board around. Where's your son?"

"Oakland County Jail. Bond's twenty-five thousand dollars. All he did was take a car out for a joy ride. I'm not defending it. I stole a pack of Juicy Fruit from a newsstand when I was eight; my old man broke his hand on my ass and I never took another thing without paying for it in my life. Maybe I should've broken mine on Roy a long time ago. But, Jesus, twenty-five grand! It's not like he took a shot at the mayor."

"Collect the bounty, huh?" Ance grinned.

Wizotsky made an exhausted smile.

"I called the Pontiac Police this afternoon," the bail bondsman said. "Your boy shoved a salesman out the passenger's door during a test drive. The salesman landed on his head. He's been unconscious for thirty-six hours. The county prosecutor is talking assault with intent to commit great bodily harm less than murder. Your son's nineteen. That's a mandatory one to five in this state."

"Fucking yuppie made more on his worst day than I did in a week frying in that plant. Roy's been working for minimum wage since he was sixteen."

"The man's a human being, Howard." Mrs. Wizotsky set a tray containing three steaming cups and a sugar bowl on the coffee table and took a seat on the edge of an upholstered chair with her hands in her lap.

"Fuck him. He's got insurance. I want my son out of that hole before he gets nailed by a bunch of fag bikers."

"There'd be a lot more chance of that if he were in the Wayne County lock-up. They get a better class of scroat in Oakland." Ance tore open three packets of Sweet'n Low and stirred the contents into his coffee. "How much can you raise?"

"I can scratch up ten percent. That's customary, right?"

"Do you have any collateral?"

"The house is paid for. I've got eight more payments to make on the car."

"Model and year?"

" 'Eighty-eight Celebrity. It's got less than forty thousand miles on it," Wizotsky added hopefully.

The bail bondsman pulled a face. "I'll need you to sign the deed to the house over to the M. W. Ance Bail Bond Service. We can do it in your lawyer's office if you want."

The couple exchanged a look. Wizotsky said, "We weren't planning on signing anything over. If we wanted to put up the house we'd've just mortgaged again."

"But you came to me instead, because you know a bank or a mortgage company can take up to six weeks processing your application and all that time your boy will be sitting in jail. I'm prepared to go straight to my bank from here, get a cashier's check in the amount of twenty-five thousand dollars, and head right up to Pontiac with it this afternoon, unless you want your lawyer present when the deed changes hands. Roy will be home in time for supper."

Another look. Mrs. Wizotsky said, "Would you excuse us?"

Ance said certainly and put his hands on the arms of his chair, but the couple got to their feet first and went through a swinging door into what Doc supposed was the kitchen. While they were gone the bail bondsman sat back, shook a cigarette out of his wrinkled pack, studied the brand name printed on one end, then put it back in the pack and returned the pack to his pocket. "Nice place," he said. "Clean."

Howard Wizotsky came back alone. The skin around his mouth was the color of a clenched knuckle. "I keep everything in a strongbox upstairs," he said without looking at anyone. He crossed the room without stopping and mounted the steps off the entryway. In the kitchen, pots and pans clattered. "My first wife was like that," Ance told Doc. "Bang, clang, kee-rash, every time we had a fight. After she left I had to throw out every pot I owned. None of 'em would hold water."

"What did you fight about?"

"Same thing I fought with all of them about. I never talked to them, they said."

Mrs. Wizotsky came out finally, looking unruffled, and freshened the cups from a glass carafe. Ance and she were agreeing that coffee never tasted as good as it used to from old-fashioned percolators when Wizotsky came down with the deed to the house and quarter-acre lot. Ance put on his glasses to read it, then produced a long stiff fold of paper from an inside pocket. Wizotsky squinted at it, patting his pockets, then accepted Ance's reading glasses and slid them down the sheet like a magnifying lens, his lips moving as he read. Finally he spread the paper on the coffee table and used a fountain pen Ance gave him to sign at the bottom. His wife was next, then the bail bondsman, and finally Doc added his signature as witness. Ance fished a notary seal out of a side pocket and clamped the lower left-hand corner. He pocketed the two documents and stood to shake Wizotsky's hand. "You'll get it back at the preliminary."

At the door he said, "Better put on a fresh pot, Mrs. W. That stuff they serve at County would strip varnish."

They got into the Coachmen. "Nice couple," Ance said. "Too bad they're going to lose the place."

"What makes you so sure they will?" Doc leaned out the open driver's door as he backed into the street.

"Desk sergeant I talked to in Pontiac said the kid was a stone puke. Everyone was a motherfucker, including his parents. He'll skip, Ozzie and Harriet will lose their house, and I'll be stuck with another fucking piece of Detroit real estate I couldn't give away if I threw in a case of Stroh's. Maybe the guy on TV is right. I should go in for the exciting life of a bartender."

"I didn't believe you when you told me how much you pay in taxes. I guess it's true."

"Sure it's true. I pay about the same amount to a firm of accountants to keep from paying twice as much to the government. Which come to think of it if I went ahead and paid, I wouldn't be spending it on accountants. I'm going to have to give this some thought. I may have stumbled on to something here." He rolled down his window, letting in a stream of sweet cool air; the day was getting nicer by the minute. "Listen, I'm not the guy in the stovepipe hat who ties the girl to the railroad tracks. That's the kid. I paid forty-eight thousand for this rig outright, but I had cosigners: Dr. Spock and Tim Leary and Asshole Abbie Hoffman and the Beatles and my late great client Wilson McCoy, may he rot in hell with his head up his sphincter. They built this generation from the ground up with that drug counterculture-civil disobedience horseshit. Without it I'd be down to my last sodomite."

"I heard on the radio Alcina Lilley may speak at McCoy's funeral."

"Maybe. The M-and-M's been trying to tie themselves to her halo for years, but she hasn't said boo to them yet. She'd rather go on as a symbol of the civil rights movement without ever doing anything but be Mahomet's widow. But I'm not knocking it, that's her angle. Mine's bankrolling worried parents of little assholes and shoveling the shit with a bucket-loader."

"The police think Starkweather Hall may show up."

"If they thought that they sure as hell wouldn't say it on the radio. Maybe they think he'll take the dare. That big an asshole he isn't. That power-to-the-brothers fist-in-the-air crap is an angle, too." Ance bared his teeth at the windshield. "I copped a peek once at his jacket down at the Federal Building. Drug Enforcement thinks he took his name from Charles Starkweather, that crazy-ass killer they fried in Nebraska thirty years back. It's the name of the chapel at Eastern Michigan University. He must've read it somewhere. He reads more than the entire population of Watts. And they're treating him like some little ghetto snotnose can't write his own name in the snow on Antietam."

"Sounds like he trusted you."

"Up to a point. I don't go get the pry bar out when they decide to clam. You never hear about a bail bondsman being found all trussed up like a pullet and shot full of holes in the trunk of his car."

"Where to now, your bank?"

"Nah, let the little scroat scratch his balls a couple more hours. We'll spring him just before feeding time. He'll stay home long enough to eat anyway. Let's go to the State Farm office, let the adjuster look at that window Taber busted." Ance fired a cigarette off the dashboard lighter and let the slipstream pull the smoke out the window.

Chapter 10

◆◇◆◇◆◇◆◇◆

Neal wasn't around when Doc walked home from the bus stop at sundown. Billie said he'd called to say he was staying late because John Deere had sold a customer a new backhoe without oil seals and the Baline brothers had promised the customer they'd have them installed before morning.

"How was your first day?" She was stirring onions and peppers in a skillet on the stove, taking grease spatters directly in her face without flinching. The spicy aroma pricked Doc's nostrils.

"Interesting."

"What did you do?"

I almost ran over a fellow employee and watched a couple trade their home for their delinquent son. "Not much. Just drove the boss around town."

"As long as it's honest."

"Not like baseball, huh?"

"We won't get into that." She took the skillet off the burner and scraped the contents into a steel bowl full of steaming ground beef.

"Where's Sean?"

"In the living room, where else?"

"We won't get into that either," he said.

She turned off the burner and used a big spoon to stir the mixture in the bowl. "Supper's in about a half-hour."

"What are you making?"

"Stuffed peppers. Hope you like them. Sean and I love them but we can only have them when Neal's not here. He says they're too spicy for his stomach."

He went into the living room. Sean was sitting cross-legged on the floor in front of the TV set, cold-cocking dragons and monsters by proxy. The green-and-blue glow of the screen was the room's only illumination. Doc switched on a lamp and sat in his brother's chair, an ivory-colored recliner worn shiny on the arms, and watched the boy, not the game. Sean was developing a roll of fat at the base of his neck.

The game ended. The boy climbed onto his knees, ejected the cassette from the machine on the bottom of the TV cart, and began sorting through the half-dozen or so cassettes he had stacked on the carpet. So far he hadn't acknowledged his uncle's presence.

"How's school?" Doc asked.

Great opening. Sean lifted and dropped his shoulders without looking up from the cassettes. "Okay."

"I guess they've got you using a computer by now."

He shrugged again and fed one of the tapes into the machine.

"Take gym?"

"Uh-huh." He picked up the controls.

Doc wondered if he should leave the chair and sit on the floor next to the boy. He decided he shouldn't. Some of his father's friends had done that with him, pretending to be interested in a child's affairs, when he was trying to watch Dick Van Dyke or something, and he had seriously resented the invasion. They had all smelled of Old Spice and Carling Black Label. "So do you, like, play games or exercise or what?"

No answer. A little figure with a bulbous head moved along the screen with the jerky gait of the stickmen Doc used to draw on the corners of the pages in arithmetic books and animate by flipping the pages rapidly. The object seemed to be to destroy as many obstacles as possible by butting them with the little guy's big head. Doc wondered if the game's designers had scored as poorly in arithmetic as he had.

"Ever play baseball?"

Sean took out a woolly mammoth. "Soccer," he said. "Some basketball."

"Which do you like better?"

"I don't play much. Mr. Anderson says the boys that don't want to can play shuffleboard."

Gym class hadn't changed. The kids on shuffleboard when Doc was in school mostly wore glasses with the waistband of their shorts hiked up under their armpits.

"When I was eight I played baseball all the time, couldn't keep me off the field. You play?"

"Sure I played."

"How many times?" He heard himself on that one, the badgering tone. Cool it.

Sean was quiet. The little guy on the screen was taking an awful walloping from a gorilla, or maybe it was a grizzly bear. He wasn't getting much help from the living room. When the boy spoke, Doc could detect the sudden inspiration. "Fifteen times."

It must have seemed like a lot to him. The actual number was probably closer to four or five. Neal's son would be that last boy left over after both captains had chosen up sides, the one the gym teacher had to assign to a team. Doc, who was usually the first pick when he wasn't captain himself, had always found it excruciating to watch. "Would you like to play with me Saturday?"

The gorilla/bear bit the dust finally. On its back it looked like Aurelio Lopez, old *Señor* Smoke. "You need more than two to play baseball."

"Your dad and I used to play all the time. We lived in the country, players were hard to find. You do a lot of running after the ball is all. It's good practice."

"The yard's too small. Mama says I shouldn't run into the street."

"There's a big empty lot up on the corner."

"Mama says stay away from there. People sell dope and stuff."

"It'll be broad daylight and I'll be with you. We'll clear it with her first, though. So do we have a date?"

The little guy brained his last adversary and captured the princess. The screen went black. "I guess so."

Billie came to the living room doorway, mopping her hands on her apron. "Kevin, I almost forgot. You had a phone call, a Mr. Battle. He wants you to call him back. The number's on the desk."

He got up and went to the shallow glazed rolltop where Neal paid his bills. The telephone was there and Doc dialed the number written on a pad with a cartoon of Ziggy in one corner wallowing in a one-size-fits-all sweatshirt. When Sergeant Battle answered Doc identified himself.

"Thanks for getting back to me. Can you come downtown tomorrow? I've got some more questions."

"I told you everything I know about McCoy."

"This isn't about McCoy. It'll only take a few minutes."

"I'm working tomorrow."

"You're in Dearborn, right?" Battle said. "It's right on my way to work. I could stop by before you leave."

He turned his back to the kitchen. Sean was sorting through his tapes. "No, I don't want to scare my brother and sister-in-law with a visit from the police. Can we meet somewhere?"

"Your call."

He thought about restaurants. He didn't know any except the Acropolis, and Greektown was out of his way. "I'll meet you on the corner. There's a vacant lot." He named the streets. "Seven o'clock okay? I have to leave for work at seven-thirty."

"You'll make it." The connection broke.

On TV, while the tape Sean had just played was rewinding, a news show—Doc thought it was *48 Hours*—was documenting the prostitution in a city that looked like Detroit but could have been any one of a dozen population centers currently going to hell: The camera, mounted on a truck or something, cruised down a broad avenue lined with women, mostly black, in halter tops and leather jackets and short skirts or skintight Day-Glo pants and spike heels watching the traffic go by. Some of them stood on the edge of the curb and leaned down to speak through open windows to drivers stopped at red lights. Doc still had an erection ten minutes later when Billie announced supper. He approached the table carrying in front of him the copy of the *Detroit News* he'd been reading in Neal's chair.

That erection had been coming since he'd read the WE EMPLOY ONLY AMERICAN MASSEUSES sign on the health spa that shared Maynard Ance's building. It didn't go away until he'd finished one stuffed pepper and started on a second. If he didn't do something about it soon . . .

"Split open," Billie said.

Doc looked up from his plate. She was dissecting her meal with her fork. The expression on her worn face was clinical. "Sorry?"

"I let the peppers boil too long. They get soft and split open when you try to stuff them."

"They're delicious." The bite he took then was the first he'd actually tasted. He was getting used to his sister-in-law's cooking, so much more pungent than what he'd been eating for seven years. Nevertheless he was losing weight, due to the nightly walks and his own metabolism. In another week he'd be his lanky self again. "Is the city going to do anything with that property on the corner?"

"Those empty lots? I don't think that's the city's responsibility. They were part of a federal housing project that never got off the ground. Neal says if John Deere was run like the government, farmers would still be plowing with horses."

"I thought Sean and I would go there Saturday. Play a little ball."

The skin around her nostrils whitened. "Did you talk to Neal about it?"

"No, I just got the idea tonight. Sean wants to do it. Right, Sean?"

The boy poked at a lump of ground beef. "Yeah."

Doc felt a flash of self-loathing; he hated bullying a child psychologically. But he pressed on. "I'll be with him the whole time, if that's what's bothering you."

"I think you should discuss it with Neal."

"You know he'll say yes."

She filled her coffee cup from the pot—Ance would have appreciated the old-fashioned percolator—and reached across to top off Doc's. "Those lots are a mess. You'll be the whole weekend just cleaning up."

"Billie, we're just going to knock the ball around a little. I'm not talking about spreading lime and building a grandstand." She didn't answer. "I'll stop by tomorrow on my way to the bus stop and take a look. A little cleanup wouldn't hurt us if it's not too bad."

"What was that phone call about? It sounded kind of official."

He considered not letting her change the subject, but Sean was staring at his plate, his face darkening. Doc sat back with his coffee. "Just something at work. Nothing to worry about."

"I do worry, Kevin. You know why." She looked at him for the first time since before she had commented on the peppers.

He met her gaze. "Everything's fine. Really."

After a moment she nodded and stood up to get dessert.

Doc had been too different from the rest of his family too long not to be able to look someone in the eye and lie.

He hoped his parole officer hadn't changed his mind.

Lying on his back in Sean's bed hours later, watching the ceiling grow lighter, he told himself again that if Kubitsky had doubts about the arrangement after rethinking Maynard Ance's relationship with Wilson McCoy, he wouldn't send Sergeant Battle to swing the axe. It was just one of those fears that crept in by darkness and slithered away with the dawn. It was a hefty slice of time out of his parole to spend afraid, and it was the one thing he hadn't foreseen all those nights when he lay like this in the constant dusk of his cell thinking about freedom. That was the thing prison taught you: Whatever they gave you they could take away, and afterward it would be worse than if they had never given you anything at all. And he thought he understood then what it was that made ex-convicts who had served half their life want to go back. It wasn't so much that they couldn't adjust to the world outside as it was not being able to stand the suspense. And just understanding that scared him as much as the other.

He had heard Neal's pickup pulling into the garage about three, then his keys hitting the kitchen table and the stairs moaning under his big feet. Later he had heard, very faintly, the metronomic stirring of bedsprings and a stifled cry from Billie, and that brought him back to the problem he'd forgotten about since supper. He had to find his own place.

He checked the alarm clock for the last time at twenty to six and got up and showered and shaved and dressed and went downstairs and made a fresh pot of coffee. At six-thirty, hearing someone stirring upstairs—it would be Billie, women in every society got up ahead of the men—he wrote a note on the kitchen pad and went out to walk around before meeting Battle.

It was a brittle early spring morning. The air was sharp and ice skinned the tops of puddles left over from the last rain. Birds strung their cold square-edged notes from branch to branch, clear enough to see. Doc could separate the songs but couldn't identify the singers; it had always been a source of embarrassment to him, a country boy, that he didn't know one bird from another and could barely tell a maple by its leaves or timothy from Queen Anne's lace. Spring in all its incarnations was just a stage set for baseball.

After circling the block he still got to the open area early. The quack grass was ankle-high and the frost, thawing, soaked through his shoes when he walked around in it, kicking up no-deposit beer cans from out of state and empty Sheik boxes and plastic six-pack carriers. The last he picked up automatically and pulled apart loop by loop because he had heard somewhere that animals sometimes got their heads caught in the loops and strangled to death. A huge ring-necked pheasant took off in a burst of copper and brilliant green almost from under his foot with a noise like an outboard motor starting, actually stopping his heart for a beat. It swung into the sun lodged red as an open sore between buildings on the east side of the street and glided down into the tall grass of the adjoining lot. It was one bird Doc knew from back home and he was amazed to find it roosting here in the heart of an industrial suburb. It was as if nature had grown impatient with the whole Detroit sprawl and was reclaiming it parcel by parcel.

Doc went to the sidewalk to let his shoes dry while he waited.

He'd been there fifteen minutes and had seen perhaps as many cars when he found himself looking at Battle, staring back at him through the window on the passenger's side of a gray four-door Chrysler LeBaron. Someday Doc would have to find out how the police managed to come up on you all at once that way in a couple of tons of automobile. The sergeant said something to the man at the wheel and got out and slammed the door behind him. He had on a charcoal double-breasted car coat on top of a gray suit and gleaming black latex boots stretched over his street shoes. The other man stayed in the car.

"Thanks for the time. How's the job?"

"Let you know when I get settled in." Doc gave him back his hand.

"I know what you mean. I never had one I wasn't ready to quit after the first day." He looked around. "I did an exchange bit with the New York Police Department last year. You don't see unused real estate like this there. That son of a bitch in the mayor's office here lets the neighborhoods go to hell while he throws up ugly buildings on the river to go bankrupt because nobody with a brain wants to run his business in Detroit."

"This is Dearborn."

"Dearborn, Hamtramck, Highland Park, downriver, it's all Detroit. Except Grosse Pointe and Birmingham. They bottle their own air."

"I've heard more bellyaching since I got out than all the time I was inside. Why is it if everybody I meet thinks Young is a son of a bitch he keeps getting elected?"

"I figured it out. It's like Barbara Cartland. The lady romance writer? My wife says she never reads her books, all her friends say they wouldn't touch 'em, but she's like one of the five bestselling writers in the world. Somebody's got to be lying, right? And somebody's got to be voting for the old turd." The two-way radio in the car spat and crackled. Battle turned his head an inch that way, listened, then turned back. Doc couldn't hear anything intelligible through the closed window. "I wanted to talk to you without Ance around. This Starkweather Hall thing is steaming up the windows down at Thirteen Hundred. It was starting to die down when McCoy suicided; now the press won't let go of it. My wife says my ass doesn't look nearly as good to her with Chief Hart's teeth marks in it."

"Why talk to me? I barely heard of Hall."

"The city has upped its reward offer for information leading to Hall's arrest and conviction ten thousand. We're targeting the leaders this season; last time it was the mules, but the junior highs turn them out like GM makes cars. With what the various parents' anti-drug groups are putting up, that brings the ante to around a hundred thousand. That's well inside Maynard Ance's loop."

"What's that mean?"

The sergeant looked out across the weedy lot. His breath made a gray jet. "Everybody in the department wanted a piece of this one when it went down, on account of the chances for promotion. Not me. If I miss I'm back in General Service, counting how many states some Circuit Court judge's brand new Jag was parted out over after it went missing. If I hit the bull's-eye I'm just another Tom fetching back one of my own for the Man and wagging my tail when he scratches behind my ears. I kept my head low, but someone in Personnel pulled my jacket, found out my Uncle Anthony was a Mahomet bodyguard after he left wrestling, and before you can say 'Officer down' I'm assigned to the M-and-M detail. Special knowledge, they called it. Like I wasn't chin-deep in textbooks sweating out the draft all the time the old man was tasting Mahomet's soup for arsenic. I almost quit." He looked at Doc. "Is Ance harboring Hall?"

"What?"

"It's a sweet deal, sitting on him till the reward jacks up high enough, then turning him in and splitting it, half to go for Hall's defense."

"Sounds thick," Doc said.

"I'd haul him in, only that'd be a day lost interrogating a brick when I could be shaking out buildings looking for Hall. Taber's an easy crack but the last time a cop got an alky to talk by tanking him forty-eight hours and waving a jug under his nose the judge flushed the whole chain of evidence on account of duress."

"But I'm a fresh parolee, and you don't even have to tell me what would happen if I refused to cooperate in a criminal investigation."

"It doesn't have to be like that. I could talk to Kubitski, get him to cut you some slack. You could take a trip out of the state or have a drink in a bar frequented by known felons."

"I like it here. And the only felons I know are locked up."

"Don't make me use muscle, Doc. My kid would kill me."

Doc picked up a twig that had fallen off a dead elm on the corner and used it to scrape wet grass off his left heel. It was like knocking dirt from his cleats while he thought about the next pitch. "I haven't been working for him that long. I think I could be working for him ten years before he'd tell me anything like that."

"You've got eyes. You've got ears. I'm just sweeping out all the closets. I don't think he's dumb enough to risk a harboring rap,

89

but his conscience sure as hell wouldn't stop him. Hall might try to contact him on his own. As far as he trusts anyone white he trusts Ance." He leaned back against the Chrysler. "My spidey sense tells me you've already got a favor lined up."

Doc threw away the twig, rotated his working shoulder. "What are you and your kid doing Saturday?"

Chapter 11

❖❖❖❖❖❖❖❖

Russell Taber sober was a different man.

Seated at Maynard Ance's desk reading the *Free Press* sports section, he swiveled a quarter turn when Doc came in and raised himself an inch off the chair to offer his hand. Doc hesitated, then grasped it. It was wrapped in white gauze secured with adhesive tape. "I had a hundred bucks down on your first game with Texas," Taber said. "You caught a line drive without stepping off the mound for the last out."

"Glad I could help."

"Help my ass. I bet on the Rangers. Who thought Detroit had anything in the bullpen?"

"I was on the d.l. with a sprained wrist for the next three games. How's your hand?"

He looked at it. "Couple of cuts. No stitches. I don't remember much about yesterday. Guess I slipped out of Park. You should've told me who you was."

"Would it have made any difference?"

"Nah. Maynard should've warned you about me, about liquor and me. I'd quit, but what'd I do for an excuse then?" His truck driver's face squinched up, as if he were staring into the sun. "How about you, still on dope?"

"I never was. Where's Ance?"

"I took him over to the garage and dropped him off with the Coachmen. While they're fixing the window he wants to go over a couple new features he wants them to put in. Gun portholes maybe. Said he'd catch a cab back here." Taber was still squinting. "What're you, six-four?"

"Six-five."

"I'm six-two. Maynard likes to surround himself with telephone poles. Can you do anything besides pitch and steal motor homes?"

"I'm a fast learner." Doc plucked a clean mug off a tree next to the complex coffee maker and filled it from the carafe. "Are we supposed to do anything while we're waiting for him?"

"Waiting, that's the job. I got plenty of experience. Twenty years sitting in a blue-and-white waiting for some puke to come along with a pinch bar and pry open some alley door. I got piles old enough to run for president."

"I heard they let you go."

Taber moved his shoulders. "This Willie took a run at me when I walked in on him during a stickup at a stop-and-rob on Chene. Shooting team never found a gun."

"Willie?"

"Them people got no imagination when it comes to naming their kids."

He went back to the sports section. Doc drank coffee and looked out at the dirt parking lot. The sun was well up now, and little curls of steam were coming off the patches of frost. A Volare hatchback with a wrinkled right fender pulled up next to the health spa canopy and a slim blonde got out, tugged down her short leather jacket, and went up the brief flight of steps carrying a gym bag. Her hair was in a ponytail and she had long legs in tight white jeans and knee-length suede boots with fringes. She unlocked the door with a key and went inside.

The coffee had a metallic taste. Doc set down the mug. "Okay if I step out for a half-hour?"

"Suit yourself. I'm just here to watch the phone." Taber was doing arithmetic with a pencil in the margin by the box scores.

The sign on the door under the canopy read OPEN 10 A.M. TIL MIDNIGHT. It was a few minutes after eight. Doc pushed the button with his thumb. A bell jangled deep inside. After a moment a woman's voice said, "Come back later."

He rang again.

Footsteps scuffed carpeting. The opaque curtain over the pane of glass in the door parted an inch, then closed. The door opened against a chain. He saw part of a face.

"We don't open for two more hours."

"I may be busy then. I've got cash," he added.

The door closed. He thought it was a rejection. Then the chain rattled and the door swung wide. He stepped inside around the blonde. She shut the door and replaced the chain. She was a foot and a half shorter than Doc, which surprised him; her proportions were those of a much taller girl. She had removed the leather jacket and was wearing one of those red printed handkerchief blouses tied under her breasts. She had an athletic build, but her face was pocked all over like a golf ball under heavy makeup. He couldn't guess her age.

"Massage is thirty dollars."

He produced his wallet and gave her a twenty and a ten. In the narrow, yellow-painted entryway she leaned through a square hole cut in the wall that reminded him of the registration desk at the Independence Motel. A buzzer sounded and she opened a door next to the hole and held it for him. "The sauna's not ready yet," she said. "Put your valuables in this and keep it with you." She handed him a flat blue canvas bag the size of a pocketbook with a key attached to the zipper, then took a thick white folded towel off a shelf and gave him that. "The showers are in there. When you're through, wrap yourself in the towel and come back here."

"I took a shower this morning."

"It's required."

He went through the open door she'd indicated into a room with a low Formica-topped bench and metal lockers against one wall. One of the lockers had a combination lock; the others were just latched. When he unzipped the bag to put his wallet and watch inside he found a small padlock. After determining that the key fit the lock, he stripped and put his clothes in the locker and secured the door with the padlock and stepped into the cavernous shower room to the left. As he lathered himself with liquid soap from the dispenser he had an idea the blonde was watching him somehow. The thought of it gave him an erection. He hoped he'd be able to get through the massage.

He rinsed himself, toweled off, wrapped the towel around his waist kilt-fashion, and found her waiting for him when he went back out. He was sure then that she'd been watching him. She led him to a curtained opening, held the curtain aside for him, and followed him through. They were in a small square room with a padded table and a bench with plastic bottles on it. Pink recessed lighting illuminated the mirrors on the walls and ceiling. "Hand me the towel."

When he complied, standing before her naked, she gave him a quick appraising glance that told him nothing. "This is how it works," she said. "I make my living entirely off tips. A plain massage will cost you another thirty dollars."

"I only have twenty."

"Visa and MasterCard are okay."

"I don't have a credit card. I guess you'll have to give me back my money."

"I can't. I already rang it up."

"Well, I didn't pay thirty bucks just to take a shower."

She chewed the inside of a cheek. "Okay, twenty. But don't tell anyone, okay?"

"Who'd I tell?"

He unzipped the bag and gave her a bill. She directed him to lie facedown on the table and went out through the curtain. When she returned a few minutes later, he saw in the mirrors that she had changed out of the blouse, jeans, and boots into a black teddy and high-heeled slippers. She had high pointed breasts and muscles in her buttocks like a dancer's.

She spread a light scented oil over his back, buttocks, and legs and worked it into his skin starting with the shoulders. Her hands were strong and she knew something about massage; his muscles responded as they had in the hands of experts when he was with the Tigers. She cracked his fingers and toes and smacked the soles of his feet and braced a hand between his shoulder blades while she bent back each of his legs in turn with the other, stretching him like a bow. Finally she applied powder, spread his legs, and grazed her palms over him with light, feathery strokes, paying special attention to the area between his thighs. He thought his erection would push him off the table.

"Turn over."

When it was finished—three minutes was as long as he could hold out—she handed him a clean towel and he showered again and dressed. Outside the locker room she met him in a yellow kimono, took the towel and the zipper bag, now empty, and escorted him to the door with her hand in the small of his back.

"Full price next time," she said. "And come back during business hours."

"What's your name?"

"Lynda, with a *y*. What's yours?"

"Keith."

"Come back enough times and we'll call each other by our *real* names." Just before she closed the outer door between them she smiled. He decided the makeup was misleading; she was younger than she looked.

At the bottom of the steps he almost ran into Maynard Ance getting out of a yellow cab. The bail bondsman had traded his overcoat for something lighter, but the industrial-strength suit beneath it was the same one he always wore, unless he had a closet full of them.

"Get a good workout?" he asked Doc.

Doc felt too good to be defensive. "Did I break a rule?"

"Not if you washed up afterwards."

"How's the Coachmen?"

"Third in line at the garage. Taber in the office?"

"He was when I left."

"Get in the cab. I'll bring him out."

"Where we going?"

"Hertz. I just called the Wizotskys. That little scroat Roy skipped last night with their car. He didn't even stay the night."

Doc sat in the backseat and contemplated an angry boil behind the driver's right ear. He felt mellow after the massage, as if he had had two beers on top of an hour in the whirlpool. When Ance and Taber came out of the building they were carrying cased shotguns. The driver got out and opened the trunk for them. Taber climbed in the passenger's seat in front and Ance got in beside Doc.

"How many guns do you own?" Doc asked.

"Not that many. We took these out before we dropped off the bus. Those mechanics are all thieves."

At the Hertz office downtown they waited thirty minutes while a Cadillac was being gassed and prepped. Taber stayed outside with the shotguns to avoid panicking a clerk. Sitting in the office, Ance said, "I always ask for Fleetwoods after the time Budget stuck me with a Toyota. Fucking Japmobiles are too small even for a sawed-off. Besides, I buy American."

It was a midnight blue V-8, not as big as they used to make them but bigger than anything else on the road. There was room enough in the trunk for everything in Ance's arsenal and a Honda Civic, and the bail bondsman could have stretched out on the fabric-covered backseat if he wanted to. Doc drove, with Taber beside him. The suspension was slushy and there was too much play in the steering wheel, but Doc liked the instant response he got from the big engine when he pressed the pedal. "Where to?"

"Ypsilanti. Wizotsky says Roy has friends there he hangs out with sometimes."

"Okay if I play the radio?"

"You can piss out the fucking window as long as you keep your eyes on the road."

He went past reggae and country and about eighty rap stations before stopping at a call-in talk show, a phenomenon he had gotten hooked on in prison; most of the people he heard there made him feel better about his own situation.

". . . twelve-seventy, all-talk. You're on the air."

"Hello?"

"Hello, you're on the air."

"Am I on?"

"Sure, go ahead." The announcer sounded patient.

"Okay, well, um, I think the City of Detroit should erect a

statue of Wilson McCoy in Hart Plaza. That's one brother who stuck to his guns, you know?"

"The ones he didn't sell to support his habit," Ance said.

The announcer said, "I get where you're coming from, and a lot of people would agree with you. But probably a lot more would say that McCoy represents a negative image of African-Americans."

"Just the white mother—" The radio crackled and he was off the air.

"WXYT Twelve-seventy talk radio, what's on your mind?" the announcer asked the next caller.

"Hey, that guy was full of it. The only thing McCoy done right his whole life was kill himself. Them Mountains of Mohammed—"

"I think you mean the Marshals of Mahomet."

"Huh?"

"Go on."

"The FBI should of burned them M-and-M's out a long time ago just like they done the Panthers. I had it with all this sixties crap. To hear some of these coloreds you'd think you was in some kind of time warp. They overcame, already. What do they want now?"

"For one thing, they don't want to be called coloreds." Crackle. "WXYT One Two Seven Oh, talk to me."

Taber reached over and turned off the radio. "Gab, gab, gab. Some people got nothing better to do than listen to their gums flap."

"Sounds like the M-and-M's are lining up another god," Doc said. "In case something goes wrong with Mahomet."

"Nothing to us, till they have to make bail." In the rearview mirror Ance ran a cigarette under his nose and sniffed both ends. That was starting to get on Doc's nerves.

Ypsilanti looked like pictures Doc had seen of Detroit in the fifties: elegant old Victorian and Queen Anne houses advertising rooms for rent and blocks of horizontal storefronts and neighborhoods showing signs of early decay. A phallic water tower built of brick dominated the skyline. At the bail bondsman's direction Doc took a succession of side streets and boated into a curb in front of a blue frame house with gables and turrets and shingles shaped like fish scales. Two of the windows had VACANCY signs in them.

They got out. Ance opened the trunk, unzipped the shotgun cases, and laid them side by side on the backseat with the butts sticking out. "No sense stirring something up if we don't need them," he told Doc. "You see one or both of us come running out of the house, have 'em ready to hand out when we get to the car." He and Taber went up the flagstone walk to the porch. They wiped their feet, opened the screen door against the complaint of a spring, and let it clap shut behind them.

Doc was starting to think about lunch when he heard the first shot. A windowpane in one of the turrets tipped out in two big pieces and fell a long way to the grass.

Chapter 12

◆◆◆◆◆◆◆◆

Doc stared at the two halves of glass shining on the lawn. The second shot got his reflexes going.

He circled to the other side of the Cadillac, placing the car between himself and the house, opened the rear door on that side, and slid out one of the shotguns barrel first. As he was shucking the case from the Ithaca the screen door popped open. An older reflex, going back to hunting trips with his father and brother, kicked in and he pumped a round into the barrel.

The man running down the walk was several inches shorter than Taber and as broad as Ance, but softer, encased in a jacket of flesh that jiggled under his sweatshirt as he ran. He had a round red face and an adolescent beard like spun sugar. Doc slung the shotgun across the roof of the Cadillac, his finger wrapping the trigger. "Stop!"

His own shout rang in his head louder than the two shots. The running man braked and had to catch himself to avoid falling on his face. He gaped uncomprehendingly at the shotgun and the man crouched behind it. Doc doubted he was twenty.

A moment crawled past. Doc wasn't sure what to do next.

The screen door opened again and Taber came barreling out. Something in his right hand caught the light. When he saw what was going on his pace slowed to a trot. He caught the fat youth by the neck of his sweatshirt and shoved him forward stumbling. The young man clutched at the roof of the Cadillac with both hands and Taber kicked his legs apart and patted him down. Doc lowered the shotgun and came around to their side.

"What happened?"

"Puke took a shot at us. He was lucky to hit the window with this piece of shit." He held up a dull black revolver with plastic side grips with a wood grain printed on them.

"I heard two shots."

"He did that when I took it away from him. That time he hit the floor."

Ance came down the steps from the porch. His face was a deep blood color and he was breathing hard. "I'm getting too old for this shit. Two years ago he'd've never gotten out of the room."

"Kid's faster than he looks," Taber said. "Doc threw down on him."

The bail bondsman nodded and held out a hand. Doc gave him the Ithaca. Reaction was setting in; he put his hands in his pockets to stop them from shaking. "This is Roy Wizotsky?"

"This is Roy Wizotsky's friend Darryl Stemp. Darryl's got a drug problem, don't you, Darryl? Can't get enough of 'em, that's Darryl's problem. While Darryl was busy showing us his marksmanship, his friend Roy rabbited out the back door and over the fence." Ance rammed the butt of the shotgun into the fat youth's right kidney. He mewed and his knees buckled but he caught himself on the Cadillac's door handle. Ance stepped around him and slammed the butt against that hand. Stemp gasped and knelt on the curb, hugging the hand to his body. Ance braced himself against the car with one hand and kicked Stemp's knees out from under him. His chin hit the door. He rolled over onto his side and curled up. His sweatshirt rode up his back, exposing eight inches of pink skin and the cleft of his buttocks.

"Where'd he run to?" Ance was puffing now.

Stemp mewed. A car turned into the street, slowed as it neared the Cadillac, then sped up. The driver was an old man wearing a wide-brimmed hat. Doc always wondered where they shopped. Ance caught Taber's eye and held out the shotgun. Taber worked the slide out of habit, ejecting the shell Doc had pumped in and racking in the next, and placed the muzzle against Stemp's neck under his left ear.

"Where'd he run to?" Ance repeated. He was leaning back against the car, mopping his face with a white lawn handkerchief.

"I don't know." It was muffled.

Taber twisted the shotgun. The skin wrinkled below Stemp's ear.

Ance said, "That's too quick. Let's take him back and lock him up for a while. In a few hours when those big purple maggots start crawling all over him he'll forget all about what a good friend Roy is."

"If he don't die first like the last one," Taber said.

"That one had a bum ticker. Darryl's is all built up from carrying around all that blubber."

Stemp said something. It sounded like "salt cellar."

"Speak up, Darryl. Don't mumble." Ance booted him lightly in the kidney he'd bruised earlier.

"Phelps-Sellers."

"What the hell's that?"

"Dormitory at Eastern Michigan," Taber said. "I was a campus cop there after I left Detroit. Not good enough, Darryl. What room?"

Stemp spoke again. Accordion?

"Custodian," said Taber. "There's a little apartment off the storage room in the basement of Phelps."

"What's Roy's connection?" Ance asked.

This time Doc heard the word "friend."

"This scroat's more popular than Trojans," Ance said. "Scrape him up and let's get going."

Doc said, "Are we turning him in?"

"And dick around half a day waiting for some Polack sergeant to take down my complaint? We'll cut him loose soon as we get Roy. It's either that or bust all his fingers so he can't use a telephone. Lessons are lost on guys like Darryl." The bail bondsman took the other shotgun off the seat and Taber lifted Stemp by the waistband of his jeans and dumped him into the back. Stemp had bitten his lip when his chin hit the door of the Cadillac; a bright thread of blood ran down onto his shirt. Taber produced a pair of handcuffs and manacled the youth to the door handle.

Ance cased the shotguns, locked them in the trunk, and got in beside Stemp. "Let's see that piece." Taber passed the black revolver over the front seat. Doc started the motor and waited for orders. In the mirror Ance swung out the cylinder and peered down the barrel. "You got an eye for the exotic, Darryl. You don't often see a gun from Bangladesh. Where'd you get it?"

"Guy in Pfleen." The split lip was getting in the way.

"Shit, nobody in Saline knows nothing about guns," Taber said. "Why didn't you go down to Toledo?"

Stemp said nothing.

Ance said, "You've been out of it too long, Taber. These days people from Toledo come up to Detroit looking for ordnance. They wouldn't make the trip for a piece of shit like this, though. Ever shoot it before today?"

Doc didn't hear the answer. Taber told him to drive to the end of the block and turn right. Doc pulled out into the street.

". . . need is an old tire and a long piece of twine," Ance was saying. "Prop the gun up on the tire and pull the trigger with the twine tied to it. That way if it blows up all you lose is the tire."

Taber said, "Better yet, let Roy shoot it. That way you save the tire."

"Pfuck you."

The directive ended in a loud grunt. Doc figured Ance had used his elbow. But when the bail bondsman spoke again his tone was friendly.

"Roy's no friend of yours, Darryl. Friends don't jump the fence while their friends are getting the crap beat out of them. A scroat like you needs a stand-up guy. 'Course, what'd a stand-up guy be doing with a scroat like you?"

With Taber directing, Doc drove across a hilly campus studded with old brick Gothic buildings with vines crawling up the walls and space-age structures that looked as if they were preparing to blast off from their foundations. Students carrying books walked along the sidewalks and sat on the grass reading and crossed the streets without looking. It seemed to Doc that the college crowd was getting younger.

"Pull in by that dumpster."

The dumpster took up part of the parking area in front of a pair of dormitories shaped like cracker boxes laid end to end; the university architecture must have been designed by a committee that never met.

"Keep an eye on Darryl," Ance told Doc. He climbed out and dropped the revolver in his overcoat pocket.

Taber, getting out, said, "You're not figuring on using that thing?"

"Only if Roy makes me. Thanks to Darryl we know it won't blow up and that it's accurate to within twelve feet at close range. Just make sure you're standing behind me when it goes off."

"I don't even know where the hell Bangladesh is." Taber slammed the door on the rest of their conversation. They entered the building.

Doc adjusted the rearview mirror to take in Stemp, slumped against the door he was cuffed to and dabbing at his bleeding lip with the front of his sweatshirt. "Are you a student here?" Doc asked.

"Go pfuck yourselpf."

He gave up and switched on the radio. They were still discussing Wilson McCoy and the Marshals of Mahomet. McCoy's death seemed to have triggered new interest in the civil rights movement of the sixties. One caller was a former Black Panther who had served five years in Marquette Branch Penitentiary for arson in the 1967 riots, where he had become a born-again Christian: He said he was less interested in McCoy's postmortem reputation than he was in the condition of his immortal soul after having renounced Jesus. When the caller began reading from Matthew, the announcer cut him off.

McCoy's funeral was announced for the following night at a private establishment in Taylor. The press was invited.

Ance and Taber returned sooner than expected. Walking stiffly between them was a young man of about Darryl Stemp's age wearing corduroy slacks and a red Windbreaker over a black T-shirt with writing on the front. He wore his black hair in a buzz cut and the general squarish shape of his face reminded

Doc of Howard Wizotsky. Doc got out and walked around the car and held open the door opposite Stemp. Taber, who had been gripping the youth's right arm behind his back, reversed the twist with an expert maneuver, shoved his head down with one hand, and pushed him into the backseat. Ance meanwhile opened the door on the other side, pulling Stemp halfway out of the car, freed him from the cuffs, and tossed them across the roof of the Cadillac to Taber, who manacled the fresh captive to the other door. The bail bondsman pulled Stemp out the rest of the way and took his place.

Darryl stood pinching his lip on the pavement. "Don't I get a ride back?"

"This ain't the People Mover." Ance slammed the door.

"Hey, what about my gun?"

Taber and Doc sat in front. Taber made a flicking motion with his hand. Doc hit the ignition and pulled out of the space. Darryl still hadn't moved when he lost sight of him behind the hill.

"Did he give you any trouble?" asked Doc.

"No, Roy ain't such hot shit when he's facing two and he doesn't have any stupid friends handy," Ance said. "He was just laying there on the janitor's sofa jerking off to M. C. Hammer when we walked in on him."

Roy said, "That's a fucking lie."

"Well, one of them dickhead rappers, anyway. I'd rather listen to my ulcers bleeding."

"I didn't do nothing. I got a right to hitch a ride out of town when I want."

"*I* own all your rights, Junior. Bought 'em for twenty-five thou."

Taber said, "What do we do with him? His hearing's three weeks off. If we take him back to his folks he'll just kick over the traces again."

"We're going to tank him."

"What for?" Roy was shouting now.

"Carrying a concealed weapon; unregistered handgun at that. You're under citizen's arrest."

In the mirror, Roy goggled at the revolver. "That ain't mine!"

"Take Washtenaw down to Hogback," Ance told Doc. "That's the Washtenaw County Sheriff's Department. They'll notify Wayne County. The judge will revoke bail, I'll get my money back, and the Wizotskys get to keep their house. At least until the next time Roy fucks up."

Doc joined the traffic on the broad avenue. Several blocks later, when Roy had quieted down, Ance said: "Some days I'm nuts about this business. Can't get enough of it."

Chapter 13

❖❖❖❖❖❖❖❖

The next day was Friday. Morning spread buttery sunlight over the dry pavement. Convertibles Doc passed in the Cadillac had their tops down.

Ance, getting into the car in front of his house, said, "What'd your brother say when you tooled in last night with the Caddy?"

"He said if I was running girls I'd get in trouble with the coloreds. I took everybody out to the Big Boy for dinner. I hope that was okay."

"Sure. I generally try to run rentals into the ground before I give 'em back. I won't be needing you today," he said. "I'm in all day. My accountant's coming in and we're going to see if he can keep me out of jail for another year."

"I guess you'll need the car." After the massage parlor Doc didn't have enough cash left for bus fare.

"No, just bring it back when you're through with it." Ance pulled out his wallet, took some bills out of it without counting them, and placed them on the dash in front of Doc. "Friday's payday. I don't want you bringing it back with the tank empty."

Doc took one hand off the wheel to riffle the bills with his thumb. There were three hundreds, two fifties, and five twenties. He wondered how Ance had managed the exact amount. "No withholding?"

"No. Shit, no. You're a contract worker. Figure your own taxes."

After Doc let him out behind the office he picked up the bills and looked at the WE EMPLOY ONLY AMERICAN MASSEUSES sign. Then he pocketed the cash and drove out of the dirt lot. A man could spend his whole paycheck in the building where he earned it.

A few blocks from the office he pulled into a metered space, bought a *Free Press* from a stand, and had a second cup of coffee at a counter manned by an Arab while he read through the classifieds. He borrowed a pencil from the Arab and circled five notices under APARTMENTS FOR RENT.

He drove past the first address without stopping. It belonged to one of a row of buildings on Antietam with plywood in most of the windows and three young black men in torn jeans, bomber jackets, and hundred-dollar Nikes leaning against a burnt-out car parked in front.

The second address, on West Grand River, looked more promising. It was a brick house with green shutters and a shady front porch built sometime in the twenties and well-maintained. But the owner, a tall handsome black woman of about the same vintage, told him she was looking for a married couple to occupy the two rooms on the second floor; she had had bad luck renting them to single men in the past. She took his name and number and said she'd be in touch if she changed her mind. The third place was in a warehouse that had been converted into lofts on Highland Park, light and roomy and the rent was reasonable, but it was right next to a mosque with a loudspeaker chanting Moslem prayers at all hours. Doc didn't leave his name.

Two of the three others he checked out were more than

satisfactory, but the owners wanted first and last months' rent in advance with a security deposit, which came to more than he had on him. He decided he'd have to postpone serious hunting until next payday, and since the last place was only a dozen blocks from Greektown he went to the Acropolis for lunch. Maynard Ance was in a booth with a man Doc didn't know. The bail bondsman spotted Doc and motioned him over.

"Doc Miller, Jeff Dolan," Ance said. "We're on a break."

Dolan had the grip—and the build—of a center for the Lions. He had red hair and bright blue eyes in a big face full of freckles. "You don't look like an accountant," Doc said.

"I get that a lot." Dolan's voice was high and soft for a man his size.

"Dolan used to make the figures jump through hoops for Patsy Orr. You wouldn't remember his grandfather, Big Jim Dolan, the Irish Pope; he died when I was a little kid. He told the fat cats who to elect for mayor."

"I've heard of Patsy Orr."

"I quit just in time," Dolan said. "Six months later Wilson McCoy dusted him and his new accountant in an elevator in the Penobscot Building."

"Congratulations." Doc didn't know what else to say.

"Sit down. Dolan was just leaving. We'll hit the books next week, same time."

"I guess that's my exit line." Dolan rose. He was as big standing as he looked sitting. "Good to meet you, Doc. Maynard tells me you played ball."

"A little."

"We should get up a game sometime. I used to belong to a softball league in my neighborhood, but everybody died."

"What position?"

"Hot corner."

"What are you doing Saturday?"

In the exchange that followed Dolan gave Doc his card and wrote down the Millers' telephone number in an alligator notebook. They shook hands again and Dolan left. Doc sat down.

"If I wasn't a hockey man I'd offer to umpire." Ance popped a chunk of roast lamb into his mouth and pushed his plate to one side. "Lucky we ran into each other. Dolan rode me down here. I've been trying to get Taber all day but I guess he's drunk again. Any plans this afternoon?"

"No." He'd been hoping to stop by a sporting goods store and pick up some stuff for tomorrow's game with Sean and Sergeant Battle and his son.

"Good. Did the state give you a dark suit when they kicked you?"

"I've got a dark suit."

"How'd you like to wear it to Wilson McCoy's funeral? I got an invitation this morning."

"Who invited you?"

"Well, you might say I invited myself. I bought the casket."

"Why?"

"McCoy wasn't my only M-and-M client. It gets around I dump them just because they're dead, I lose half my revenue. The Marshals have been paying my mortgage for years. Anyway the six grand was just a drop in the bucket after the fifty he cost me when he flushed himself down the toilet. Where's the suit, at home?"

Doc said it was.

"We'll swing by there after lunch. Funeral's at two-thirty. We'll be late, but these colored revolutionaries don't go by the clock. White man's invention, don't you know, to keep the slaves in line. Try the shishkebab; it's my own recipe."

The Brown & Kilmer Funeral Home on Sherman was a two-story house built sometime in the twenties with a fresh coat of white paint and a red brick front that looked as if it had been added on. As Doc slowed down in front, a mixed group, all black, in dark suits and gray and blue and lavender dresses was climbing the front steps, one of the men holding the arm of an old woman in a flowered hat. A black Cadillac hearse was parked in front and a number of limousines with smoked windows and other cars of various makes lined both curbs. One was a powder blue van bearing the News 4 logo on its side.

A young black in pinstripes approached the rented Cadillac carrying a handful of small red flags with suction cups attached and leaned down next to the open window on the driver's side. If Doc's white face surprised him he gave no indication. "Will you be joining the procession?" he asked.

Doc looked at Ance, who shook his head. Doc said no and the young man directed him to park in the alley that ran next to the building. As they came back around the corner on foot they passed the van, where a bald-headed black man built like a professional wrestler was fooling around with a video camera and a small spare white man Doc thought he recognized from TV was looking at his reflection in the window on the passenger's side. He had on a trenchcoat, although the temperature was in the upper fifties and there was no sign of rain.

The entryway was done in soft grays with a mauve carpet that extended into the other rooms wall to wall. There was a lighted portrait in a heavy gilt frame, a photograph tinted with oils, of a middle-aged black man with a tabby-cat smile in sixties lapels with an engraved plate reading ELROD BROWN 1921–1970. The lighting was indirect and so was the manner of the bearlike man in a black suit and French cuffs who took their hands in a warm, enveloping grip while steering them firmly toward a room on the left. This room, separated by gray curtains from the rest of the ground floor, contained rows of folding chairs with an aisle down the center, a dais supporting the casket, and murmuring guests seated and standing about in groups. There were some white faces among them. Doc thought he could tell the undercover police officers, each of whom stood alone in a different part of the room. He looked for Sergeant Battle but didn't see him.

The recorded organ music was turned so low in keeping with the rest of the proceedings that it was several moments before Doc realized the tune being played, albeit in half-tempo, was "My Guy."

"You'd think they were burying a Methodist." Ance was almost whispering; Doc had to stoop slightly to hear him. "In the Depression my old man took work as a gravedigger at Mt. Elliott Cemetery, and he was there when they planted this big black numbers boss the wops iced. He said he could've retired on the diamond rings and gold teeth that showed up for the graveside service."

"Times change."

"I'm glad as hell I don't."

Ance circulated, shaking hands and introducing Doc. None of the mourners seemed pleased to see them, but Doc didn't sense real hostility. McCoy had left no family and it was clear he hadn't many friends. Doc mentioned this to Ance when they moved out of the others' hearing.

"Hell, he didn't have *any* friends," the bail bondsman muttered. "McCoy was a stone asshole. Only reason the Marshals put up with him at all was his reputation. He should've been glad he was born black or *nobody* would've hung around him more than five minutes. Well, let's go pay the son of a bitch our respects."

The casket was polished mahogany, almost black, with brass handrails and an eggshell satin lining. McCoy, dressed in a brown leather Windbreaker and blue silk shirt with the collar spread to show off a gold chain around his neck, was lying slightly propped up on a pillow with his hands folded atop a paperback-size book resting on his sternum. Doc twisted his head to read the title stamped on the black Permabound cover. *Mahomet: The Life and Death of a Negro Prophet,* by Clinton Baedecker.

"The Little Black Book," Ance said. "I don't know if the cocksucker could even read."

Brown & Kilmer had worked miracles with the shrunken corpse Doc had seen in the Independence Motel a few days earlier, filling in the caved cheeks and doing something with putty where the flesh had puckered to the bone. The temple wound was only a faint outline, filled in and covered with makeup. The rest was paint and lighting; a fixture in the top of the arch over the dais shed dusky pink light on the deceased, eliminating harsh shadows and softening the atrocities of years and drugs. Doc thought he looked better than he had in recent newsreels.

Ance echoed his thoughts. "Cashing in was one smart career move. I just wish he'd done it before he got so far into my wallet."

Mourners were still filing in. Most of the latecomers were young, in their late teens and early twenties, and the nearest most of them had to a suit was a matching black leather jacket and pants with skinny Michael Jackson neckties. The haircuts ranged from conservative flattops to geometric designs razored into their heads. Their talk was noisier than the earlier arrivals' but less raucous than it would have been on the street. There was something about the presence of a dressed and painted corpse that knocked the edge off people.

The largest group had formed around a chair in the front row by the aisle. This was occupied by the elderly woman Doc had seen entering the building when he was looking for a place to park. She sat with her ankles crossed and her hands folded in her lap, answering remarks politely but without looking up. The flowered hat, set on a pageboy that was too straight and too dark to have grown on her head, was the brightest thing about her. Her tailored suit was ash rose and she had on plain black pumps and glasses with heavy black rims that Doc suspected had been selected to cover the crepe under her eyes. She looked seventy. She could just as easily have been ninety.

"Beatrice Blackwood," said Ance when Doc asked about her. "After Mother Waddles and Alcina Lilley she's just about the most respected black woman in this town. Her whorehouses were cleaner than most of the restaurants."

"She's a madam?"

"Was. Well, halfway; word is she's semi-retired, sold all her cribs and massage parlors and comes in a couple of times a month on a salary basis to make sure nobody's skimming too much. Place you got your tie straightened in yesterday? One of hers."

"I thought you said it belonged to the mayor."

"I said the feds think that. Anyway she sold it along with all the rest. Come on, I'll introduce you."

The group was gathered in a kind of ragged reception line, each person taking her hand and saying something to her in obsequious tones as if she were the widow. Doc and Ance took their place behind the well-upholstered trousers of a man Doc was sure he recognized as a city official or a leading businessman or a minister he had seen a few times on local television.

When the overstuffed man stepped out of the way, Ance moved forward and spoke to the woman. Doc wasn't paying attention to the words. He was watching the way she didn't offer her hand, sheathed in a gray kid glove, until she heard his voice, the way he reached over to take the hand, and the way her heavy-lidded eyes, magnified behind the thick glasses, remained fixed on the middle distance between them, not lifting to meet his gaze. Doc wondered how much she could see. Perhaps Ance was just a shadow between her and the light.

"Maynard, how long has it been?" Her speech was youthful and almost musical, the consonants crisp. Jamaican? "Contributing to the delinquency, wasn't it?"

"Five counts. Four girls and the queen, straight flush. Fifteen thousand for each of them, sixty for you. I was down to bread-and-butter sandwiches that month."

"Don't complain, you got back every penny. Beatrice never stiffed anyone. How much did Wilson beat you out of?"

"Fifty."

"That boy. I could have told you he was a bad risk."

"This is Doc Miller. He works for me."

Her grip was surprisingly strong. "I hope he's paying you. Maynard wouldn't do anything he asks his people to do."

Doc said he was pleased to meet her. She smiled, showing a perfection of teeth not found in nature, groped, and laid a hand on Ance's wrist. "Come see Beatrice after she gets the cataracts off. Bring this charming boy with you. I'm going in next week."

"It's a date."

They stepped away. "You'll be old a long time before you meet another woman like her," Ance said. "She delivered thirty thousand votes to the mayor last year."

"And they still arrested her?" Doc asked after a moment.

"That was three elections ago. It takes a couple of terms in office to find out where to oil the machine. Oh, they crack down from time to time, to keep the whores from going out and stopping traffic, but those misdemeanor pops are petty cash, and they're a lot cheaper than breaking in a new administration. So she gets out the vote."

Ance had been right about the casual timing. At 2:45 guests were still arriving, and the bruiser in the black suit who had greeted them at the door was setting up a tripod at one end of the casket bearing a blowup photograph of Wilson McCoy inside a black wreath, a shot Doc remembered from a period poster of the young commando in the black beret and fatigue uniform of the Panthers with gloved fist raised and a predatory light in his eye. Another black suit brought in a lectern and stood it in front of the first row of chairs. The hum of conversation began to level off. Doc and Ance found seats in the back row near the curtain.

One of the young men in black leather sat down next to Doc. "Excuse me, did I hear somebody say you're Doc Miller? The ballplayer?"

He was a lean youth sprouting a silky moustache. On either side of his head a barber had shaved quarter-inch squares set corner to corner in an elaborate checkerboard. There was no hostility in the young man's expression, only curiosity. Doc admitted he had played ball. He couldn't keep his eyes off the haircut.

"I knowed it! I cut school and snuck into the park to see you pitch to the Brewers. It was a doubleheader, and you come on in the ninth both times. My mama whomped the shit out of me when she found out, but it was worth it."

"The only time I relieved back to back against Milwaukee we lost both games."

"Wasn't your fault. Petry went all to hell in the sixth inning of the first game and Kirk Gibson choked with the bases loaded in the top of the eighth in the second like the motherfucker always done till he went to California. You walked Robin Yount in the first game. Nobody else got past you."

"You must've been what, twelve years old?"

"Ten. Epithelial Lewis. My friends call me Needles." He stuck out a hand that looked too big for his wrist.

Doc took it. "You play, Needles?"

"I catch some out on Belle Isle. First base too, when it's open, but I'm better behind the plate. This here is Yarnell and Creed; they's some of the ones I play with."

Doc stretched his neck to nod at the two men who had sat down on the other side of Needles. Yarnell shaved his head. Creed wore his hair in dreadlocks and sported a diamond on the left side of his nose. Doc was pretty sure all three were M-and-M's. He was about to ask them what positions they played when the lights came up.

Actually it was just one light, a bright one on a stand erected by the News 4 cameraman, standing to the side of the curtained entrance supporting the camera on one shoulder. The reporter Doc thought he recognized stood next to him holding a microphone. The object of their attention was the Reverend Somebody-or-Other—Doc never caught the name—from the Second Baptist Church, who donned a pair of Ben Franklin glasses to read from a Bible spread open on the lectern; something from Luke. The oration that followed was brief and entirely forgettable. Maynard Ance's head slid forward after a minute and Doc wondered if he'd gone to sleep.

He wondered too why the Marshals of Mahomet had invited the press. He'd expected pyrotechnics, but so far Needles' checkerboard and Creed's diamond seemed to be it.

The minister finished speaking and the guests began to stir. Just then a woman came through the curtain past the cameraman and the reporter and walked up the aisle without looking right or left, not slowing or stopping until she came to the casket, where she placed a small bouquet on top of the closed half of the lid, paused for a beat, then turned and went out the way she had come. Doc got a good look at her then, a trim tall handsome black woman in a knee-length blue dress caught at the waist with a wide black belt, no other accessories, and straight hair tied behind her head. But for some pale lipstick she wore no makeup. She appeared to be in her middle thirties. She'd been gone a full second when the TV reporter seemed to come to life and went out after her, hesitating only to say something to the man with the camera, who followed him, leaving his light behind. Only then did the first of the mourners rise from his chair to turn and stare at the curtain.

"Shit."

Doc looked at Ance, wide awake, who tilted his head toward the exit. "Alcina Lilley. Mahomet's widow. Just when you think the show's a bust."

GRANNY AT THE BAT
By Leon "Bud" Arsenault
(continued)

In 1968, when Loyola MacGryff was 65, she became determined to cheer her beloved Tigers to victory in person over the St. Louis Cardinals in Detroit's first World Series since 1945.

Opportunity knocked during the American League playoffs.

Confident that a lineup including Al Kaline, Jim Northrup, Stormin' Norman Cash, and Willie Horton, together with a pitching staff headed by Denny McLain and Mickey Lolich, would lead the team to a pennant, Mrs. MacGryff entered a contest sponsored by Vernor's Ginger Ale.

First prize? Two tickets to Game 2 of the Series.

Challenged to write an essay in 25 words or less entitled, "Why the Detroit Tigers and the Taste of Vernor's are Unbeatable," the Queen of Fandom, by then thrice a grandmother, declined all offers of familial assistance and locked herself in her house for two days, subsisting on coffee, doughnuts, and the enigmatic whispers of the Muse.

At length, from a Vesuvius of discarded sheets of crumpled notepaper, she excavated her masterpiece: an ode to coaches, catchers, and carbonation.

After laboriously two-finger-typing it on her old Reming-

121

ton, she sealed it up and sent it off, the best pitch in her repertoire.

And it was a strike! Within ten days, she received her tickets by return mail.

"Oh, it was a grand day," rhapsodizes Mrs. MacGryff, who brought her daughter-in-law with her to the stadium. "We sat in the old green seats, you know, and I can still smell the sun and the old mustard stains on the fabric. It was especially sweet that day.

"Willie and Norm and Mickey all hit homers with men on. It was Mickey's first home run in the majors—I almost caught it, but I forgot my glove that day, and the ball went through my hands and bounced up into the higher seats. We won, eight to one."

But the glow of victory was short.

When the die-hard rooter returned to her old house, she found it empty.

In her absence, neighbors reported, a moving van had backed up to her front door and two men in coveralls had carried out furniture, rugs, appliances, even clothes, until all six rooms were as bare as that turn-of-the-century day her parents had moved in.

Acquaintances on the block expressed surprise that she was leaving the neighborhood after so many years.

Mrs. MacGryff had not won the Vernor's contest; someone else had. The burglars, whom police surmised had local ties, took advantage of the scuttlebutt that Mrs. MacGryff had entered the competition, purchasing and sending her the tickets so they could work most of the day undisturbed.

After all these years the octogenarian is philosophical.

"If I had just caught Mickey's home run ball it would've been worth losing all those family pictures and things."

(to be continued)

PART THREE
Screwball

❖❖❖❖❖❖❖❖❖

Chapter 14

◆◆◆◆◆◆◆◆◆

O kay, so baseball wasn't like sex.
Nothing was. What Doc felt when his hand closed around the small hard sphere, wrapped in soiled white leather rubbed shiny and held together with stitches as tight as old scar tissue (and stamped *Made in Taiwan*), wasn't what he had felt when the blonde who called herself Lynda first placed her palms on his naked skin in the massage parlor. It just made him think of it. And the release when he wound up and followed through and the ball whistled over the plate and struck Needles Lewis' mitt with a report like a muzzled shotgun wasn't orgasmic. It was more like stepping off the bus, hot and tired and aching all over, in front of his own house after a long time away. It was a cold drink and a familiar bed and a broken-down pair of loose shoes all rolled up into one.

"Ball one!" bellowed Neal.

"Ball, hell! I split the plate."

"Another inch lower and you would've."

"You ought to clean the grease out of your eyes before you leave work."

"Play ball," Neal said.

Doc's brother, who worked only a half-day Saturdays, had come to the empty lot just in time to umpire the game. Before that, Doc, young Sean, Sergeant Battle and his son Charlie Junior—a reedy youth in a flattop and Fat Boys sweatshirt with the sleeves cut off who looked older than his fourteen years—the three young M-and-M's from the funeral parlor, and Jeff Dolan, who arrived last, had spent four hours raking the cans and broken bottles and other less identifiable trash into a big pile off the playing field. Battle, dressed comfortably but carefully in a gray sweatshirt without lettering, stone-washed Levi's, and black Nikes, had hesitated when he saw the three Marshals, all of whom he had seen around 1300 during drug sweeps, but Doc had talked him into staying on condition that Needles, Yarnell, and Creed stand for a frisk with their hands on the roof of the sergeant's Chevy parked at the curb. Battle relieved them of a clasp knife with a five-inch blade, a set of brass knuckles which the owner, Creed of the dreadlocks and nasal jewelry, claimed was a paperweight he carried for luck, and a hypodermic syringe.

"This why they call you Needles?" he asked the youth with the checkerboard haircut.

"I'm a diabetic."

"Where's your insulin?"

"What's that?"

"Two concealed weapons and drug paraphernalia," Battle said. "With priors, you might all be out in time for basketball season. Hell of a team you got here, Doc."

Doc said, "That's kind of chickenshit. You didn't find any drugs."

"Shit. Shit." Battle snapped the needle off the syringe, crumpled the barrel, and pocketed it along with the knife and brass knuckles. "With my luck the chief'll drive by."

"Tell him you're undercover. He's got his own problems." A federal grand jury was investigating an alleged connection between Chief Hart and $2.6 million missing from a secret police fund.

They walked away from the car. "You might've told me who I'd be playing with."

"*I* didn't know until yesterday," Doc said. "I can't send them away. They brought the equipment."

"This could cost me a lieutenantcy."

"That mean you're staying?"

"I'd go home, but my wife would make me put up the screens." The sergeant picked up his fielder's glove.

Since they had only eight men—nine, when Neal showed up—it was less a game than batting practice; but since the thing had started as a one-on-one baseball lesson for Sean, Doc wasn't complaining. With a complete rotating outfield playing in close to monitor the bases, it beat chasing the ball through the tall grass most of the day.

The diamond they had laid out reminded him of the weekend sandlot games of his boyhood. First base was Needles' Pistons warm-up jacket, stripped off during the heat of the cleanup and raveled in the cuffs. Second and third were broken shingles and home plate was an old rubber car floor mat. The pitcher's "mound" was level with home and Doc had used up half his warm-up pitches learning to compensate.

Jeff Dolan was batting when Neal made his "ball one" call. The big Irishman had on sweats, worn Reeboks, and a Tigers home cap, team issue, not one of the mesh-backed adjustable jobs they sold at the concession stands. He had a crouching stance and choked up high on the bat. Doc blew two past him after the first call, then delivered a split-finger that connected and would have been no problem with a professional outfield and a shortstop, but took a slow loop and dropped in between second and third. Yarnell was still chasing it in from left field when Dolan reached first. For a giant the accountant could run.

Battle was next up. Doc went fishing with his first two pitches, got him to swing at a duster, went to first to keep Dolan from stealing—no chance for the pitchout, since he had to telegraph the move to allow Charlie Junior to come in from right field— caught the sergeant looking on the next, and fanned him out when he went for another one in the dirt. He stalked away cursing himself.

Sean stepped up reluctantly. The boy was wearing a dumpy madras shirt with the tail out and elastic jeans stretched tight across his large buttocks. Neal spent some time showing him how to hold the bat, which drooped in his son's hands the moment Neal let go of it, then stepped back behind the catcher looking worried. Doc thought that if his brother had been that unsure of himself when he and Billie were discussing whether Sean should be allowed to play, the boy would be home right now annihilating enemy spacecraft.

Doc fed him an easy one waist-high, slow enough to read the lettering on the ball. Sean swung, missed, and sat down on the plate. Creed, out in center field, laughed.

Neal and Doc both took a step toward the boy and stopped. Sean got up and looked at the ground. The bat dangled.

"Play ball," Neal said.

When the bat came up, Doc tried to hit it and succeeded. The ball bounced up and landed in Needles' mitt.

Neal hesitated, then: "You're out."

"All right, another Cecil Fielder!" Creed called.

Sean dropped the bat and shuffled away.

The outfield rotated. Battle went out to cover left field and Charlie Junior came in from right to bat, tossing his father his glove on the way. Doc supposed that the amount of energy the elder Battle might spend putting his son out depended on what kind of relationship they had.

His curiosity wasn't satisfied that time, however. Charlie Junior jumped on the first pitch, a fastball up around the letters, and knocked the ball over the roof of the house next door. He and Dolan both scored while Creed went to look for the ball. It was the only one they had.

Doc pitched most of the afternoon, quitting the mound just before five o'clock when his arm started to ache. Sean struck out four times, hit a ground ball finally that bounced and rolled to a stop ten feet in front of the mound, and was thrown out while he was waddling toward first. Creed had a laugh and a comment for every failure until Neal went out for a talk with the M-and-M, who was silent afterward; the mechanic outweighed him sixty solid pounds, and Creed was weaponless. When it came Sean's turn to play right field, Doc had a talk with Dolan, who was next up, and the accountant hit another looper that dropped almost at the boy's feet. Doc wasn't sure which one of them tripped and fell the most times, Sean on his way in to tag the runner out or Dolan on his way to first. At that it was still a near thing when Sean dropped the ball with one foot on the base. Dolan, fresh out of subterfuges, waited patiently for the tag.

That was the last play of the game. Sean, flushed with exertion if not excitement, came in holding the ball, and Doc took it from him with a "Good work." He suppressed the urge to make more of a fuss. The boy was clumsy, not stupid.

"What did you say to Creed?" Doc asked his brother.

Neal rolled his thick shoulders. "I said if he didn't shut up I'd rip that fucking diamond out of his nose and ram it up his ass."

Needles announced there were cold drinks in the cooler in the box of his pickup, a green 1976 Dodge club cab parked behind Battle's Chevy, rusted as holey as antique lace around the wheels and missing its tailgate. The sound system inside the cab had cost more than the truck, and after a couple of minutes Battle reached inside and switched the radio from the rap station Needles had turned on to one that played Motown. The sergeant had stripped off his sweatshirt early in the game. Slabs of muscle jumped and twitched under his soaked undershirt when he used the heavier garment to mop the sweat from the back of his neck. He opened the cooler. Cans of Stroh's, Coors, and Coca-Cola stuck up like the prows of bright-colored submarines through the ice.

"How old are you?" he asked Needles.

"Sixty-two. I take care of myself."

Battle handed him a Coke.

"Shit. I *paid* for the beer."

"Who sold it to you?"

"I ain't your snitch." He popped the top and walked away from the truck.

The sergeant gave Cokes to Creed and Yarnell and got out a Stroh's for Neal and a Coke for Sean, but Neal said they were going home to wash up for supper. He held up a hand and left with the boy. For a second Doc thought that his brother was going to drop the hand to Sean's shoulder, and so did Neal, but after hovering in the vicinity for a beat it fell to his side. Their father had never been one for displays of affection either.

Battle offered a beer to Dolan, who pleaded an evening appointment to do someone's taxes, shook hands with Doc and the sergeant, and started across the lot to where he had left his car. As Charlie Junior approached, his father tossed him a Coke and the youth spun around and caught it behind his back. Grinning, he sat down on the Chevy's front bumper to drink.

"Kid's a hell of an athlete," Doc said. "Any aspirations?"

"He's even better on the court. Wants to be the next Isaiah, but I don't know." Battle handed Doc a Stroh's and opened a Coors for himself. "I had a shot at a baseball scholarship at Michigan but I put myself through the U of D."

"Why?" After his ignominious first time at bat, the sergeant had hit a double, forced in two runs, and scored all the way from first on a sacrifice by Dolan. He had a good eye and fast reflexes.

"I don't know. My uncle was a pro wrestler, that qualify as an athlete? He was always bitching about cheap hotel rooms and rotten food. He raised me. I guess some of it took." He chugged down half his beer and belched, a good deep one. Guy thing; Doc figured he didn't get to do it at home. "I wouldn't try too hard to make that nephew of yours into a player. Some kids just aren't cut out."

"He stinks, all right. I just couldn't stand watching him rotting in front of the tube. That's not healthy."

"You jocks are all the same. Lots of people lead perfectly normal lives without ever knowing what a locker room smells like. Kid'll probably discover a cure for AIDS. Maybe he'll invent another pet rock and you and your brother get to retire before you're fifty."

Doc let it slide and drank. He only liked beer when he was hot and it was cold and he was in the company of guys. He'd heard a psychotherapist on *Donahue* refer to it as male bonding. Leave it to the shrinks to ruin a good thing with a sissy name.

"What were you and Ance doing at Wilson McCoy's funeral yesterday?"

Battle was looking away when he asked the question, tipping his can. Doc's experience with the police during the investigation of the death in his suite at the Westin had taught him that they were most dangerous when they didn't seem to be paying attention to their own words. He nodded. "I thought I saw some of your men. I drove Ance there. He was invited."

"What'd you think of Beatrice Blackwood?"

"She was okay. Everybody's nice at a funeral."

"What'd she say?"

"She said she's having her eyes operated on."

"Anything else?"

"Starkweather Hall's name didn't come up, if that's what you're asking."

"Is that what I'm asking?" He was looking at Doc now.

"I don't think Ance knows where he is. What am I supposed to do, ask him?"

"Just look and listen. He had some reason for introducing you to that circle. I wish I knew what it was. Anyway, you're doing fine. Yesterday you didn't know any Marshals, and today here you are playing ball with three of them."

"They're just kids."

"Your boy Needles was in for questioning just last month on a drive-by shooting in Ferndale. Somebody put a bullet in a six-year-old girl's head from the backseat of a '68 Impala. Turned out it was the wrong neighborhood. They were looking for an eleven-year-old runner who lived in the next block. Yeah"—he emptied the can, crushed it, and tossed it into the pickup box—"they're just kids."

"Did you look into the ownership of these lots like I asked?" Doc said after a moment.

Battle wriggled into his sweatshirt. The late-afternoon air was cooling. "City property. The federal funding was for the two houses they tore down to shoo out a crack operation. Buying land from the city is like digging a trench in quicksand. No civic grunt's going to put himself out to profit the treasury."

"I don't want to buy it. I don't have enough for a security deposit on an apartment. I'd just like to know if I decide to clear the space for a ball field that some guy in a hard hat's not going to march in and turn it into a parking lot. I want official sanction."

"Going to blow away evil with the clear cold redeeming wind of baseball, that it?"

"I wasn't thinking that, but look at the M-and-M's. They're not running dope when they're running bases."

"Cute," Battle said. "Make it your slogan. You penitent ex-jailbird ballplayers give me a pain. They must have some world-class chaplains in stir."

"Penitent hell. Last week on the news some judge decided a guy that strangled his wife was unfit for trial and turned him over to Ypsi State. The shrinks held him three days, said he was sane and let him go. All I did was throw a party and they put me away for seven years. I just want to have something to do with the game."

"I'll look into it. If you will."

"I wish I knew what I was looking for."

"If you don't know, you haven't seen it." He scrubbed a sleeve across his thick-boned forehead. "I wonder what Alcina Lilley was doing slumming with a bunch like the Marshals. She never acknowledged their existence before."

Doc said, "Maybe it was McCoy she was there for. You said he shot up the Sicilians for what they did to Mahomet."

"Yeah, well, I got that wrong. I looked it up. McCoy offed Patsy Orr *before* Mahomet got his. That may have even been the reason the Sicilians killed him. Which makes her showing up at the services a big-time mystery."

"Ask her."

"She doesn't talk to cops. Cops and her late husband didn't get along. And we can't apply pressure to the widow of a saint."

"He's been dead what, twenty-five years?"

"Twenty-four this August. Some people want to make it a holiday. Nobody knows what day he was born."

"She doesn't look a day over thirty-five."

"I don't think she's forty," the sergeant said. "She was just a kid when they married, I mean a *kid*. No one even knew he *had* a wife until she came forward after. They married somewhere down South where it was legal then."

Doc wanted to ask him more questions about Alcina Lilley, but Charlie Junior had joined them. "Dad, the movies. You said I could go."

"Yeah, okay." Battle laid his hand on his son's shoulder; no hesitation there. To Doc: "Just do what Ance tells you to. He's got plans for you. Whatever they are, if they don't include Hall, I've wasted thirteen years on this job. I should've put up with the shitty hotels.

"Thanks for the game," he added. "Next week *I'll* bring the beer."

Chapter 15

❖❖❖❖❖❖❖❖❖

Whatever plans Maynard Ance might have had for Doc, they weren't evident early in the week. On Monday Doc drove him in the Cadillac to a house in Hazel Park, where a woman who didn't want her husband to know what she was up to arranged bail for her sister, who had been taken into police custody when her fingerprints showed up in the apartment of a young man being held for the armed robbery of the 7-Eleven where she worked in Romulus. On Tuesday, after a slow morning spent reading George F. Will's *Men At Work,* borrowed from the Detroit Public Library, Doc was given the afternoon off and spent thirty minutes of it in the massage parlor next door. He drove Ance to Jeff Dolan's house in Corktown Wednesday and watched Jack Morris give up a six-run lead to the Indians—a team he'd loathed ever since Dickie Noles set a park record for beaned Tigers in 1986—on the forty-eight-inch set in the living room while Dolan went over Ance's 1040 return in the study. The big Irishman's wife was a tiny woman a few years older than Doc with tightly curled hair, the iron smile of the born hostess, and cups and saucers apparently growing out of both hands. Said Ance later: "These micks always marry Stepford women."

The house itself was as old as the century but very clean, smelling of lemon-scented furniture polish and one of those subtle air fresheners that managed not to remind Doc of a Christmas tree or lilacs gone berserk in the parlor, and was in excellent repair, unlike the rest of the decomposing neighborhood around Tiger Stadium. Dolan's grandfather, the legendary Big Jim Dolan, had lived there the last thirty years of his life, electing mayors and governors and dispensing influence for favors even as the great political machine he had built on a platform as solid as the Vatican choked and shook itself to pieces on the rich mixture of brash new Prohibition money. (The tattered ends of the so-called Dublin Mafia, Jeff Dolan said, still gathered once a month at the Irish Saloon around the corner on Trumbull to swap stories of the glory days and plot the overthrow of Coleman A. Young, secure in the support of the fifteen percent of Detroit's population that was still white.) A portrait of the Irish Pope, big and beer-bellied in white muttonchops and black cutaway, thumbs in vest pockets, hung from the mahogany paneling over the fireplace, its subject looking like a piece of heavy carved furniture in a room full of Plexiglas and plastic.

Ance was in a sanguine mood when they pulled out of the driveway, resting his arm across the back of the seat and humming something tuneless. Doc asked him if the news about his taxes was good.

"I got ripped. But that fifty large I dumped on McCoy kicks me into a lower bracket this year, so my estimated's less. Looks like the cocksucker did me a favor after all. Not here," he said when Doc started to turn onto Woodward Avenue. "I talked to the garage this morning. The bus is finished."

"What do we do with the Cadillac?"

"Leave it at the garage. I'll have Taber pick it up and drop it off at the agency. It'll be good to get out of this nigger deisel and look down at traffic again."

The body shop was on Cadieux in Grosse Pointe and looked like an antique shop in front, a square yellow brick building with beveled glass in the bay doors and a sign on the lawn suspended by chains from an iron stanchion. The Coachmen barely cleared the top of the bay when the mechanic drove it out. A Mercedes, two Cadillacs, and a green Porsche up on the hoist were in various stages of assembly inside. Doc tried the window on the driver's side. It rolled down and up without a hitch. Stepping down, he told Ance he couldn't figure out why it had taken so long just to replace a window. The mechanic, a tall gray-haired man in clean coveralls, banged the door with the side of his fist. It made a dull sound like lead.

"Kevlar panels," the mechanic said. "Bullet-resistant up to forty-five calibers at twenty yards. That means almost a thousand extra pounds up front, so we had to put in heavy-duty shocks. That was last spring. The new window's bullet-proof and three-quarters of an inch thick, which calls for a whole new gear assembly in the cranking system to handle the weight. I had to install it myself and there were two cars ahead of this one. Now, one bullet-proof window's not much good unless all the others are too. I was just finishing up the one on the passenger's side this morning when Maynard called to ask when it'd be ready. Windshield should be in next week," he told Ance.

"Call me then." The bail bondsman was playing with a pack of cigarettes.

"Every time Maynard has it in we have to add something else. Last time it was bars."

Doc said, "I can't figure out how you did it so fast."

The mechanic laughed. "The day after the first time he came in here I bought subscriptions to *Police Times*, *Soldier of Fortune*, and *The Whole Survivalists' Catalogue*. When he starts daydreaming out loud I put in an order."

"What do I owe you, Dick?"

"Fifteen hundred ought to do it. It takes three people to handle one of those windows."

Ance put away the cigarettes, got out his old wallet, and counted fifteen bills onto the mechanic's palm. The bills were folded into a breast pocket of the coveralls and the flap was snapped shut. No receipt changed hands.

Doc felt a new respect for the smooth glide of the motor home as they drove away. He would never have known about the armor plating if he hadn't been told, although he'd wondered why the vehicle averaged only eight miles to the gallon. "Does everything he does for you stay off the books?" he asked Ance.

"Only the big jobs. He discounts for cash. If I told you what a grease monkey in Grosse Pointe lays out in taxes you'd shit your pants. I used to deduct every cent until some son of a bitch at the IRS disallowed the two grand Dick soaked me to install those bars. Like I'd ride around in a fucking hoosegow on wheels if I wasn't in the business I'm in."

They drove most of the way to the office without speaking—a feat of which Doc would have thought his employer incapable. He decided the bail bondsman was preoccupied.

A dozen blocks short of their destination Ance spoke. "How'd you like Beatrice Blackwood?"

It was the second time Doc had been asked the question. He made the same noncommital answer he'd given Charlie Battle.

Ance didn't seem to have been listening. "She's a hummer. In her own way she's made a deeper dent in this community than the last three administrations. When the local N.A.A.C.P. raised a hundred grand for the lobby to have Martin Luther King's birthday declared a national holiday, she matched it. She knew King personally. *How* personally is her own business."

"Wasn't she a little old for him even then?"

"You didn't see Beatrice twenty years ago. Even in her fifties she could make a sock stand up straight."

"Still, I wonder why she settled for being a madam."

"I don't guess the GM board of directors had any openings for poor black island girls when she was young. Anyway it's honest work. Nobody ever carried away a dose from one of her joints. When the AIDS thing broke, she shut down for three months, had her girls tested, and paid all the medical bills for those that got infected. It broke her. That's why she sold out."

"I hope her operation comes off okay."

"She had it Monday. They're kicking her out of Receiving today. I said you'd pick her up, that all right?"

"You're the boss."

"I never get tired of hearing you say it. How'd the game go Saturday?"

Doc adjusted to the change of subjects. "My arm got tired. My arm didn't used to get tired."

"Yeah, well, thirty-three ain't twenty-two."

"Tell that to Nolan Ryan."

"Right after you tell it to Mark Fidrych. The money's big because you're washed up at forty. What kind of a player is Charlie Battle?"

"Good hitter. Fair fielder. His boy's better. I guess Dolan told you he was there."

The bail bondsman didn't reply. "Charlie never took a minute off work in his life. He pump you?"

"He asked me about Starkweather Hall." Entering their

block, Doc decided to tell some of the truth. "He thought you might have him stashed somewhere."

"The idea doesn't stink. Hall and I could split the reward and he could pay his lawyers with his half."

Doc pulled into the dirt lot and stopped. The extra thousand pounds didn't sway more than a fraction of an inch. "Was I wearing a bug?"

"Doesn't take a computer whiz to put it together. Don't think I didn't give it some thought. Only those rewards are never paid. Ask the lady who dropped the dime on Dillinger; they deported her for prostitution. Battle knows that and he knows I know it."

"So why'd he bring it up?" He kept his hands on the wheel and gazed through the windshield at the sign reading WE EMPLOY ONLY AMERICAN MASSEUSES.

"What'd you tell him?"

"I said I didn't think you were dumb enough to risk a harboring charge."

"Did you mean it?"

Everything Ance said sounded offhand, but Doc had been with him long enough now to recognize his grilling technique. He made eye contact. "I'm on parole. If I didn't mean it I'd have to quit."

Ance opened his door. "He's fishing. When you don't have bait or a hook or a line you throw in the rod." He hopped down and turned to look back in with one hand on the door. The floorboards were level with his sternum. "Room 411. She's expecting you any time." He swung the door shut.

Doc wondered if he should stop and buy flowers.

Chapter 16

◇◆◇◆◇◆◇◆◇

A fter taking his first step through the open door of 411,
which was nearly as wide as it was tall to leave room for
wheelchairs and gurneys, Doc reversed himself and double-
checked the number on the wall outside.

He had half-expected to find the impoverished madam in
a ward, or at most a semi-private room. Number 411 was
equipped with a small sitting room containing a sofa, love seat,
and chairs upholstered in gray tweed and oil paintings on the
walls, with a connecting door to a corner bedroom with windows
on two adjacent walls looking out on the city. Beatrice Blackwood, in her pageboy wig and a pink bed jacket with a spray of
rhinestones on the left shoulder, was sitting up in bed reading a
large-print edition of Countee Cullen's *Copper Sun*. Behind her
glasses she had an egg-shaped perforated aluminum patch
taped over her left eye. Her face was made up lightly and
expertly. She looked younger than she had at Wilson McCoy's
funeral, but then here she controlled the light. The reading
lamp was switched off and the sunlight coming between the
vertical louvers over the windows was obsequious. Doc felt a flash

of certainty that he had just stepped onto a stage set for his entrance.

"My stars, is it that time?" she asked when he greeted her. "I guess I *am* getting old. Give me ten minutes, please."

"Do you need help?"

"Beatrice has been dressing herself for more than seventy years." She swung two long ruby-nailed feet, slightly wrinkled, out from under the covers and into a pair of furry white slippers on the floor.

He retreated to the sitting room and closed the connecting door. The room was filled with flowers, small bouquets of peonies in throwaway vases and big displays of roses and orchids that reminded him of gangland send-offs in the movies. He recognized the names of some Detroit city councilmen and a judge or something on several of the cards. Most of the rest ran along the lines of Captain Jack, Mighty Dee, and the Rap City Ring. The splash of colors was enough to make him forget he was in a hospital.

In scarcely more than the promised ten minutes, the door opened and the woman stepped out wearing a mauve suit that caught her below the knees and flared out at the shoulders. Doc suspected the jeweled butterfly perched on the side of her head belonged to a pin securing the wig to her own hair. The piratical eye patch should have clashed with the Victorian gray kid gloves and gold jabot at her throat, but it didn't. A word came to mind, shimmering to the surface from the dim depths of his forgotten education: *courtesan*.

From the flowered hat she'd had on when he first met her to the muted gaiety of her appearance in this room full of blossoms, Doc was beginning to associate Beatrice Blackwood with a universe of color, and to consider the scale of the tragedy should modern medical science fail to restore her sight.

"Does Beatrice look that bad?" she asked, showing her sculpted teeth. "Never trust a woman who wears a uniform to hang up your clothes for you."

"You look great."

"You're a gentleman. I look old. Would you bring out my suitcase? I'm not allowed to lift anything heavier than five pounds."

It was white pigskin with two straps, very old but beautifully kept, like its owner. When he carried it out into the sitting room, a black nurse with big hips and orange hair was folding down the footplates on a wheelchair.

"Beatrice almost invested in this hospital." She allowed the nurse to help her into the chair. "Then she decided that the kind of mind that would get you up and walking as soon as possible after surgery, then forbid you to walk out the front door, couldn't be trusted with her money."

The nurse laughed, a not unpleasant bray. "Sending someone back for the flowers, sugar?"

"Distribute them to the other patients. I can't stand to watch things die."

"Very generous. You want a receipt for your taxes?"

"Of course."

Down in the lobby Doc left them to get the Coachmen and bring it up under the canopy. He was a little worried about getting the old woman up into the passenger's seat, but using the toolbox from the back for a stepping stool and taking one of her hands and supporting her back with his other palm, he lifted her in with little effort. She looked tall when standing on her own, but he towered over her by more than a foot and she weighed almost nothing. She told him she lived on McGraw.

The afternoon rush hour was under way, and for several

streets he was too busy maneuvering the great towering rectangle among cars desperate to get out of the city before the sun
went down. Leaving behind the commercial district and gliding
through neighborhoods of old houses with missing shingles,
burnt-out lawns, and a shiny orange basketball hoop attached to
every garage, he relaxed. "How'd the operation go?"

"Well, I'm reading street signs. I couldn't do that before. In a
couple of months I'm going back to get the other eye done. I
haven't finished a book in one sitting in two years."

"I guess you're used to being independent."

"I'll never get used to that," she said; and Doc had the impression that that conversation had ended. But he thought about it
all the way to her place.

It was a brownstone in a block of them separated by common
walls, five stories high with plywood in some of the windows and
crushed cans and broken bottles tossed behind wrought-iron
railings designed to enclose gardens in genteel days. A trio of
black youths in parachute pants and sweatshirts with the sleeves
cut off at the shoulders looked up from the stoop they were
sitting on as the motor home drifted to a stop against the curb.
The twin speakers of a boom box perched on top of one of the
railings gargled and coughed in rhythm with rap's kidney-
crushing beat. Doc felt them watching as he climbed the steps of
the place next door, his free hand on Beatrice Blackwood's
elbow. He carried the pigskin suitcase in the other.

The foyer smelled of mildew and old urine. Doc rested his
thumb on the soiled white rubber call button next to the old
woman's name on the directory. "Anybody there?"

"Try it."

He pressed. A buzzer razzed and he pushed open the inner
door. They rode a clanking old brass-plated elevator to the
fourth floor, where he had to give the doors a nudge when they

stuck halfway open. The hallway, lit by unshaded electric bulbs spaced too far apart in the ceiling and painted dark green over the plaster and wainscoting, smelled like the foyer, but someone had added Lysol.

Stopping at her door, he heard music inside. It sounded like Otis Redding. The door opened away from his knuckles and a broad black male face confronted his at a level, something that didn't happen often. Doc recognized one of the men who had escorted Beatrice Blackwood into the funeral home. He had on what looked like the same dark suit and conservative tie, as if he had just returned from another service. Doc felt a flash of suspicion and hostility between them like an electric arc: the race thing. Then the man's eyes went to Beatrice and his face metamorphosed into something Doc would never see directed at him.

"You look like a pirate," was the first thing he said.

Doc could have done better than that.

The man's name was Truman. Doc never found out if it was his first or his last, because she only introduced him by the one name. He didn't shake Doc's hand, but he opened the door wide enough to let them both in with no show of reluctance, and Doc assumed that he was just socially awkward. He was carrying around thirty pounds more than he should have, but he moved them well enough to have had some training as an athlete. Doc guessed boxing; flat scar tissue glittered like pieces of Scotch tape at the corners of both eyebrows.

He didn't have much time to think about it, though, because in the next second bright light flooded the dim apartment and a lot of people were yelling something all at once that might have been "Surprise!" The timing was off, as it always was, and some people started early and one or two others missed the moment and it ended in untidy tatters.

Doc's was the only white face in the room. The guests—it seemed at first there were a hundred of them, but it was more like twenty—had been seated and standing around the room with the curtains closed and most of the lights off, and the sudden illumination as the switches were turned had dazzled him, but it was just normal lamplight in a room full of tobacco smoke. Unlike Truman, the others were dressed anything but conservatively, in bright colors and jewelry that clanked and sporting an occasional gold tooth. Doc looked around to see if Needles and his friends were there, but he soon determined that he was the youngest person present by at least ten years.

Beatrice made no attempt to look surprised. She smiled and stood still and turned her cheeks this way and that for kisses and allowed herself to be embraced. There seemed to be a kind of protocol in the order in which the others came forward to bestow their affections, but it didn't seem to be according to age, as some of the grayer heads came later, and he decided he didn't know enough about the hierarchy to follow the pattern. He was largely—but not pointedly—ignored.

The room was more of a surprise than the party. The furniture was dyed leather and polished wood and chrome, the hardwood floor buffed to a satiny sheen, and underneath the cigarette odor the place smelled of citrus wax and regular airing. Books lined built-in shelves in a wall papered in bright yellow. Beatrice Blackwood had managed through no small effort and expense to construct a moat between her home and the squalor of her neighborhood without abandoning it.

Beatrice's queenly reserve shattered in a squeal that prickled Doc's skin under his clothes. She tottered forward, arms out, dividing the crowd, and bent to embrace an old man seated in an easy chair in the corner. Completely bald to the narrow brim of his Tyrolean, he had the dark gaunt look of an African wood carving. The lenses of his gold-rimmed half-glasses were opaque and the cane his long bony hands were folded on was bamboo with a broad white band halfway down its shaft in the universal symbol of the blind. His suit was electric blue, cut extravagantly, and he wore black silk socks and alligator shoes. He unfolded one hand to pat her on the back.

"Gidgy, I heard you was dead and buried." Her Jamaican-accented speech had slipped from cultured third-person to street argot.

"Buried, anyways. Croakers won't even let me smoke the weed no more."

"That ain't no Chesterfield there in the ashtray."

"Sweet thing, I done turned eighty last month. I was running out of things to do that I ain't supposed to."

"You still selling?"

"No. Hell, no. That damn crack has gone and roont the drug culture. I only deals in Acapulco and Asian and I can't get my price. *You* still selling?"

"No. That AIDS thing got everybody staying home pulling they own chain. You hear about Quincy?"

"I heard he died."

"Well, you knew him, how he was built. He didn't weigh no more than ninety pounds at the end."

"I always told that boy he'd fuck hisself to death." He pointed the cane in Doc's general direction. "Who's that white boy you got with you?"

"Can you see him?"

"Somebody looked out the window. He one of them Libber Als?"

Beatrice remembered her manners then, disengaged herself from the old man, and came over to grasp Doc's arm. "This is

147

Doc Miller, he drove me over from the hospital. He works for Maynard Ance. You all know Maynard." The sculpted tones were back.

Doc felt a general lifting of the atmosphere then, as if a window had been opened. He wondered how many digits that assembly totaled in past bond. Beatrice went off to mingle. Doc was offered a drink by a woman with her hair cropped close to her skull and a forked scar on her left cheek that crinkled the skin around that eye when she smiled. He accepted a vodka and water. Somebody else offered him something to eat, and he became aware then of the sweet smell of hot grease. One minute later he was holding a paper plate weighted down with ribs in a maroon sauce. The volume on the old-fashioned cabinet stereo was turned up, and it was straight Lou Rawls, Stevie Wonder, and Martha and the Vandellas from then on. The woman with the scar was talking to Beatrice when the music got louder. She raised her voice. ". . . another surprise. Truman?"

The big man in the dark suit set his paper plate down on the stereo, rapped gently at a side door, listened with his ear to the panel, and pushed it open. Alcina Lilley came out.

Chapter 17

◇◆◇◆◇◆◇◆◇

I was born in Kingston, that much I know," Beatrice Blackwood said. "I think in 1914, but I don't know what month. I was the eighth girl in the family. When I was about six months old my father sewed me up in a tobacco sack and threw me in a river. I don't know which one; Jamaica has more rivers than it has girl children."

She paused to break a two-inch column of ash next to a row of them in the saucer on the kitchen table. She only used it twice per cigarette, a trick that fascinated Doc. With at least six Bacardis in her system, she had stopped referring to herself by name, but she showed no signs of loss of coordination or concentration. Her cataracted right eye looked milky behind her glasses. Doc had no idea how much she could see with it, or through the holes in the patch over her left. There were sixteen of them arranged in a star, like a Chinese checkerboard.

Doc had had only the one vodka, after which he kept refilling his glass from the tap in the apartment's clean little kitchen, but he was getting sleepy. It was dark out and the tobacco smoke burned his eyes. The music from the living room improvised all around the rhythm of his pulse.

Beatrice went on. "A policeman fished me out. By the time the police tracked down my father he had himself barricaded in the house. He shot my mother and five of my sisters with an army gun; the other two were in school. He'd have shot himself too, probably, but he was out of bullets. The police did it for him.

"I got artificial respiration, but no one knew how long my brain had gone without oxygen, so I was registered as an idiot at the orphanage. I must've thought they were right, because I didn't start talking until I was four years old. After that they couldn't shut me up. I was adopted by a couple named Thornton. He was a retired British Army officer. I was eleven or twelve when he took me to bed the first time. Mrs. Thornton found out and threw me out of the house." She sipped Bacardi. "When I was sixteen a man named French Bill took me to Detroit with four other girls. He sold me to Hattie Long and I went to work for her."

"Sold you?"

"Well, my work card, but it came to the same thing. They called me a domestic. The first time you tried to run away Bill bruised you up. If you tried again—well, nobody ever made a third try. Hattie was a woman ahead of her time. She ran the first integrated house in Detroit. Some of those big auto men liked their meat dark, you see, and that black trade got big after the Rouge plant opened, but none of the other white places would touch it. She took a special interest in me. She taught me how to dress and talk and which fork to use and where to hide a knife where I could get to it in a hurry. 'Ruby,' she said—Ruby Sandoval, that's my birth name, my great-grandmother was a Spanish slave—'Ruby, don't ever lose the accent. There's lots of girls prettier than you, but the second they open their mouth they might as well be out on Michigan Avenue giving out hand jobs at a buck a throw. When you've got something nobody else has, hang on to it.' I cried like a baby at her funeral. By then I had my own place. I met them all: Joey Machine, Jack Dance, Frankie Orr. You're too young to remember those names."

"I remember Frankie Orr."

"His boy Patsy lost his cherry at my place on Twelfth. Personally I don't believe it, that boy was crippled in more than just his legs, but I didn't ask my girls any questions as long as they came through with the house cut and the customers left looking satisfied."

She shook her head, smiling. She didn't look as old when she wasn't showing the perfection of her dentures. "The sixties, now, that was the time to be on Twelfth Street. Those were our Roaring Twenties: blind pigs, rib joints, our music coming out of every open car window. Quincy Springfield ran the numbers. You should've seen the *shirts* that boy wore, all the colors of Life Savers. They made parks out of some of the buildings that burned down in the riots and boarded up the rest, so you wouldn't know it to look at the place now, but for a little while there we owned the town."

"You own it now. The mayor's black and so's the chief of police and most of the population."

"That's not owning it." She laid a fresh column next to the last. "That's being owned by it."

He drank some of his water. "Who's Gidgy?"

"Theron Toussaint L'Ouverture Gidrey." The name rolled grandly off her experienced tongue. "Nobody ever got poisoned on his merchandise, although some OD'd because they weren't used to the pure original. He had a half-interest in the Morocco Motor Hotel on Euclid. Maybe you heard that name."

"There was a Morocco Motel incident."

"STRESS cops broke down the door in '73 looking for a liquor-store robber. They shot and killed three people. One of them was Gidgy's sister's son Richard. Gidgy had a stroke the next day. He never did get back his eyes."

"Was the robber there?"

"No, the police in North Carolina arrested him about a week later. Richard wasn't in the business, he was just staying there while he was going to Wayne State. Well, Gidgy had to expect something like it in his line of work. Anyway nobody around here cried when Young took office and disbanded STRESS. Some of those white cops went around with notches on their guns. Seriously."

The air changed in the kitchen, stirred by the two-way door. Doc knew—and was aware that he knew—that Alcina Lilley had entered behind his back. He stood. Her head came above his shoulders, which made her almost six feet tall in her moderate heels. She was wearing a beige skirt that should have hobbled her at the knees but didn't, and a matching jacket with a double row of big cloth buttons. There was no blouse; the diamond-shaped expanse of medium brown flesh that was her bosom and the neck that grew up out of it were without lines or blemishes except for a small mole just above the shadow where her lapels met. She had full lips, small eyes set far apart, and a short nose and long upper lip that colluded in the overall impression of youth. As at McCoy's funeral, her only makeup—almost an afterthought—was a touch of lipstick. He couldn't believe she had been married to a man dead twenty-four years.

"It was a lovely party, Beatrice," she said.

Beatrice drew a fresh cigarette out of her pack and smiled. "You should tell Truman. Would you believe it was his idea? He's starting to develop an imagination. Thank you for coming. I was afraid we were only going to see each other at funerals from now on."

"Poor Wilson. I can't think of anything good to say about him."

"Neither could he. I suppose that's why he shot himself." She leaned forward while Doc lit the cigarette from a throwaway lighter, thanked him, and sat back. "Are you ready to go home? Truman will drive you."

"I don't think so," Alcina Lilley said. "He passed out about a half-hour ago."

"That boy never will learn how to drink. He's Sebastian Bright's youngest, you know. When he gave him to me for protection he didn't tell me I was supposed to finish raising him. Doc—I hate to ask."

"Where do you live?" he asked the younger woman.

"Birmingham." She couldn't prevent a light drawl from seeping into certain words and names.

"Mind riding in a motor home? The man I work for calls it a bus."

She smiled, briefly lighting the grave arrangement of her features. "As long as you don't put me in the back."

Beatrice separated a finger from her glass to beckon. When Doc leaned down she kissed his cheek. "Tell Maynard thanks. He knows Beatrice can't get along without her handsome young men."

He touched the back of her wrist. "Like hell."

Gidgy was sitting in the same place when Doc and Mrs. Lilley crossed through the living room, his chin on his chest and his face hidden by his hat. Doc paused to watch the old man's chest rise and fall a couple of times, then moved on.

Mrs. Lilley's legs, veneered in sheer hose, were nearly as long as Doc's, and the pressure of her hand on his was very slight as she mounted to the passenger's seat. The warm nights of late spring and summer were more than two months off and she clutched her light wrap at the throat. Doc slid the heat levers all the way to the right. When he felt warm air coming out of the vents he turned on the fan. The wipers skinned a light mist off the windshield. Lighted windows hung on the night like ripe yellow pears, delineating the neighborhoods less by the lights themselves than by the dark spaces in between. To the southeast, the glow of downtown and Coleman A. Young's riverfront reflected off the man-made overcast of factory smoke and auto exhaust.

"Nice party," Doc said after a few minutes. He couldn't think of anything else.

"Yes, it was." She was looking out her window.

"Beatrice has a lot of friends."

"Beatrice is a lot of friend."

"Have you known her a long time?"

"She was part of the Twelfth Street scene in the sixties. I knew most of them."

"Through Mahomet, I guess."

"No, I met them after he died. Most of them didn't know he was married. I was sixteen, the youngest of the batch." She made a throaty sound. "I still am. It's funny how few of the young ones are left, and how many of the ones who weren't young even then are still around."

"Those early models last."

"This town eats its young," she said.

He took the ramp onto the Jeffries Freeway. The slipstream squealed around the edges of the new bullet-proof windows. "You wonder how someone like Wilson McCoy lasted as long as he did."

"A lot of people thought he was already dead. They were right."

"Did you go to the funeral because of his connection with the Marshals of Mahomet?"

She turned her head to look at him. Bursts of light from the gooseneck streetlamps stuttering overhead found the bones of her face, making it look illuminated from within. She turned back. "I thought I recognized you. No, McCoy never understood Gerald, what he stood for. The Marshals represent a big part of what he was trying to overcome. He died trying to stop a riot that McCoy was doing his best to start. I didn't go to the funeral of Wilson McCoy the M-and-M. I went to pay my respects to the man who gave Mahomet his first chance to speak to his brothers and sisters about what was eating him from inside. Gerald was just another unemployed Negro with a taken name until McCoy asked him to address a meeting of the Black Afro-American Congress. I went because Gerald would have gone himself without having to think about it."

"Oh."

She made the throaty sound. "I speechify when I'm tired. I'm sorry. Gerald used to use me as his test audience and I guess some of it took. It comes in handy when I'm asked to say a few words at rallies and fund-raisers."

"You speak beautifully."

"Not as beautifully as he did. He was a gospel singer, and he had the voice. But what you mean is I don't speak like a city black. I can do that too. Most of us switch back and forth. Most of you do, too, depending on who's listening. I dropped out of high school to get married. Beatrice made up for what I missed."

"She learned from a madam too, she says."

"She told me the same story. Maybe it's true. I think she dramatizes herself a little. I'm pretty sure her father was still alive when I knew her on Twelfth Street. She used to get these letters in an old man's shaky scrawl from Jamaica, addressed to Miss Ruby Sandoval. Probably asking for money."

"I thought that story about him trying to drown her and shooting the rest of the family was fishy," he said. "It sounded more like something that would happen in Detroit."

"The older you get the fewer people there are who can call you a liar."

They exited the Jeffries and rolled through well-lit blocks of large homes with clipped lawns and beds of flowers. "Truman is Beatrice's bodyguard, such as he is," Doc said then. "Why don't you have one?"

"I have three. The N.A.A.C.P. pays for them. I sent them home this afternoon. Freedom is supposed to be what it's all about." More of the deep South was veining her speech, as if she were too tired to fight it back. "If they could stuff me and stick me in a glass box, they would. Being a symbol is a tough way to make a living."

"Why don't you quit?"

"How do you quit what you never started?" She shifted on the seat. "That's my house there, the third one."

It was a brick split-level on a quarter-acre lot, with a fence of cedars along one edge of the yard and an arched window in front that reminded Doc of church. He parked in the asphalt driveway, filling it, and got out to help her down, but she was already standing on the ground when he reached her. He walked with her to the front door.

"Thank you, Kevin. Or do you prefer Doc?" She used her key. A T-square-shaped section of light tipped out onto the porch.

"I can go either way."

"Kevin, then. Doc sounds too much like a street name." On the other side of the threshold she turned to smile back at him. "Good night, Kevin."

"Alcina, that you? I just—"

Beyond her shoulder, a young black man in mottled jeans and a green tank top stained black with sweat had stepped into the lighted entryway through a side arch, saw Doc, and drew back out of sight.

Mrs. Lilley moved quickly and gracefully, filling the space between the door and the frame with her body. "My nephew," she said. "He has a key. Good night." The door closed.

Doc hesitated, then stepped off the porch. On his way across the grass to the Coachmen, the tail of his eye caught a movement of the curtain in the arched window, but he didn't turn to see which of them was watching.

Neal, Billie, and young Sean were sitting at the dinner table when he got home. The house smelled of cooking. It sat heavily on the vodka in his stomach. Neal said to his wife, "Told you I saw that big box going past the window. Hope you didn't block my truck," he told Doc.

"I parked on the street. Ance said I could take it home when I called him from—when I called him. I don't feel like eating," he said when Billie got up to set another place. "I think I'll go upstairs and lie down."

She said, "You smell like an ashtray. You're not supposed to go to any bars."

"It was a party in an apartment. I'll tell you about it later." His head was hurting, too. All the smoke and too much conversation were catching up with him.

The telephone rang as he was climbing the stairs. Billie answered.

"Kevin, it's for you. I think it's your boss."

A TV set was mumbling in the background on Ance's end. Doc recognized the percussive theme and looped soundtrack of that irritating cold-medication commercial inspired by rap. "Want me to pick you up in the morning?" he asked.

"Fuck that." The bail bondsman's voice had an edge. "You watching Channel Two?"

He glanced at the dark set and said no. Ance said, "Put it on. I'll call you back."

The picture blipped on just as the commercial ended. He waited through another almost as bad, then the TV-2 News anchorman's moisturized and barbered face looked up from the sheaf of blank sheets in his hands and announced that an undercover officer with the Detroit Narcotics Squad had been shot to death while on assignment. Doc thought that couldn't be what Ance had wanted him to see. Then, following a picture of the slain officer taken in uniform, a front-and-profile mug shot came on. The anchorman's professional-mourner voice continued:

"Police suspect Starkweather Hall, a prominent member of the Marshals of Mahomet group of African-American activists, believed to be a front for one of the city's biggest crack cocaine operations. Hall, sought since last December on drug charges . . ."

Doc didn't pay much attention to the rest, which was mostly file information he had heard before. The photo of Starkweather Hall showed a combative face with wide-set eyes, short hair, and black fan-shaped side-whiskers underscoring the hollows under his cheekbones. Clean-shaven, the face would look fuller and younger and somewhat less sinister. That was how Doc had seen it less than thirty minutes before in the entryway of Alcina Lilley's home in Birmingham.

Chapter 18

◆◆◆◆◆◆◆◆◆

Saturday's game took place under a gray steel sky like the doors of the old solitary cells in Jackson, now used for storage. And it was three-handed.

Charlie Battle was pulling extra duty in the investigation into the death of Sergeant Ernest Melvin of the Detroit Narcotics Squad, whose body dressed in civilian clothes had been found leaking into the grass behind an empty crack house on Dragoon. Needles Lewis and his two fellow Marshals didn't show up, and Doc guessed they had been taken in for questioning. Neal was working, and just before Doc and Sean left the house Jeff Dolan called to say he had clients coming in all day to have their taxes done. At that point Doc had suggested canceling, but Sean surprised him by saying he needed batting practice. The boy looked bright-eyed on the way to the corner and almost rugged in a new pair of jeans and a sweatshirt he had cut the sleeves off himself. He carried the bat and fielder's glove Doc had bought for him.

"That ain't no way to throw. You got to snap your arm."

Doc, stepping forward to retrieve the ball Sean had tried to throw back at him while he was warming up, looked up as

Battle's son Charlie Junior came trotting across the lot. He was wearing the same cutoff sweatshirt and Levi's he'd had on the week before. Doc suspected from Sean's similar outfit that some bonding had been going on outside his notice. "Hi, Charlie!" The boy sounded ecstatic.

"I thought your dad was working," Doc said.

"He is. I walked." Junior pulled on his glove and turned the palm Doc's way. Doc threw him the ball. "Sean, you ever see a gladiator picture, they bust down a wall with one of them catapults? That's how you got to use your arm. Here, I'll show you."

The ballfield was shaping up. Doc and Sean had cleared away a lot of debris during the week, stuffing it into trash bags and carrying it to the curb. Doc made a note to ask his brother if he could borrow his lawn mower next week.

Things had been quiet since the day of Beatrice Blackwood's homecoming party. When Ance had called back after the news report on Starkweather Hall and the murder of Sergeant Melvin he had asked Doc to come to his house.

The woman who had answered the door was nearly as tall as Alcina Lilley, trim, blonde, and younger than Doc. She wore a gold open-necked blouse tucked into beige slacks that hugged her hips and high-heeled sandals on her bare feet with vermilion paint on the toenails.

"Hi. I'm Cynthia, Maynard's wife. You're Doc Miller. What are the Tigers' chances for a .500 season?"

"About five hundred to one against." He shook her strong hand. "Better if Sparky has a stroke or Monaghan fires him."

"Not much chance of that. I think Sparky has evidence that Monaghan worships Satan, or maybe that he's allergic to pepperoni. I'd have canned him after the '85 season. Maynard's downstairs."

It was a full basement with a seven-foot soundproofed ceiling and pegboard panels on the walls loaded with tools. It contained a workbench with vise attached and shelves of how-to books arranged alphabetically according to subject and a drill press and bandsaw mounted on stout frames and cans of stain and varnish on steel utility shelves. Doc was no great observer, but during the short walk across the thick carpet from the stairs to the big recliner where Ance sat reading the evening *News*, he decided that the tools had never been off their hooks and that the lids had never been pried from the cans. The only things in the room that showed signs of use—besides Ance himself— were the recliner, split at the seams with foam rubber bulging out like pale flesh, and a scarred kitchen table leaning in a corner covered with empty brass cartridges and cans of smoke- less powder. A bare metal revolver frame with neither cylinder nor side grips lay atop a stack of *Shooters' Bibles.*

"My workshop, where the cares of the day fade away whilst I'm painting a shithouse for hummingbirds," said the bail bondsman without greeting. "My third wife sprang it on me when I got back from eleven days in Wisconsin looking for an arsonist. Her psychotherapist told her I needed a hobby. I filed the next day."

"Your new one seems nice."

"I've been married to her longer than the first four put together." He folded the newspaper and scaled it onto the bench. "How was the party?"

"Dull, except for the conversation. I was the youngest one there not counting the bodyguard, and he passed out early."

"Beatrice the one you had the conversation with?"

"She's had an interesting life."

"Several of 'em. Which one she tell you about?"

Doc pulled a stool out from under the bench and sat down. "Just out of curiosity, do you tell Taber any more than you tell me when you send him on an errand? It'd help if I knew what I was supposed to find out. Truman or any one of a dozen people at that party could have driven her home from the hospital. She didn't need me."

"She asked for you."

"Bullshit."

"Okay, but she did. I wanted to send Taber. I should've guessed how it'd go when I couldn't find him to take me to the funeral. You two hit it off pretty good there."

"Has it got something to do with Starkweather Hall?"

Ance had gotten out a cigarette and was playing with it. He glanced beyond Doc's shoulder. "Hit that switch, will you? It goes to the vent fan."

Doc reached over and flipped it without getting up. The fan, mounted behind a screen in the wall near the bandsaw, whirred. Ance struck a kitchen match off the edge of the bench and lit the cigarette. "I promised Cynthia she wouldn't catch me smoking. If you want to keep a wife you've got to keep your promises first." He batted at the smoke until he was satisfied it was drifting toward the screen. "If it wasn't for Beatrice Blackwood I'd have gone bust years ago. You know what it's like for a white man in my racket to get information in a place like Detroit?"

"She's your snitch?"

"That's TV talk. Street skinny is merchandise just like everything else. There's no shame in selling it. A good intelligence broker gets more respect than a surgeon."

"Is that what you're grooming me for?"

The question went unacknowledged. "I can't do the digging myself. It's got to look good. This is a sports town. A professional jock like you carries his own bona fides. It'd be better if you were black, but maybe not; that's kind of obvious. They don't mind being pumped so much if it doesn't look like you think you're putting one over on them. It's complicated when you try to put words to it."

"Who's *they*?"

"The brokers. The boys and girls with the poopy. The big-eared hookers and the grifters and the smart fellers in the stick joints that know it all except how to hold a job that doesn't pay in old bills. They know how much what they've got is worth, and they like it when you ask them with respect. That's where you figure in. You treat everybody like people, you know it? Must be that southern upbringing. With Taber it's asshole this and scroat that. Me too, but we've seen more of the world than you. Anyway, if you and Beatrice got on okay today I was going to suggest hiring you out to her, but this thing with the undercover cop fucks up my timetable. What'd you hear?"

"Nothing about Hall. If you'd told me all this before, I could have asked."

"That's just what I didn't want. Jesus. How'd you survive seven years in Jackson?"

"I'm too big to bugger." He'd had that one ready. "Why are you interested? You said those rewards are never paid."

"Those community pool jobs never are. He's a cop killer now, though. That changes everything. The cop union, the D.P.O.A., will match them or better, and they have a reputation for making good on their offers. The sons of bitches think when one of their own goes down it's a bigger deal than when it's just a citizen. That's bad for democracy but good for me. An extra hundred grand would keep me in lightbulbs and envelopes for the next six months."

"You didn't know he was going to be a cop-killer when you lent me out."

"Let's say I was speculating in Hall futures. He's got a hot head and every blue bag in town smelled promotion all over him." Ance pinched out his cigarette half-smoked and laid it on the bench. "This undercover, this Melvin, was moling his way into the M-and-M's. His last message out said he had a line on Hall. Two days later some kid looking for a connection or an open window stumbles over Melvin's body, and Hall's the biggest catch in town since Jack Dance."

"I'm nobody's idea of a mole. Everything shows on my face."

"That's why people trust you. Even Charlie Battle. He's got you spying on me."

Doc knew better than to hesitate. "If that were true he'd be wasting his money. I told you I had nothing to tell him."

"Don't get sore. I said there's nothing wrong with selling what you know. Who was at the party?"

"You've got a bad habit of accusing people of things, then backing off," Doc said. "I told Battle I'd keep my eyes and ears open. If I didn't he could screw my parole down so tight I'd be happy to go back to prison. I think I just quit."

"A speech like that is usually made standing up."

Doc stood up.

"Sit down. Everybody knows how tall you are. I believe you."

Doc sat down.

"Better. Trouble with ballplayers is they all think they got to live up to the numbers on the back of their card."

"I never had a card."

"Who gives a shit? Some kid winds up trading eighteen Doc Millers for one Boog Powell and there you are with a price sticker on your ass."

"Boog Powell? Give me a break."

"I don't see you doing beer commercials. Anyway, fuck that. What counts is what you're worth to me. You're there when I call. I'd dump Taber, but he knows too much about the way I do business. Who was at the party?"

"I didn't get most of the names. Truman at the door. A woman with a scar on her cheek."

"Bonnibelle Rudge. The Sicilians gave her that scratch when they knocked over Joe Petite's place in '66."

"Someone mentioned Sebastian Bright."

"Dead for years. Come on. Anybody who can memorize all those fancy signs ought to be good at names."

"Theron Something Gidrey. Gidgy, Beatrice called him."

"Old guy? Weak eyes?"

"More than weak. Blind. She said he used to own the Morocco Motor Hotel."

"Owned a hell of a lot more than that before the riots. Jesus, I was sure he died. Who else?"

That time he hesitated. "Alcina Lilley."

"No shit, you talk to her?"

"I took her home."

"Yeah?" It had a leer in it. "No wonder you're zonked."

Doc was in the middle of a bitter yawn. His headache was better but his bones felt heavy. "She's a little old for me. I was nine when her husband got killed."

"A man can learn a lot from an older woman. I'm kidding. What did you talk about?"

Now, watching Charlie Junior showing Sean how to cock his arm with the ball in his hand, then straighten it out with a snap, following through after the ball was in flight as if directing it with an invisible rod, Doc wasn't sure why he had said nothing to Ance or anyone else about seeing Starkweather Hall at Alcina Lilley's house in Birmingham. If it was Hall. He had seen the man only briefly and with the light behind him, and as often as Doc had talked himself into accepting that Sergeant Melvin's suspected killer was staying with Mahomet's widow, he had talked himself out of it just as often. He was pretty sure that wasn't the reason he had kept silent. He didn't know if he would have done the same before Jackson. The Kevin Miller who had never been to prison had nothing to discuss with the Doc Miller who watched life on the outside as if it were still framed by the nineteen-inch screen in the TV room. Paralyzed by the terms of his parole, he was no more a participant in the world than Sean was in front of his everlasting video games. Even his sex was brought to him and applied literally at arm's length for a fee.

"Heads up, Doc!"

Junior's warning penetrated as a wild throw from Sean sent the ball spinning at Doc's head. He pivoted, caught it in front of his face, then followed through in a full turn, knifing it at Junior with everything he had. It struck the boy's glove with a sharp crack. He held on to the ball a fraction of a second, then dropped it, flung away the glove, and doubled over, hugging his hand between his thighs. "Ow. Shit. Jesus God. Ouch."

Doc ran up to him in a chill of remorse. "I'm sorry. You okay? I'm really sorry."

Junior straightened, shaking the hand and blowing on the fingers. "Who'd you think you was pitching to, Reggie Jackson? Jesus."

"I wasn't thinking. I uncorked the heat. Let's go to the house and put it in ice. You want to go to the emergency room?"

"I don't think nothing's broken." He flexed his fingers. He had a red patch on his palm. "Man, you're wasting your time here. You ought to be back with the Tigers."

Sean's eyes were as big as bases. "You were a Tiger?"

Before Doc could answer, a gray stretch Lincoln as long as a throw to center field drifted into the curb behind home plate. Its horn flatted.

"Watch it!" said Junior when Doc started walking that way. He sounded like his father the cop.

"If it's a drive-by, the gangs are coming up in the world." But Doc slowed his pace. The driver was a large black man in a blue serge suit. Another black man was seated on the passenger's side. The windows in back were smoked. As Doc drew near, the dark window on his side glissed down.

"Who's winning?"

Alcina Lilley had on a dark blue dress with a yellow-and-red scarf knotted at the side cowboy fashion and because it looked like rain a belted car coat of a shade of white that Doc guessed was called eggshell. A yellow silk carnation was pinned to her hair two inches to the right of the part. It made him think of a picture he had once seen of Billie Holliday. By daylight he could see tiny lines around her eyes.

"Nobody's winning or losing," he said. "We're just fooling around."

"I stopped at your house. Your sister-in-law told me you were here." She looked apologetic. "Are you committed? I'd like to borrow you for the day. Part of it, anyway."

He glanced at the two men in the front seat. "I don't play golf."

She made introductions. The pair nodded their beachball-size heads infinitesimally. Their names slid out of Doc's grasp like glycerine. "I want to take you to lunch," she said.

"Am I dressed for it?" He looked down at his flannel shirt and corduroys.

"The dress code is whatever turns you on. Are you free?"

"I'll find out."

Junior, still working his stricken hand, goggled at the woman in the car. "That who I think it is?"

"How would I know that?" Doc said. "Okay if I leave you guys? Sean needs practice hitting the low ones."

"He needs practice hitting the ground with a bat. He'll be Cecil Fielder when I get through with him. If it don't rain first."

Doc turned toward the car. Junior called his name. He looked back.

"Use a condom."

Doc threw him his glove.

The backseat, upholstered in heavy-duty tweed with leather reinforcing, was like a divan, wrapping itself around Doc's hips

167

and shoulders as the car ghosted out into the street. Alcina Lilley touched his knee briefly. The gesture was warm and natural and over too quickly to be sexual; but suddenly he was very far away from the ballfield.

"I got the feeling I was abrupt with you the other night," she said. "I'm sorry. I wasn't expecting a visit from my nephew. It threw me off."

He murmured something about not having noticed. He felt a sudden strange sadness. He had just about talked himself out of believing that it was Starkweather Hall he had seen. Her bringing up the other night said different.

"Is that younger boy your son?" she asked.

"My brother's. I'm not married."

"Notice how subtle I was about asking."

She was looking out her window as she spoke and probably didn't notice the glance that passed between the two men in the front seat. Darkened by the tinted glass, the sky looked more threatening than it did through the clear windshield, but there was a dark fringe beyond the downtown skyscrapers in the distance that looked like the brown curling edge of a diseased leaf. Doc hoped Sean would have the courtesy to invite Charlie Junior home before the rain started.

"Where are we eating?" he asked Mrs. Lilley.

"The National Guard Armory."

He was glad he hadn't dressed.

By Leon "Bud" Arsenault
(continued)

The parlor of the house on Trumbull that has seen Mrs. MacGryff from infancy to old age contains enough Detroit Tigers memorabilia to fill a wing at Cooperstown.

Here is a pair of scuffed and curling high-topped athletic shoes said to have been worn by Ty Cobb, which if a good forensic pathologist were to put them to the test would probably yield up the blood and tissue of a hundred third basemen from the cleats; here, on a stand, a ball scribbled all over with the faded signatures of the Detroit 1940 World Series team, including Greenburg and Gehringer; up there on the wall, cancer-spotted with mildew and gnawed by moths, a pennant found in a junk shop, advertising a forgotten team known as the Detroits.

Dregs, sighs Mrs. MacGryff.

The bulk of her collection was never recovered after the 1968 burglary.

"I had a complete set of Rudy York cards from 1934 to 1945," she laments, "and a scorecard signed by Schoolboy Rowe. It was hard to read because it was the year he hurt his shoulder. Anybody who didn't know what it was might have just thrown it out. So many things. But I still have my memories."

Seized with a sudden inspiration, the rotund matron

bounces out of her padded rocker and stands on tiptoe to take down a wooden bat from atop a bookcase crammed with Tiger Yearbooks. It is smeared with pine tar and bears the famed Louisville trademark.

"It was presented to me personally by Lou Whitaker in 1984. It wasn't his favorite; he asked for that one back after he hit me in the mouth with it."

The occasion was spring training for the Tigers' remarkable championship season. Mrs. MacGryff's children and grandchildren pooled their resources to send her to the Florida camp as an early Mother's Day present.

Swinging at a Dan Petry fastball, Sweet Lou missed and lost his grip on the bat, which spun end over end into the stands and smashed into Mrs. MacGryff's jaw.

While recovering from emergency oral surgery at Lakeland Memorial Hospital she received a visitor.

"Lou brought me flowers and this bat. I was groggy from the anesthetic and my jaw was wired. I don't know now if I thanked him properly at the time.

"Whenever I look at the bat, or take out my upper and lower plates, I think of that wonderful spring. I'm just sorry I was too busy going in and out of hospitals that season to watch most of the games. I missed the play-offs entirely."

Lou still sends her a Christmas card every year.

(to be continued)

PART FOUR
Heat

◆◆◆◆◆◆◆◆◆

Chapter 19

❖❖❖❖❖❖❖❖

The Detroit National Guard Armory was a great Gothic limestone pile that took up a city block downtown and served as its own gargoyle. A triumphantly ugly building, it was cratered on the outside with moldy arches like suppurating sores and on the inside looked as desolate as a scorched foundation in an empty field. The big dank ceilingless rooms echoed with the sense-memory of a thousand swap meets, book-and-author luncheons, and desperate circuses with their elderly elephants and sinister clowns. Entering through a side door next to Alcina Lilley with the two bodyguards stationed fore and aft, Doc kicked something that rattled across the concrete floor; a bone, perhaps, from the skeleton of some forgotten delegate to an old political convention. The air, never entirely still in buildings of that size and vacancy, rustled like cast-off cocoons in a ruin.

Beneath the rustling, or perhaps over it, Doc heard a hum of voices. It grew louder as they approached the main room, and when they were inside, looking around at what must have been several hundred people seated at long tables draped in white cloth, the voices retained a disembodied quality, washing around among the rafters twenty feet above while the speakers' mouths moved silently in a kind of mass ventriloquism. Most of those present were black, and every one of them was dressed better than Doc. There was a general shifting of seats when Mrs. Lilley entered. When she paused to allow Doc to help her off with her coat, their attention went to him, and he was living an old dream in which he found himself standing stark naked on the pitcher's mound before a capacity crowd. Certainly his presence here was just as inexplicable.

At the end of the big room near the door stood another long table on a dais, and behind the table on the wall with drapery gathered around it like an enormous window hung a photograph fifteen feet by ten of Gerald W. Lilley, known best to the world as Mahomet. The handsome, straight-haired black man, who bore a slight resemblance to Nat King Cole, was shown from the waist up in one of his trademark white suits, posed characteristically with arms aloft, his face illuminated from some unseen source. For Doc the image contained all the best and worst qualities of one of those trick paintings of Jesus whose face moved with the angle of scrutiny or an Elvis portrait on black velvet. It would have seemed riotously out of place anywhere but among the Wagnerian proportions of that room. With a jolt, Doc recognized Detroit City Councilwoman Maryann Mahaffey and State Senator John Conyers seated among the dignitaries at the head table. They too were watching the two new arrivals.

For a moment Doc had a horror that they would be conducted to the head table, but when a bodyguard pulled a chair from the end of the one nearest the door for Mrs. Lilley, Doc responded gratefully to a gesture from her to take the seat next to hers. He was relieved to be out of the line of sight of most of the assembly.

Mrs. Lilley sensed it. "They wanted me to sit up there, but I can't stand having everyone in the room watching me eat. I'd be sure to spill something."

"I expected something more casual." Doc's place setting looked like a silver-plated hubcap.

"You look fine. They're just staring because I had the nerve to choose my own escort."

"A white escort."

"Don't be a bigot. I attend these things about four times a year and I was getting just a little tired of being steered around like someone's crazy rich aunt."

"A necktie at least."

She wasn't listening. "This time they're raising money to lobby the legislature in Lansing to have Gerald's birthday declared a state holiday. He'd have been fifty-six next Tuesday."

Doc said nothing. He didn't know whether to offer congratulations or condolences. He was sure Mahomet was staring down at him from the picture.

The bodyguards had retreated to the near wall, where standing with feet spread and their hands folded in front of them they made no attempt to look like anything but what they were. Looking around, Doc saw others he knew on a more personal basis than Mahaffey and Conyers: Dick "Night Train" Lane, the former Detroit Lion and now director of the Police Athletic Program, whom Doc had met a long time ago at a banquet honoring yet another sports legend with his eye on local politics; a number of conservatively dressed men spotted around the room whom Doc eventually identified as police officers he had seen at Wilson McCoy's funeral; and, seated kitty-corner from him at the far end of his own table, talking with a fat man in a bad hairpiece sitting on the other side, Sergeant Charlie Battle. He made brief eye contact with Doc but there was no recognition in it, and he appeared engrossed in the discussion, which Doc decided from the other man's gestures had to do with the Pistons' performance in last night's NBA play-off game. Either that, or the man was having some kind of fit.

175

"See anyone you know?"

Doc realized Mrs. Lilley had been watching him watching Battle. "A few," he said. "Who's minding the store?"

"The clerks and secretaries, just like always. That's why you never see them at these things."

The room was stirring again. A flying wedge of anonymous humanity in dark double-breasted suits had entered on the stride with Mayor Coleman Young in the center.

Frustrated would-be visitors and newsmen who had failed to track down the peripatetic politician complained that he moved around like a man with a price on his head, as if a lifetime of dodging grand juries, process-servers, and old girlfriends with new babies had forced him into a shell game in which even the shells—his office in the City-County Building, his Manoogian Mansion residence, the shifting headquarters of his Detroit Technologies investment firm, various hotel suites throughout the city and its suburbs—changed with the daily calendar. The way he moved suggested that same restless energy. The group, charged by the industry of its central component like a vehicle its engine, knifed in without pausing and made straight for the table where Doc was seated with Alcina Lilley. The effect of the Presence on the room's occupants was physical, turning their heads and bodies in a kind of wave as if an inverse wind had blasted the door open from inside and tried to suck them out into the corridor. Doc felt it and was rising from his seat— whether resisting it or succumbing to it, he wasn't certain— when the group stopped and Young glittered forward out of its center to take Mrs. Lilley's hand in the two-handed grip universal to office-holders everywhere. " 'Cina, if you was to bottle them good looks and put them on sale in Hudson's you could buy the whole God damn city."

She smiled. "I didn't know you were selling."

Young reacted with that silent, shoulder-shaking laugh often seen in press conferences (until the wrong question was asked), watching her closely through the large square lenses of his featherweight glasses. He wasn't as tall as he looked on television. Built like a truck on a short wheelbase, round-faced and graying above nine hundred dollars of haberdashery, he had skin almost as light as Doc's, against which his white Clark Gable moustache came close to disappearing under the overhead lights. But his blackness was unquestionable, particularly in his urban drawl and seemingly unconscious use of gutter language in unexpected surroundings. The precision of his "God damn"—not "goddamn" as it was frequently written, or "*got*damn" as it appeared in articles by journalists who fancied themselves authors—convinced Doc that it was anything but unconscious. "Motherfucker," another favorite Colemanism, still escaped publication in the family-oriented press. The dirty-old-man twinkle in his eyes when he swore couldn't quite mask an increased intensity in his gaze as he observed the effect on his listener.

Now the gaze shifted Doc's way, and he broke off his own analysis to grasp the large smooth well-manicured hand that was offered him. "You're Doc Miller," Young told him. "Where were you in '87 when the Twins took the play-offs away from us with their God damn domed stadium?"

Doc just smiled. They both knew where he'd been. The mayor's grip was strong, too strong. It seemed to be yet another test, but it tightened spasmodically with the words "domed stadium"; Young had been wanting to pull down the venerable and historic Tiger Stadium—the oldest of its kind and the site of the first major league game in baseball history—and replace it with a sprawling cupolaed multipurpose coliseum along the lines of those in Houston and Minneapolis–St. Paul for as long as he had been in office, preferably with his own name etched in granite over every entrance. From his advantage of height and leverage, Doc gave back as good as he got in the handclasp. The contact was broken with an approving duck of the mayoral head. There was nothing subtle about the expressions and gestures of this diabolically subtle man.

"How long you know our 'Cina?" he asked then.

Doc had a flash of complete certainty that it was a question to which Young already knew the answer. Indeed, his recognition of a ballplayer whose face he could not have seen since his third term had been too fast to be the result of anything but a recent briefing.

"We met just this week." He wondered how long he had been under investigation. It was an open secret in Detroit that an entire detail of the police department existed only to run errands for Coleman A. Young.

"Well, you be sure and look after her good, son. She's a one-woman campaign chest." And he moved off in the direction of the head table, shoulders shaking. His entourage closed around him like bow wash around a fast-moving destroyer.

The food, catered by the exclusive (and dear) Lark restaurant in West Bloomfield and brought by waiters and waitresses in spotless livery, was excellent, light-years removed from the common banquet fare of embalmed turkey, superannuated mashed potatoes, and despicable peas. Doc commented on this to Mrs. Lilley, who said, "It better be, at five hundred dollars a plate. Coleman doesn't change his shirt for anything less."

Doc paid special attention to his London broil after that.

Dessert was chilled peaches cloaked in heavy cream, followed by speeches. Doc's old friend from Wilson McCoy's funeral, the Reverend Whatsizname from the Second Baptist Church, hooked on his Ben Franklins and read a benediction from a prepared text with the leaden intonation of an eighth-grade English student reciting Shakespeare, while Doc bowed his head and studied a gravy spot on the tablecloth. The emcee was Dave Bing, former Detroit Piston and rumored protégé of Young's to succeed him in office, who told a joke about the black folks being in charge of the armory, then as the laughter rippled away introduced the mayor. At that point a Channel 7 news crew moved down the aisle trailing its tentacled infinity of equipment and a bolt of hard white light lifted the new speaker out of the human condition onto the bright antiseptic plane of the public platform. The applause rocked the huge old building on its foundation. This self-described "Cadillac mayor" was one of theirs: labor activist, war hero, belligerent survivor of the congressional witch-hunts of the 1950s, former blue-collar incorrigible who had slugged his way—with a monkey wrench, according to an old police complaint—out of the pipe-sweating, acetylene-splattering, man-made labyrinth of this working-class town into a silk-lined office twice the size of his parents' apartment, and never let the suburban white establishment forget either his color or his street-soiled past. His low forehead and chubby cheeks had supplanted the austere green cast-copper face of the Spirit of Detroit the way the cylindrical cigar-case towers of his Renaissance Center had changed the skyline along the river. Neither the Justice Department nor the federal grand jury system nor the Detroit Yacht Club—altogether a far more formidable society with its own concept of government and a memory going back to before Mr. Ford's five-dollar workday darkened the city's complexion—had been able to tip him out of the wingbacked tufted-leather swivel chair of power; no amount of garbage-contract scandals or plundered police funds or paternity suits or personal traffic in South African Krugerrands could even force him to shift his weight on the springs. He had planted himself so solidly that even an assassin's bullet could do no more than remove his almost redundant physical presence from the upholstery. His aura had scorched its stocky outline onto the surface of Detroit like a garish pattern onto an early color television lens, to glow there like some mocking Banquo long after the person who wore it had passed out of the frame.

Young's opening remarks were surprisingly tame, confining themselves to platitudes on race, equality, and Mahomet's brief career as a public spokesman on their behalf that Doc had heard from more conservative sources. The subject of race seemed to make the mayor uncomfortable when he wasn't employing it as a bludgeon to pummel his detractors and bring the largely white-owned Detroit media into line. His experiences as an unfriendly witness before the House Un-American Activities Committee had taught him the power of labels, and in the painfully socially sensitive atmosphere of the 1990s, to be branded a racist by the most volatile black politician in America was as potentially devastating as to be termed a communist by Senator Joseph McCarthy in the time of Eisenhower. But before a sympathetic audience, most of whom had suffered from the effects of true racism at one time or another, all his best ammunition went off with the hollow plop of blank cartridges in a mock battle staged for purposes of training. Nevertheless he was forced to pause at intervals while geysers of applause spouted and died.

Police Chief William Hart had entered the room behind the mayor and his people and taken a seat at the end of the head table by the door, where he sat in his customary heap of inert ugliness, stirring only to put his hands together along with the rest of the audience whenever his superior remade a point established as far back as *Brown vs. Board of Education.* A disconcertingly homely man whose wide-set eyes glimmered through fissures in a face like a collapsed balloon, Hart had made few public appearances

recently and seldom spoke when he did. He left during yet another noisy interlude, slipping out the door without fanfare. Doc
wondered if he was reluctant to stay away from his office for fear
it would be rifled by federal investigators. The probe into his
connections with much-indicted civilian Deputy Police Chief
Kenneth Weiner showed no signs of letting up; currently, can-
celed checks indicating that Weiner had used public money to
pay the rent on an apartment for Hart's daughter were appear-
ing on television and in facsimile in both local newspapers. The
daily soap operas faded like pressed flowers beside revelations of
these and other investments made by Weiner in the name of
Mayor Young's Detroit Technologies corporation, of which he
was general manager. It was a Young blessing that a large part of
his constituency was incapable of following so intricate a fraud
and thus continued to re-elect him with spasmodic regularity.

"... person best qualified to speak of Mahomet's life and
work. His widow, Alcina Lilley."

The mayor's concluding words slid under a fresh detona-
tion of palms throughout the auditorium. Doc stood and—
somewhat maliciously, for one of the N.A.A.C.P. bodyguards
had left the wall to reach for Mrs. Lilley's chair—presented his
own services, blocking the aisle with his body. She rose with a
slight pressure of her hand on his and left the table silently on a
cushion of encomium. Young steered her to the lecturn. By this
time everyone was on his feet. She waited, smiling, while the din
washed away. Flashguns lit her face in a sputtering volley.

"Thank you." Her voice, keyed slightly above the middle
register, went out into the room without the electronic booming
that had accompanied Young's. "Gerald—Mahomet—would
have been proud to see this day. Not because of the attention to
him, but because of the pride that is present and which he gave
his life trying to instill in all of us." She paused and seemed
to turn away from the microphone; a single pair of hands

smacked. Then: "I might add that he could have bought five suits for the price of the meal I just had. Thank you."

The simple speech and the quiet joke at the end brought the audience back out of its seat, and as she left the podium with a kiss on one cheek from the mayor, the noise reminded Doc of thirty thousand fans stamping their feet on the grandstand. He joined in the applause. He couldn't hear his own hands clapping.

"Mahomet is God! You're eating the body and drinking the blood of Mahomet!"

Doc had the impression that the same words had been shouted over and over again before anyone heard them over the general tumult. They came from the direction of the door, where a group of young black men dressed as he was, in old shirts and faded trousers, surged against the arms of the two bodyguards extended to keep them out. "You're eating the body and drinking the blood of Mahomet! Mahomet is God!"

On the dais, Mayor Young had inserted himself between Alcina Lilley and the intruders. At the other end of Doc's table Charlie Battle, backing into the clear space in front of the lectern, lifted his hands to signal to the plainclothes officers stationed around the room, unconsciously mirroring Mahomet's pose in the huge photograph behind him. Some of the officers were already tunneling their way toward the door with their hands inside their coats. One almost knocked over the Channel 7 cameraman, who had turned to record the disturbance. All this time the apparent spokesman for the uninvited guests continued to assure the assembly at the top of his lungs that Mahomet was God and that they were eating his body and drinking his blood.

He was almost out of sight, obscured by the broad backs of the converging detectives, before Doc recognized the young man as Needles Lewis, one of his acquaintances from Wilson McCoy's funeral and the best catcher he had had in a long time.

Chapter 20

◆◇◆◇◆◇◆◇◆

W ake up, Kevin! Telephone!"
Doc had been Doc so long he almost never thought to answer when his Christian name was called. This time he seized it as a hand up out of his old naked dream, in which he had been pondering how to conceal his tendency toward erection whenever he got set to throw his fastball. He awoke with a real-life erection, and pretended entanglement with the bedclothes until his sister-in-law pulled her head out of the doorway. For a minute he sat in his pajamas on the edge of the mattress, thinking thoughts of the deaths of loved ones, and when he was flaccid enough to present himself put on his glasses and padded downstairs. The light coming through the living room window was gray; it was just past dawn Sunday morning. "Hello?"

"Is this Mr. Miller? Doc Miller?"

He woke up a little. He had thought it might be Ance, but this was a woman's voice. Billie, wearing a blue quilted housecoat and furry open-toed slippers, scuffed across the room without looking at Doc, opened and closed the front door, and went back toward the kitchen, unrolling the Sunday *Free Press.* "Yes?"

"Mr. Miller, my name is Joyce Stefanik. I'm sorry to bother you so early in the morning. I'm a reporter with the *News*. I'd like to do a story on you for the Sunday magazine. Would you be available for an interview?"

"What on earth for?"

"Well, I understand you were quite the local celebrity before you—before your bad luck." Listening, Doc thought there was something calculated about the substitution; that the woman was not as unsure of herself as she tried to appear. "I apologize for not having heard of you, but I was away at school when you played for the Tigers, and I'm afraid I've never been much of a baseball fan. What I want to do . . ."

"Kevin?" Billie came back in from the kitchen, staring at the front section of the *Free Press*.

". . . along the lines of a former all-American hero trying to put his life back together," Joyce Stefanik went on.

Doc excused himself and put his hand over the mouthpiece. "What?"

Billie turned the section over and held it out by the edges. *Young greets former Tiger pitcher Kevin "Doc" Miller at Saturday's event honoring Mahomet,* began the caption under the two-column color picture centered near the top of page one. *Alcina Lilley, widow of the slain civil rights leader, looks on.* Indeed, she was standing as far off to the side as possible without being left out of the shot entirely. The angle at which the photo was taken diminished the Mutt-and-Jeff effect of Doc's reaching down to grasp the mayor's hand. He hadn't known a camera was anywhere near.

"Mr. Miller?"

He asked the reporter to call back later and fumbled the handset into the cradle. Billie watched him as he took the paper, skimmed through the portion of the article that appeared on page one, and turned to the concluding columns near the back of the section. There was no mention of him anywhere in the article. The headline read MAHOMET RALLY SUCCESSFUL DESPITE PROTEST.

The story reported that $21,000 had been raised for efforts to have Mahomet's birthday made a state holiday. The attempt by seven men identifying themselves as Marshals of Mahomet to disrupt the proceedings had ended peacefully enough when the interlopers were arrested and charged with disturbing the peace and trespassing. They were expected to be arraigned on Monday.

Doc shook his head distractedly. He would never understand either politics or religion. Why the M-and-M's should want to prevent their god from having his own holiday eluded him.

"You didn't tell us you met the *mayor*," Billie said. "What were you doing—I'll get it." She answered the telephone. "Hello? Oh, hello, Roberta. Yes, that's Neal's brother; your Nicole met him last time she sat with Sean. Well, it didn't come up. No, we haven't been hiding him. Listen, Roberta, can I call you back? We have to get ready for church." She hung up. "Honestly, Kevin, why don't you ever tell us anything? Are you afraid we'll embarrass you in front of your friends? Neal said you were kind of stuck up when you played ball, but I always defended—darn it." She picked up the telephone and spoke with another neighbor who had read the *Free Press*. Doc went back to bed.

He was up again in a half-hour. The ringing of the telephone every five minutes made sleep impossible. He had just finished shaving and was buttoning his shirt when Billie tapped at the bathroom door. This time it was Ance on the line.

"Hobnobbing with politicians and the high-class coloreds," greeted the familiar broken-gravel voice. "I guess he don't hardly talk to no bail men no more."

"I didn't know that picture was being taken. I didn't even know about the banquet until we walked in the door. Mrs. Lilley dragged me away from a ballgame." Doc turned his back on his brother, sprawled on the sofa in his old plaid bathrobe with the newspaper spread around him like entrails. Neal was unshaven and surly-looking at that hour on a Sunday morning. The Miller family hadn't been to regular church services since Kentucky.

Ance said, "Yeah, I bet she goes a hundred and thirty stripped. You ought to carry a piece to protect you from these renegade widows. Hey, I'm not bitching. Didn't I say I wanted you to worm your way into that crowd? I just wasn't expecting to see my worm kissing the mayor's butt over my morning stack and tomato juice."

"If I kicked it instead of kissing it I wouldn't be here to answer the phone."

"He wouldn't've felt it as long as it wasn't in the pocket where he keeps his wallet. Just stay low, okay? You're no good to me you become a celebrity, drag a shitload of reporters behind you every time you go to the can."

He remembered the reporter he'd spoken to. "I got a call from a woman named Stefanik."

"Shit. Joyce Stefanik? Shit."

"You know her?"

"Do I know I got a prostate the size of Ohio? She's a pain-in-the-ass feature writer at the *News*, gets in my face every time a client takes a hike. I think she fucks somebody down at the City-County Building is how she finds out. She used to be food editor, but I guess you can only straddle so many zucchinis before it starts getting old. What'd she want?"

"An interview for the Sunday magazine, she said. I guess I should refuse."

"Fuckin'-A you should refuse. Tell her to parade it straight up her—no." He was silent for a moment. Sean came in yawning in his pajamas and turned on the television in the middle of a religious program. Doc stuck a finger in his ear to shut out the organ music. Ance said, "No, you better do the interview. You start playing hermit every snoop in town'll be at your door trying to find out what you're hiding."

"Any other instructions?"

His tone was lost on the bail bondsman. "Try not to be too fucking fascinating." The connection broke.

"Look! Uncle Kevin's on TV!"

Doc turned toward Sean, who was sitting cross-legged on the floor in front of the set. Neal looked up from the sports section. The boy had switched stations to a local news program. Doc saw himself sliding out Alcina Lilley's chair and helping her to her feet in the armory auditorium. As his profile came into view the news reader's voice laid in over the scene. "Mrs. Lilley's escort for the afternoon was Kevin 'Doc' Miller, a former pitcher for the Detroit Tigers. His major-league career ended in 1983 when he was convicted on felony charges in the death by cocaine overdose of a teenage girl at a party he hosted in the Westin Hotel and sentenced to prison. Mrs. Lilley took the opportunity to tease the guests for spending more on the luncheon than—"

"Oh, Christ!"

His sister-in-law's blasphemy shook Doc more than the spectacle of seeing himself on television. She had charged in past him wiping her hands on a dish towel and clonked off the set. Sean continued staring at the screen while the picture folded horizontally and vertically and retreated into the center of the tube. Doc couldn't see his expression. Billie's was furious.

"You just stood there and let him watch!" She rolled the dish towel into a hard ball. "You want to talk to him?"

Sean was looking at him now. "Uncle Kevin? What they said?"

Billie said, "It's not true, honey. Remember what we talked about when you saw that scary program? It isn't real."

"Sean, how about a game of catch?"

Even as he said it he became aware that it was raining outside. Big drops like blobs of glue smeared the living room window and thudded on the roof. Sean got up in one motion and ran out of the room. Feet drummed the stairs, an upstairs door banged shut.

"Kid needs his butt paddled." Neal scaled aside the sports section and braced his hands on the sofa cushions.

Doc said, "Sit tight. I'll talk to him."

"Leave him alone," said Billie. "He'll come down later and I'll talk to him then. You've done enough."

"Bullshit."

She flinched. "What?"

He repeated it. "It was your idea not to tell him anything about me. The kid didn't even know I was a ballplayer until somebody mentioned it yesterday. How long did you think you could keep him ignorant?"

"He's eight years old! How much did you understand when you were eight years old?"

"He was bound to find out. It should've come from one of us. I'll go up and talk to him."

She looked down at Neal, still braced on the sofa. "It's your son and your brother. Don't you have anything to say?"

"The hell with the whole damn bunch of you. It's my only day off." He got up and went into the kitchen. The refrigerator door thumped. Something plopped and hissed.

"I'll be upstairs." The statement dropped into the silence between Doc and his brother's wife. He left her.

Sean had gone to his uncle's room, probably from old habit because it had been Sean's room first. Doc had been age eight and thought he could picture it: the look of horror when his impulsive retreat placed the boy among the effects of the very person he had fled there to avoid; the turn back toward the door; then the stubborn angle of the young jaw with the decision to stay put. Doc rapped at the door and when there was no answer he let himself in. There was no lock, a common safety feature in houses of that vintage where the smaller bedrooms were likely to be occupied by children who were sometimes a liability. He caught Sean returning a soiled baseball to the top of the bureau. It was the last ball Doc had pitched in his last game at Jackson and had been presented to him by Blaize Depardieu, team manager and convicted rapist. It was plastered with signatures in felt-tipped marker. The inscribers weren't allowed to have ballpoint pens.

It seemed as good an opening as any.

"Did you read the autographs?"

Sean, looking out the window at a blighted maple blocking the view, was a long time responding. "I don't know any of those names."

"No reason you would, unless you hung around the post office. They're all convicts."

"What's a convict?"

"A guy in prison. You know what a convict is."

"You were one." It was almost inaudible.

"Yeah, I was one. You know what the difference is between the guys that signed that ball and your Uncle Kevin? They all did what they were in for."

He didn't turn from the window. "You didn't do what they said?"

"I threw a party. A girl died. I didn't know there was dope there."

Doc stopped. He was listening to himself with Sean's ears. Under his breath he said, "Oh, shit." He sat on the bed. Across from him on the wall hung a framed picture of him in his old uniform. The picture had cost him forty dollars in a downtown studio with a hundred wallet-size prints. "I don't like talking to people's backs. You don't have to look at me if you don't want to. I'll let you know if that tree starts growing."

The boy turned. He focused on the bedding accordioned against the footboard. Doc wiped his palms on his pants.

"I knew there was dope there, Sean. Every time the bathroom door opened someone was in there doing lines. No," he said when the boy cut a glance toward him, "not me. I tried it once and it made me feel like I could pitch the world, but I felt that way when things were good on the mound and that didn't make me feel like—didn't make me feel rotten afterwards, so I left it alone. But I knew it was there and I knew the batboy who brought the girl worked for a dealer and that meant she was one of the ones who kept going into the bathroom. I could've stopped it, but nobody ever stopped it before, I wasn't going to be the first. I just told you more than I ever told anyone, even your father." There was more: Someone finding the girl unconscious on the tile floor, laughing and trying to wake her up by pouring beer on her; someone else finally getting the message and shoving the clown aside to give her CPR; the girl's eyes all rolled over white and glittering when the samaritan tipped her head back to clear her esophagus, the green-marble look of her skin that told Doc she was a corpse even though she wasn't declared one until they got her to Receiving. He remembered thinking at the time—groping for answers through a fog of Cutty and panic for answers to the stale-sounding questions asked by the police in their preoccupied way—that the cunt couldn't have picked someplace else to snort the rest of her life up her nose, no, it had to be there.

Later, at his trial, he had seen the girl's mother sitting in the same seat every day and looking too young to have a daughter almost grown. It was the first time he had considered that you didn't have to be very old to be the parent of a sixteen-year-old. And then he had felt something of her loss.

To Sean he said, "I could throw a ball better than anybody I knew. I guess when you can do that you start to thinking you don't have to do anything else. One thing I learned, just because you didn't do anything doesn't mean you didn't do anything wrong."

The boy was looking at him now. His eyes had a rubbed look. "Charlie Junior said you were a Tiger. That's all he said but if he didn't say it I wouldn't know."

"I'm sorry. It wasn't my decision."

"But you just said—"

He put up his hands. "You got me on that one. I took too long a lead and you picked me off. Your Uncle Kevin's stupid, Sean."

Sean nodded as if he'd just been given the correct answer to a tough problem. "Dad said that. I heard him say it to Mom. Before you came."

"Your dad's smart." At that moment he realized he meant it. He'd always thought of Neal as a big dumb mechanic. Even after prison he thought he was smarter than Neal, the one who had stayed home because their father didn't hold with chasing clouds. He was living under his brother's roof, out on parole because his brother had stuck his neck out at work to get him a job, and Doc had thought he was a buffoon. He stood. "Make you a deal. From now on we tell each other the truth. No matter what we tell anybody else."

After a moment Sean grinned and put his hand in Doc's big one. Doc thought the boy was developing a callus.

The telephone rang then and Billie came up after a minute to announce it was that Stefanik woman from the *News*.

Chapter 21

❖❖❖❖❖❖❖❖

The waiter who greeted him at the Acropolis, a genuine
Mediterranean type with olive skin and long thick eyelashes
and the arms of a Greek fisherman, bulging like thighs below
his rolled-up shirtsleeves, welcomed Doc like an old friend and
steered him to a booth where a young woman sat contemplating
the typewritten specials clipped to the menu. Doc was pretty
sure he'd never seen the man before. He was aware that most of
the diners in the restaurant were watching him. He heard his
name whispered.

"Thanks for seeing me, Mr. Miller." Joyce Stefanik, shoulder-
length chestnut hair and alert brown eyes under bangs and a
square jaw that was the only mannish thing about her, lent
him a cool hand with no rings and withdrew it. She had on a
pink jersey top that hinted at a black brassiere beneath and a
rose-colored silk scarf secured with a gold signet ring bearing
her initials. Whatever else she was wearing was hidden by the
table. She looked twenty-five, but might have been older; the
bangs were misleading. "You seem to be pretty well-known
here."

"I've only been here twice." He sat down. He thought the waiter was still standing next to the booth but when he saw that the Stefanik woman was looking that way he glanced up. It was a young man in a Dick Tracy T-shirt and cutoffs.

"Doc, could I have your autograph?"

Doc looked down at the ballpoint pen and paper napkin in the young man's hands and back up to his face, thinking it was a joke. The face looked earnest and a little unsure of itself behind a struggling moustache. Doc scribbled his name on the napkin and gave it back. The young man thanked him, hovered there a moment, then thanked him again and joined a group of men and women his own age seated in the corner booth. The napkin was passed around and looked at and chattered over.

"I haven't signed one of those since the Minnesota game," Doc told the Stefanik woman. "Even then I wondered what they do with them."

"Sell them. Or trade them for something else. There aren't any collectors any more. They're all speculators."

"You sound like you know something about it."

"I did a story once about an eleven-year-old kid who bought a Lou Brock rookie card for eight dollars and sold it for a thousand. My editor thought it would be amusing to assign someone to the story who didn't know anything about baseball. I thought it was going to be a cute piece about a lucky kid. That boy was the most cold-blooded businessman I ever met, and I interviewed Roger Smith and Lee Iacocca. I'll just have the squid." She handed her menu to the Greek fisherman, who had rematerialized by the table.

Doc ordered moussaka and coffee. His companion had a full cup in front of her. The waiter took his menu and lumbered away. "I guess kids don't flip cards any more," Doc said. "Maybe mine, if I had one. Do you really eat squid?"

"I like it best cold for breakfast the next day. Are you sorry you never had a card?"

"It's the single greatest tragedy of my life."

She smiled. The expression softened the cut of her jaw. "You seem to have adjusted fairly well."

"I haven't." He glanced down at her hands. The nails were short—he supposed because she did a lot of work on keyboards—and the hands were smoothly tanned, like her face and neck and what he could see of her bosom. Her arms too, whose smoothly defined muscles said she worked out. "Don't you take notes?"

"I haven't started the interview yet."

The waiter came by with Doc's coffee and the carafe, which he used to replace the quarter-inch she'd sipped from her cup on his way to the other tables. Doc said, "What kind of story are you planning to write? Has-been jock recalls his life?"

"I let the interview suggest the angle. The other way is backwards. Do you consider your life over?"

"I did when my appeal was denied and again the first time I was turned down for parole. Now I'm not sure. Can we come back to that question?"

"Will you be able to make up your mind by then if you haven't so far?"

Inwardly and outwardly, he shrugged. Before that morning the answer to the question of whether he thought his life was over might have been yes. Something had happened during his conversation with Sean, though, and he wasn't quite sure what. He was experiencing a queer tingling and spreading warmth starting at the floor of his stomach that might have been evidence either of dead cells replacing themselves or of live ones blinking out.

She seemed ready to press the point, but just then the food

195

arrived, interrupting the volley. Cutting up the rubbery-looking squid she said, "Have you known Alcina Lilley long?"

"About four days. We met at a party at Beatrice Blackwood's house. Beatrice is a friend of the man I work for."

"Maynard Ance." When Doc looked at her: "I have contacts at police headquarters. What do you do for Ance?"

"Fetch and carry. What did Sergeant Battle say about me?"

She swirled a bit of tentacle on the end of her fork in a pool of black juice on her plate. "Even if I were to identify him as a source, that would be confidential." She chewed and swallowed. "He said you play baseball Saturdays with his son. Are you getting up some sort of neighborhood team?"

"Nothing so organized. There's a pair of empty lots on the corner of the street I live on. Where I was brought up, if you could afford a bat and a ball, you didn't let a thing like that go to waste."

"That could be an angle. Is Mrs. Lilley involved?"

"No. What makes you think she would be?"

"Three of the boys who play on your field are Marshals of Mahomet. If Mrs. Lilley's appearance at Wilson McCoy's funeral means anything she's in the midst of a reconciliation with the M-and-M's. I thought there might be a connection."

It had started raining again in big drops. His back was to the window but he could hear the drumroll against the glass. "This doesn't sound like a piece for the Sunday magazine. If you're fishing for the front page, I can't help you. All I know about politics is which lever to pull to vote the straight Democratic ticket."

She smiled and set down her coffee cup. "I notice that Tennessee twang—"

"Kentucky."

"—gets more emphatic whenever we close in on something you don't want to talk about. You've got that Clem Comes to the Big City routine down cold."

"Okay, so I know a little more. I know you're barking up the wrong tree if you think Alcina Lilley is throwing in with the Marshals. Those three you mentioned were with the group that came to protest the Mahomet dinner yesterday."

"I know. It's a smokescreen of some kind. They worship Mahomet. Why interrupt a banquet in his honor?"

She still wasn't taking notes. He said, "Am I being interviewed now?"

"Not if you say it's off the record."

"It is, then. I wondered about the same thing. I think the M-and-M's have staked out Mahomet for themselves and don't want any other group claiming credit for whatever gains are made in his name. Especially not at five hundred bucks a plate with the mayor invited."

"It's a point," she conceded. "It still doesn't explain what Mrs. Lilley was doing at the McCoy services."

Technically it wasn't a question, so he didn't attempt to answer it. What Mrs. Lilley had told him about Wilson McCoy and her husband struck him as confidential. "How's the squid?"

"Just like eating surgical gloves. I love it. Would you like wine? Retsina? It's on the *News*."

"Make it ouzo."

Her eyebrows rose. "Isn't that kind of heady for an ex-convict?"

"It's raining. If I lose the rest of the day it won't be that much of a loss."

"A liter? Or doesn't ouzo come in liters?"

"Even if it does, let's make it a bottle. If you're planning on joining me."

"I don't have to report to the office until tomorrow anyway." She got the waiter's attention.

The clear liquid—Doc knew enough about spirits to recognize that transparency meant potency—poured slowly and smelled like molasses. When they introduced water from the pitcher the waiter had brought, the contents of their glasses clouded over and turned milky. She held up hers. "What should we toast? Freedom?"

"Freedom is an abstract concept." He liked the sound of it and wondered where it had come from. Talk radio, probably; he'd become hooked on it all over again since the McCoy controversy. "A pennant for the Tigers."

"No, toasts should be about something that could conceivably happen."

"Meanwhile this stuff is setting up like concrete."

"Impossible. It'd hold its consistency at two hundred below." She shrugged. It was a masculine gesture, but not when it involved her bare tanned shoulders. "Oh, hell, here's to the rest of the day."

They touched glasses. Doc thought the heavy licorice taste would take some getting used to. Joyce—she had become Joyce the moment she ordered ouzo—licked her lips and set her glass down. "Seriously, if you're interested in putting together some kind of youth league, I could help. You'd be surprised how many donations a mention in the paper could bring in."

"I wouldn't know what to do with them. The whole thing started because I wanted to get my nephew away from his video games." He took one last bite of his moussaka and pushed the plate away. It didn't go so well with the ouzo. "I could use permission from the City of Dearborn to convert the corner into a ballfield. The person I've got looking into it hasn't been having much luck."

"I don't know anyone in the Dearborn city government."

"There is no Dearborn city government. You know as well as I do that Coleman Young calls the shots in all the suburbs stuck inside Detroit."

"Young shoves the press around. It doesn't work the other way.

But I can ask. What's in it for me?" She rested her chin on her palm.

"As good an interview as I can give. I used to be pretty good at it." Which was true. Whenever Sparky Anderson said something that the reporters couldn't make any sense out of, which was after practically every game, they had generally gathered in front of Doc's locker. The southern aphorisms he'd grown up with and hadn't thought very special were fresh meat for the yankee press.

She took her chin out of her palm. "Gloves are off?"

"You mean they've been on?"

"You haven't seen me at bat." She groped in a white vinyl purse for a notebook and gold pencil. "Just how bad was it in prison? Were you raped?"

He hesitated with his glass halfway to his lips, then drank and set it down. "No. Too big. That kind of thing doesn't happen as often as you might think. A lot of the guys inside have their steadies."

"Did you?"

"No."

"What did you do for sex?"

He was about to say *I made do,* then remembered she was writing everything down. "I didn't."

"Come on."

He met her gaze. He was used to batters trying to stare him down. A columnist in Cincinnati had written about Doc Miller's "blank, owl-eyed stare."

She looked down at her notes, then back up. "Were you impotent?"

He laughed and sat back. "You're a woman. I guess a lot of guys hit on you when you were a teenager, all that stuff about urges and how it's painful for a man to go too long without sex. Maybe that's true for some, but the rest of us can hold out for as long as any of you. Let's say I thought about it a lot. I had a lot of experience of showering with other guys when I went in. They just never appealed to me."

"That's a good quote."

"It's true."

"Are you still going without?"

"What are you doing this for, the *News* or the *Enquirer?*" he asked after a beat.

She clipped her pencil to the spiral of the notebook, put it down on the table, and folded her hands on top of it. He saw his reflection in her pupils. "Let's say I'm curious."

In the little silence that followed, a dish of combustible cheese went up at another table with a poof and a hoarse cry of *"Opah!"* from the Greek fisherman. Doc picked up his glass and stroked a flaw in the rim with his forefinger. "Ms. Stefanik, are you trying to pick me up?"

"I prefer *Miss* Stefanik. When I'm trying to pick someone up."

He became aware that someone was standing next to the booth. Expecting another autograph collector, he turned to take the pen and paper. The man's hands were empty. They were large hands and blocky, with coarse dark hair on the backs and a netting of healed-over scars stretched across the knuckles of the right. Russell Taber grinned down at him. He was swaying a little and he smelled like the alley behind a bar.

"I thought that was you I saw coming in," Taber said. "You're hard to miss."

Doc said hello and that it had been a while. He kept his hands on the table. There was a kind of dangerous glow on the ex-cop's face that he'd seen in the parking lot of the Kingswood Manor Apartments when Taber had tried to push his hand through the window of the Coachmen.

"Ance fired me yesterday," Taber said. "On the phone."

"I didn't hear. I'm sorry."

"He said he didn't need two drivers. He said I'm unreliable." He had trouble with the last word.

Joyce said, "Excuse me. I think I'll visit the ladies' room." She slid toward the edge of the booth. Taber put a hand on her shoulder. It dipped under the sudden weight.

"You sure can pick 'em for looks." He petted her with his eyes. "Funny, I thought you went for that dark meat."

None of the other diners seemed to be aware of the scene. The big waiter was preparing to ignite a dish of cheese for the table across the aisle. Doc said, "Let her out, Taber."

Taber squeezed. The skin of Joyce's shoulder yellowed under the pressure of his fingers. She unclipped the gold pencil from her notebook and fisted it like an icepick.

"Baseball Joe ought to be sharing the wealth. He's got my job and two girls. He can keep the nigger. I'll just—"

Flame gushed up in the tail of Doc's eye. He swept the dish off the cart and sidearmed it into Taber's face. The ex-cop shrieked, more from fear than pain, and cupped his face in his hands. Doc came out of the booth, barking a hip on the edge of the table, hooked his foot behind Taber's near ankle, and shoved him with both hands. The cart fell over and he went down in a tangle of limbs. Doc pulled Joyce to her feet by her wrist and headed for the door.

The Greek fisherman called after them, "Your bill!"

Doc pointed at the man trying to get up off the floor. "It's on him."

"My hero," said Joyce under the awning. The rain ran off the canvas in a sheet.

"I was rescuing him, not you. Were you really going to stab him?"

"The pen is mightier—"

"Shut the hell up." He waved at a passing cab. Two cabs later he got a driver to stop.

201

Chapter 22

◆◆◆◆◆◆◆◆◆

When Doc entered the office Monday morning, Maynard Ance was poking through an ashtray with the eraser end of a pencil looking for a smokable butt. Finally he found one an inch and a quarter long, sniffed at it, made a face, and threw it and the rest of the contents into his wastebasket. Spotting Doc then he grunted and fished inside a side pocket of his trousers. His arm went in almost up to the elbow. "Count that." He tossed a roll of bills the size of a softball at Doc.

Doc reported thirty-two thousand in hundreds and fifties.

" 'Kay, go down to Frank Murphy Hall and bail out those M-and-M's the cops arrested at the armory. Bring back what's left." Ance poured himself a cup of coffee.

"They're clients?"

"As of about twenty minutes ago, when their p.d. called. Drug dealers are a good risk, generally speaking. They can raise the cash in a hurry, and they don't stiff you on account of they may need you again. 'Course, they stand about a seventy-two percent better chance of getting dead at an early age than your average citizen, but the payoff's worth the gamble and it's all in cash. No sense bothering Uncle Sam."

Doc pocketed the bills, then switched them to his other pants pocket. They made too big a bulge on the side where he carried his keys. "Have they been arraigned?"

"No, otherwise I'd know the amount. Here are the names." He tore a page off his telephone pad and gave it to Doc. "Wait till they're all out of the courtroom before you pay the clerk. That way you won't have to give any of them a ride. I need you back here in case something comes up." He studied Doc's face. "Doesn't look like Taber laid a glove on you. I heard you mixed it up yesterday."

Doc was a little in awe until he remembered that Ance owned half of the Acropolis. "Just a scuffle. He's a mean drunk. He said you fired him."

"I've fired him before. This time I mean it to take. I can't go around picking up jumpers in cabs because my ride didn't show. It makes me look like an amateur. How'd it go with Joycie?"

"Fine." He couldn't help grinning.

Ance read him immediately. "I hope you took precautions. We don't need any little Stefaniks running around taking all the fun out of the bail business." He sat down at his desk and picked up the telephone.

A gray-haired bailiff taking a cigarette break on the steps of the Frank Murphy Hall of Justice directed Doc to the courtroom where the arraignments were taking place. Doc dawdled over a cup of coffee in the cafeteria, then went on up and found a seat in the last row of the gallery. The seven members of the Marshals of Mahomet who had been arrested for attempting to disrupt the fund-raising banquet were brought out one by one. Doc knew only Austin Yarnell, George McClellan Creed, and Epithelial Lewis, none of whom looked particularly cowed by his circumstances; it would take more than the dowdy blue coveralls of the Wayne County Jail to take the strut out of Needles Lewis with his wispy moustache and checkerboard haircut. Standing by the public defender waiting for the large black judge to look up from his papers, he craned his head around, spotted Doc, and grinned fit to split his head in two. Doc couldn't help smiling back.

Doc couldn't help smiling, period. On the way in to work he had remembered to stop at a florist's and send roses to Joyce Stefanik's apartment in Royal Oak, where they had spent all Sunday afternoon and part of the evening listening to the rain stroking the roof and trying to match it with some strokes of their own. The sex had been awkward and sloppy and embarrassing like sex everywhere, and even more so because Doc was out of practice; and immensely satisfying. Joyce had an athletic body, tanned all over—she said she spent more time at the tanning parlor in the next block than she did at home—and, so far as Doc could determine from an exhaustive inventory, no inhibitions. Afterward they had showered, gone to dinner in Royal Oak, and parted in the foyer of her building with a long kiss and an agreement to go out again next week. He didn't know whether he had Taber to thank for tipping the balance. Retracing these things the next day you never knew where they would have led had one or two items been out of sequence.

He wondered if Joyce would still write her article.

Needles was the last of the M-and-M's to be arraigned. Bail was set at twenty-five hundred dollars. As the officer was leading him out, Doc went up to the clerk, got an accounting of the total bond for the seven Marshals—it came to $25,000, including Yarnell, who had had a bench warrant out for his arrest for failure to appear on a cocaine possession charge and whose bail was consequently set at $7,500, and a member Doc didn't know who had five thousand slapped on him for an incident in the police van on the way to headquarters—and armed with his receipt climbed into the Coachmen and drove down to the jail, a slab of gray granite covering an entire city block that made no attempt to look like anything but what it was. The black-enameled bars in the windows were as big around as Doc's ankles.

His instructions from Ance had ended twenty minutes ago. He waited another half hour for Needles. When he appeared, having traded his county blues for khaki parachute pants and an old green corduroy shirt unbuttoned to expose his smooth hairless chest, Doc offered him a ride. He shrugged, handed the clerk a receipt for his gold watch, chains, and a couple of hundred dollars in folded tens and twenties, and accompanied Doc out the door.

"Where can I drop you?" Doc asked, turning the key in the ignition.

Needles directed him to a men's clothing store on Gratiot. "Buying a suit?"

"I live there." He slouched down and rested his head on the back of the seat.

Doc cracked the window on his side. His passenger smelled of that sweet dispenser soap they used at the jail.

The store occupied the ground floor of a two-story brick building of thirties vintage and had the look of a place that had always been there, acknowledging the changing scene by replacing the old baroque cash register with a computer and cautiously adjusting the lapels and cuffs on the mannequins in the windows. Illuminated indirectly by tracks aimed at the walls and not at all through the plate-glass front in the perennial shade of taller buildings on all four sides, it was a cube of gently bred silence sandwiched between a deep pile carpet the color of the blood of an earlier generation and thick cork panels in the ceiling. When the door opened a gong sounded that might have been under water. Entering with Needles Lewis, Doc felt the same muting sensation he had felt upon stepping across the threshold of the Brown & Kilmer Funeral Home.

A beautiful old man almost as tall as Doc in a gray flannel three-piece that looked as soft as smoke, with a mane of thick hair to his collar and a spade-shaped beard, both too white not to have been helped along chemically, started their way across the carpet, then saw Needles and stopped. Doc was sure he bowed. Needles passed him without saying anything, embroidering a path between racks of suits and shirts stacked on shelves and trousers hung by their cuffs in rows like hanging files, and went through a door at the back marked EMPLOYEES ONLY. Doc followed hesitantly. He wasn't sure he was expected to, but Needles had made no sign of farewell.

Behind the door the store's elegant facade disintegrated rapidly. A twelve-foot hallway with brown linoleum worn down in patches to the concrete slab beneath led past tall fly-specked windows that Doc realized when he looked through them were the backs of two-way mirrors offering a view of the dressing rooms. He had heard that such things existed in some establishments to prevent shoplifting, but this was his first evidence of them, and he resolved never again to try on a pair of trousers in a store.

Around a corner and up a steep flight of stairs with a rubber runner that looked as if it had been used to sharpen knives, and Doc stopped abruptly on a dim landing to avoid colliding with Needles, who had paused to knock on a door without markings. The knock was a complicated one; Doc was still working it out when the door opened two inches. No light came out from the other side.

"Me," Needles said. "I brung someone."

"Who?"

"A friend. His name's Doc."

Doc was aware he was being scrutinized. After a moment a switch snapped and light knifed out onto the landing, dazzling him. The door opened the rest of the way. Doc followed Needles on through.

The apartment, if that's what it was, took up the whole second floor, with doors leading to what were probably a bedroom and bathroom. A buff-and-blue rug that looked Eastern and expensive covered the hardwood floor to within four feet of the walls, which were painted a luminous blue that hurt Doc's pupils, still adjusting from the gloom of the landing. The sofas and upholstered chairs looked new. There were two refrigerators, a stove, microwave, and two-basin sink, a TV with a forty-eight-inch screen, a CD stereo on a shelf with four six-foot speakers spotted around the room, and a waist-high counter with a Formica top covered with beakers and a Bunsen burner and other items Doc had seen in old mad-scientist movies. He was a moment figuring that one out. He didn't have to figure out the folding card table in the corner with its assortment of semi-automatic pistols and what looked like an Uzi knocked down into a dozen components. There were boxes of cartridges everywhere, even on the sofa cushions.

The man at the door closed and locked it. He was black, not much taller than five feet, with a large, close-cropped head and the compact hard-muscled frame of a circus acrobat in a blue knit polo shirt, gray twill slacks, and what looked like alligator shoes dyed to match the slacks. Doc figured the shoes alone had cost more than either of his own two suits. The man was holding a square black MAC-10 machine pistol that looked something like a toaster on a handle. He was perhaps nineteen.

"Sure he ain't wearing a wire?" he asked Needles.

"Sure. Whyn't you clean this place up? You expecting a fucking war, spicks gonna come up here from Colombia and tip over the block?"

"I seen him someplace. Thirteen hundred, maybe."

"Jesus Christ, he bailed me out. He works for Maynard Ance. This here's Doc *Miller.* He played ball." To Doc: "Sylvanus got busted once on account of a snitch was wearing a wire. Now he frisks his mama."

"Wire caught fire, that's why they didn't get enough to keep me." Sylvanus was showing all his teeth. He had a lot of jaw and it looked like the grille of an old Buick. "Jump around and slap his chest like a big old bird. His cop friends thought he was getting done. Bust in and throw me down and kneel on top of me and screw they pieces in my ears, call me nigger and motherfucker. Judge threw it all out. No probable cause, he said. I had sixteen kilos in a suitcase under the bed." He changed hands on the MAC-10 and stuck out his right. "I'm Silly Dee."

"That's his rap name," Needles said. "Sylvanus Porter don't rhyme so easy."

Sylvanus broke off the handshake, deposited the machine pistol on the card table, and moved to a more formidable weapon, the stereo, switching it on. The floor thumped to the beat of recorded synthesizers. Bouncing with it, he sang: "I'm Silly Dee / and it seems to me / crack's just the way / we stay in the play / 'cause the white man barks / we can't play his park / 'cause we're just too dark / 'less we gots the green / to make his team."

He was starting a second chorus when Needles flipped off the machine. "Sylvanus got M. C. Hammer scared shitless. Meantime he's the best cooker in town."

"Cooker?"

"We don't grow that shit." Sylvanus jerked his thumb toward

the chemical apparatus on the counter. He'd retreated into his earlier dark mood. No musician liked to have his performance interrupted.

Doc asked, "Do they know downstairs what you're doing up here?"

Needles had opened one of the refrigerators. He offered Doc a Stroh's, got turned down, and took one for himself, using an opener under the sink. "What they know don't mean shit. M-and-M's own this building." He put away a third of the bottle's contents in one swig.

"I didn't know the Marshals had that kind of money."

Needles and Sylvanus laughed. It was almost as loud as the synthesizers had been. Needles carried his beer through one of the doors, leaving it open behind him. A moment later clothes started flying out into the room: suits and shirts and leather jackets, silver Windbreakers and silk blazers, flocks of knits, schools of sharkskins, herds of ankle-length fur coats. Eelskin boots and Italian shoes with buckles and pointed toes, Reeboks in every color and size from nines to double-digits like basketball players wore, Nikes for muddy days, patent-leather pumps for evening in a town that had no nightlife. In a couple of minutes the rug was covered, colors splashed all over like a light show. Needles came out in a pair of red bikini underpants, pulling on an Adidas T-shirt and swilling Stroh's, kicking clothes. "I growed up on Mt. Elliott," he said. "Sylvanus was Erskine. Summers we went barefoot. Winters—winters was big; then we got to wear our brothers' shoes that didn't fit them no more. I was twelve the first time I seen anybody wearing a suit and tie outside of television. He axed me for directions. You got a father?"

"Just barely," Doc said.

"I never did. Sylvanus didn't neither. Yarnell's old man been locked up in Marquette since Yarnell was six. Creed's old man bust his heart working at Ford's. Closest thing I ever had to a father called himself Fly. He said he seen *Superfly* twenty-six times. He was fourteen when I met him, had him a green Testarossa with blocks tied to the pedals because he couldn't reach them with his feet from behind the wheel. You could cut your finger on his lapels. Cash? Used to give it away in handfuls like hard candy because he said the bulge broke up the line of his suit."

"Glittered when he walked, huh?"

"Yeah. Yeah!" But he didn't get the reference. "When the sun come out and hit his rings that boy shined like a new car. Oh, Fly was something to see."

"Was he selling crack?"

"No, that wasn't around so much then. He was dealing that Mexican brown heroin. Trouble was, so was somebody else, and they couldn't get together on who was to do his dealing where. One day this old rusty piece-of-shit El Camino come round the corner on Mt. Elliott and sprayed metal all over. Fly got one in the neck, he bled dry before the ambulance ever come. They hit a little girl, too, and my best friend, Jimmie. The doc at the free clinic pried the bullet out of his leg, Jimmie carried it around for a good luck piece."

"What about the girl?"

"Oh, she was meat before she hit the sidewalk. That's what done it, you know what I'm saying? I mean to me." Needles had selected a pair of jogging pants with a silver stripe on one side from the pile on the floor and paused as he was stepping into them. "It wasn't them clothes or the rings or that car of Fly's. I figured if the same bullets that done for him didn't know any better than to do for that girl too there wasn't no sense in nothing. So I might as well have the clothes and the rings and the car."

He pulled up the pants and tugged his T-shirt out over the elastic waistband. "Let me tell you something about that El Camino. I was there and I seen it coming for just the longest time, like it was just hanging there. Floating, you know what I'm saying? Fly and that little girl, they never seen nothing. If you can see it coming, don't worry about yourself. It ain't for you."

Doc remembered to look at his watch finally. "I better go. Ance expected me back a long time ago."

"Tell him thanks. We be around in a week or so and square up."

"I was wondering about that. How come if you've got so much cash you couldn't put up your own bail?"

Needles stuck a bare foot inside a Reebok Blacktop and sorted through the pile for its mate. He was grinning. "That's the thing about cash. One day you got more of it than you got pockets to put it in. Next day it's just gone. Clean up all this shit, will you, Sylvanus? You could lose a woman in here."

Chapter 23

❖❖❖❖❖❖❖❖

"M om, why does Grampa take his food out of his mouth after he chews it?" asked Sean.

"Shhh! He'll hear you."

Which was a total lie. The old man was getting deaf, and he always ran the water in the bathroom sink full blast when he used the toilet, forgetting to turn it off afterward. Doc, seated with the others at the table, could hear him bumping around in there.

"But why does he?"

"Because he doesn't have enough teeth to chew it thoroughly," Billie said. "You won't either, if you don't brush often enough."

"I bet he brushed all the time. I bet he brushed them so much he wore them all out and that's why he can't chew anything. Right, Doc?"

"Uncle Kevin," corrected Billie.

"Right, Uncle Kevin?"

"Nice try, kid," Doc said.

The boy grinned and attacked his corned beef and cabbage. Sean had been opening up lately, and it seemed to his uncle that the boy was losing weight, or at least that his weight was losing ground to his vertical growth. He still fooled around with his video games, but as the weather warmed and the days grew longer he was spending more time outside after school. Coming home from work Doc often found him bouncing a baseball off the wall of the garage and catching it in his glove. He was getting to be a pretty good fielder.

When the toilet flushed, Neal got up and pushed the wheel-chair into the bathroom and came out a few minutes later pushing the old man. If Sean was getting trim, it seemed to Doc that the boy's grandfather had become even more of a shapeless blob since his last visit; his chins overflowed his collar and there were gaps between the buttons of his shirt where flesh showed. The flesh was pale and spotted like old cheese. Doc thought it would have that same consistency, and that if he poked a finger into it the dent would remain. He had trouble connecting this inert pile of useless protoplasm with the robust father of Doc's youth, working with his back sixty hours a week and spending his weekends carrying heavy car batteries up thirteen steps from the basement to sell them to the local junkyard.

Now, watching his sister-in-law bending over the old man's plate to cut up his meat—meat he would make an unsuccessful attempt to masticate and then line up on the outer edge of his plate in faded pink pellets—Doc felt a twinge of guilt that he was not particularly saddened by his father's extremity. Doc remembered being closer to his mother, a small thin woman of frontier ancestry with a flair for painting that she might have made into a profession but for marriage to Keith Miller, the third son of a blue-collar family where the women stayed home and the men went out to work and generally exerted themselves to death before they were fifty. But in the kind of gentle rebel-lion that Doc imagined was typical of her, it was she who had died when her younger son was barely old enough to appreciate her presence. The small stack of watercolors, seascapes mostly, executed in dreamy pastels by a woman who had lived her entire life in a landlocked state, had gone along with her clothes and shoes and sad collection of costume jewelry, given or sold or thrown away by the sort of neighbors who always did the neighborly thing whenever a neighbor was beyond need of them, while Doc's father submerged whatever he felt—grief, Doc supposed charitably—in boilermakers and fat women with saffron hair and Rexall perfume in the cement-block bar across from the factory where he worked. Neal had had the paternal faith. He was up to his ears in auto shop class learning a trade his father could identify with while his second son was throwing rocks at the hole in the *O* on passing B & O boxcars down at the freight yards, preparing his arm for the Lord knew what—smashing department store windows, maybe. There had never been much to say between Doc and the other Millers.

"See you're hanging around with nigras now."

Doc looked up from his meal. His father was staring at him, head turned a little to bring his good eye into line.

Neal looked pained. "His roommate's TV is on all the time. They keep showing those pictures of you and that Lilley woman."

"It was just a friendly thing," Doc said.

"You work with 'em sometimes 'cause you got to. Fuck them if you ain't got nothing better. You sure as hell don't go out in public with 'em."

"Grampa said—" Sean was delighted.

"Be quiet," his mother snapped. "Father Miller, we don't use language like—"

Neal said, "Don't bother. He won't remember. Eat your corned beef, Dad. It's tender."

215

The old man pointed his fork at Doc. "You know what you get when you shake hands with the devil? You get your hand burned."

"That's original," Doc said.

"Black people and white people go out together all the time now, Father Miller. A lot of them get married. There's this couple down at the supermarket—"

"That's for trash. That's where high yellows come from. I can get along with nigras until one of 'em gets it into his head he's as good as white. Shake hands with the devil. Get your hand burned."

Doc excused himself and went out for a walk.

It was a shirtsleeve day, with a touch of humidity as the sun coasted down and a stillness that suggested the stagnant summer days to come. The puddles left over from Sunday's rain were in remission and would be gone by morning. Rush hour was over, the tinkle and clatter of flatware and crockery and the smells of cooking came out through the window screens as families sat down to dinner. Doc's footsteps were the only sound on the street.

A new set came up behind him. His brother touched his arm. They faced each other on the sidewalk.

"His mind's gone," Neal said. "Half the time he doesn't know what he's saying or who he's talking to. He thought I was Uncle Roy in the car. He's been dead thirty years."

"I'm okay. I just had to get out."

"He won't be with us long."

Doc said nothing.

"Billie says some TV people called." Neal was making conversation.

"Channel Seven," Doc said. "No, Seven was yesterday. Today I think it was Channel Two. I guess nobody got killed this week."

"How you handling it?"

"One at a time. I'm doing a talk show next Friday."

"No, I mean how are you holding up?"

"This is nothing. When I was pitching I did interviews all the time."

"Then you were a pitcher. Now you're an ex-jailbird. Some kind of freak for them to have fun with until they get tired of you."

"I know that. Don't you think I know that?"

"So why let them?"

Because I need it. Because if playing ball were all of it, or even half of it, the corner lot would be enough. But if you've never had thirty thousand pairs of eyes on you when you were reading signals or using the resin bag or toeing the rubber, you can't understand. Aloud he said, "I don't mind. It keeps me busy."

"Fuck them. You're better than them."

Doc was stuck for an answer. Neal had never said anything like it before. To say it, he would have had to think it, and the idea that he might think that Doc was better than anybody would have been like expecting one of the heads on Rushmore to ask him to reach up and scratch its nose.

The expression on his brother's face was Rushmore-like. Doc began to wonder if he'd said what Doc had heard. "Still looking for an apartment?"

"I may have found one." It felt good to be talking again. "It's in Taylor, back half of a duplex. It isn't too far to visit. I could catch a bus here for the Saturday game."

"Need cash?" Neal reached for his hip pocket.

"I'm covered. Would you believe I was walking around with thirty thousand bucks in my pocket yesterday?"

Neal's hand dropped to his side. Doc could hear the alarm horn. In his brother's world, too much money was a carcinoma come to the surface. "You're not getting into something you can't climb out of?"

Doc laughed. "I spent seven years in a place like that."

"Quit fucking around."

"I'm not in any trouble, Neal."

A breeze came up, freshening the street. A radio clonked on next to an open window, and Ernie Harwell's voice drifted out like the first green scent of spring. Frank Tanana was warming up at the mound.

"Maybe it's for the best," Neal said. "You leaving. Things are getting kind of crowded at home."

"I guess Sean will be happy to have his room back."

"He's *my* son. The last time you saw him he was just learning to walk."

The harshness startled Doc. Neal's heavy features were drawn tight, as if someone standing behind him had gathered up a fistful of his scalp and pulled. Doc knew then why they were talking about his moving out.

"He's a good kid, Neal. You did a good job. You and Billie."

The tautness went out. His brother nodded. Then his right hand came forward. They made contact. When Neal grinned the years slid off like a veil. "You know what you get when you shake hands with the devil."

Doc smiled. The contact broke.

"I'm taking Saturday off," Neal said. "The whole day. So I can umpire."

"They're talking about rain Saturday."

"It wouldn't goddamn dare."

They turned around and walked back to the house.

Chapter 24

❖❖❖❖❖❖❖❖

The office of Parole Officer Peter Y. Kubitski wasn't shafted for air conditioning. Street noises came through the window propped open behind his desk, but little air, it being mostly static at that level. It was helped along a little by an oscillating table fan of a model Doc hadn't seen since childhood, and that left over from another epoch, with a green cast-iron base and a stainless steel housing shaped like the nacelle of a B-52. The blades were off pitch, causing the unit to shift its position a fraction of an inch to the left each time the head swung that way. Kubitski was aware of this and without looking up from his desk would reach out to push the fan back to the right just when another revolution or two would have tipped it off the edge of the file cabinet. Doc, who appreciated control, was impressed.

Aside from that he did nothing for Doc's pulse. Same salt-and-pepper hair teased out at the sides to divert attention from the thinning top, same long white face and crooked nose, same stingy little eyes parked under the mantel of his forehead. It might even have been the same knitted tie and blue Oxford shirt. Doc was sure Kubitski didn't own two identical mohair jackets. Even hanging on the back of his chair it retained the general shape of his angle-iron frame.

He finished reading the letter of employment signed by Maynard Ance, then drummed the pages together and went through them again quickly. Finally he unscrewed the reading glasses from his face and folded them on the blotter, lunch-stained and strewn with the apple-soaked pipe tobacco that made the tiny room smell like a neglected orchard. "Ance pays you this much just to drive him around?"

"It isn't that much compared to what I made when I played ball."

"Hm. What sort of man is he to work for?"

"I don't have to remind him to pay me."

Kubitski stroked the bend of his nose with the stem of his pipe. The bowl had deteriorated further since Doc's last visit; soon it wouldn't hold a ten-minute charge. "You have an irritating habit of giving answers that have nothing to do with the questions," he said. "Is there a reason you're evasive?"

"I'm not sure what kind of answers you want."

"No one's trying to trap you, Kevin." He picked up his glasses and held them above the rest of the papers before him. Doc found the routine nature of the monthly interview, which required him to complete a form while waiting for his appointment as if the place were some kind of outpatient clinic, morally crushing. "So you're moving?"

"The address is there," Doc said. "I put down a security deposit. I move in next week."

"Trouble at home?"

"No. Now that I can support myself there's no reason to depend on my brother."

"Was that your decision or his?"

"Mine."

Kubitski turned over the sheet and read the other side. The other side was blank. He put it down and slid his glasses into the imitation alligator case clipped to his shirt pocket. His pipe had gone out in the ashtray. He picked it up and relit it, wasting half a book of matches. "I saw your interview with Bill Bonds last night."

Doc waited. The officer didn't pursue it.

"I'm a little concerned about these weekend baseball games," he said after a little silence.

"Did someone complain? We get a little noisy." He hoped the city hadn't been in contact. During the most recent game a couple of Dearborn police officers in a scout car had slowed down to watch on their way past.

"Nothing like that. Do you know who you're playing with?"

Doc saw where he was going now. He tossed a warm-up. "Some pretty good athletes. If I'd had a couple of them in my last game in Jackson I might've had a no-hitter."

"You almost did." Kubitski pulled a yellow sheet from under the pile on the desk. "Your catcher has an arrest record going back to junior high school. That's if he ever attended junior high school. He and two more of your all-star team were brought in just ten days ago for creating a disturbance during a dinner at the National Guard armory. I understand you were there."

"Not with them. I was a guest."

"The terms of your parole are clear on the subject of fraternizing with known felons."

Doc feinted with a curve. "Are you sure they're felons?"

"I just told you about Epithelial Lewis' record. Austin Yarnell has two juvenile convictions for possession and aggravated assault and George M. Creed spent two years at the Boys Training School in Whitmore Lake for selling two grams of crack to a police officer."

He threw his fastball. "Were there any adult convictions? I did a lot of legal reading my first two years in prison. A juvenile record isn't in point of fact a record at all. So they're not felons."

"Your first two years in prison. I see. You haven't been brushing up on it just recently." He took the stem out of his mouth, smacked his lips in distaste, and returned the pipe to the ashtray, where it smoldered out. "I'm not crazy about your attitude, Kevin. Frankly, I don't think you're adjusting all that well to life outside."

Doc felt some of the blood run out of his face. It was as if he had split the plate at the knees only to have the umpire call it a ball.

Kubitski went on. "One of the purposes of the penitentiary system is to prepare the inmates to rejoin society. Whatever bitterness and distrust of authority they may feel must be left behind the gates. I sense that you've taken a good deal of it out with you. I don't feel comfortable about filing a satisfactory conduct report with the parole board at this time. You know what that would mean." The hard little eyes caught the light.

"What rule did I break? Tell me."

"I didn't just happen to catch that interview on television last night. I've watched all of them and read the ones that appeared in the papers." Without taking his eyes off Doc he corrected the drifting fan, then dived into the pile of papers again and came up with a sheaf of cuttings held together with a clip. One of them was the Sunday piece by Joyce Stefanik. Doc thought he had come out of that one sounding arrogant, unregenerate. It wasn't a hatchet job, as she could have mentioned the scuffle with Taber in the restaurant and made enough out of it to get him in serious trouble, but the tone puzzled him and he hadn't called her or taken the two calls she'd placed to the house when he was home. "The picture I get is not that of a man who's ready to get on with his life. I assume you've read the articles and seen some of the tapes. What picture do you get?"

"If it's the interviews I'll stop giving them." In fact the requests had begun to fall off. Doc suspected he'd had his fifteen minutes. Chief Hart, Kenneth Weiner, and the manhunt for Starkweather Hall had shoved him and every other story west of the margins.

"It's not the interviews. It's the man who's giving them. I can't ask the penitentiary system to free you if you won't free yourself."

"Call Sergeant Battle."

Kubitski hadn't finished speaking. He went on for several more phrases, then stopped and rewound. "Who?"

"Charlie Battle. He's a detective sergeant. I guess whoever you've had watching the Saturday games didn't notice he plays almost every week. He'll tell you how I'm adjusting to life outside."

Watching the parole officer pick up his pen and write down the name, he had the feeling he'd betrayed a confidence. He hadn't planned to mention Battle at all. Listening to Kubitski drone his moldy platitudes about rehabilitation and society, he'd smelled the disinfectant powder the trusties used when they swept the corridors between the cells, felt the mildew damp of the gray concrete blocks that bled through the modern painted drywall on rainy days. And confidence was only a word.

I could talk to Kubitski, get him to cut you some slack.

"I'll speak with him," Kubitski said. "I'm not an ogre, Kevin. There are parole men, bitter men, who enjoy threatening their cases with reincarceration. I'm not one of them. Each revocation is a failure." He shifted the fan. "Just to be safe, I wouldn't sign a lease on that new apartment."

Sweat pricked like burrs on Doc's forehead. As the fan

swooped back the other way the breeze frosted his face. The intercom buzzed. Kubitski switched it off.

"That's my next appointment. I'll call you before I take any action."

Doc took the stairs down to Major Crimes. The elevator was too closed in.

He felt a flush of hope when he found the door to Charlie Battle's office standing open and the desk lamp on inside. In the doorway he paused to rap on the frame. And didn't rap. A young white plainclothesman was seated at the sergeant's desk in a striped shirt and one of those floral ties that were beginning to crowd the more conservative prints out of the men's stores. He looked up. "Yes?"

"Sergeant Battle," Doc said.

"He's on vacation. Anything I can do?"

"I need to get in touch with him."

"I think he went out West with his wife and kid. I don't know where."

"Will he be checking in?"

"I don't know. Maybe. I'm new here myself. They yanked me off General Service to hold down his desk. I don't even know him except sometimes from the elevator. Are you reporting a crime?"

Yes. Aloud he said, "If he checks in, ask him to call Doc Miller. It's important." He gave the young man Neal's telephone number.

"The baseball player?"

"No."

But he doubted the young man heard him.

Chapter 25

❖❖❖❖❖❖❖

S ay hey, Mr. Mays!"
    Having left 1300 Beaubien, Doc was walking along
Macomb toward Randolph, where he hoped to catch a cab;
downtown Detroit was no place to try to park a motor home, and
so he had left the Coachmen at the office. At the cry he looked
around and spotted Joyce Stefanik leaning against the fender of
a silver Trans Am. She had on a white nylon thing with a scoop
neck and no sleeves, one of those pleated skirts that turned out
not to be a skirt at all when the person wearing it mounted a
horse or a motorcycle or something, red with yellow Van Gogh
flowers, and black platform sandals. Her hair, gathered into a
loose ponytail, was red in the sunlight. He went over and
stopped a couple of yards short of her, hands in his pockets.
"Willie Mays was a fielder," he said.

"Whatever. I told you I didn't know much about the game. I
see they let you go."

"Who told you I was here?"

"Your sister-in-law. I called the house for about the eighteenth
time. I was beginning to think you thought I had AIDS."

"I've been busy."

"Everything was okay until Sunday. Was it the story?"

"You're a good writer."

"That's what my editor says just before he tells me he's not going to use something I wrote. I thought it was a good piece. The file picture of you pitching to George Brett was a nice touch."

"It was Jose Canseco. And you made me look like a cocky son of a bitch."

"Interesting choice of words. Cocky." She was smirking.

He took his hands out of his pockets. "You fucked me over twice, lady. The second time wasn't nearly as much fun."

"You're serious. You didn't like what I wrote."

The naïveté of it made him gasp. He started to shake his head, but that reminded him of the fan in Kubitski's office. He turned and resumed walking.

Her sandals clickety-clicked behind him. "I said you had 'a quiet kind of self-possession bordering on impudence.' That bothered you?" She was striding alongside him now, trying to keep up with his long legs.

"Not impudence. Insolence. Bordering on insolence."

"That's bad?"

"It is to parole officers."

"Insolence is a turn-on. *I* was turned on."

"I could tell. You said I was aloof and sly. You must've had a real thing for Nixon."

"Well, it's true."

He glanced back at her then. She had started to fall behind.

"Not about Nixon," she said. "You. You look at people like you're watching them from a tower or someplace where you can see what they're heading for and they can't."

"It's called eye contact."

"Reportorial interpretation."

"Bullshit." At the corner of Randolph he saw a Yellow Cab letting a passenger off by the opposite curb and started to cross against the light. A SEMTA bus flatted its horn and blew past an inch in front of his nose, lifting his hair.

"Maybe it's the glasses." She was shouting over the drumroll of the diesel. "Have you ever considered changing frames? The ones you wear make you look like a bird of prey."

The cab had pulled away while the bus was passing. Doc said shit and leaned against the lightpole on that side.

"Did I really get you in trouble with your parole officer?"

He looked at her. The slipstream from the bus had tangled her bangs, and she had almost lost a sandal crossing the street. Hopping on one foot, she tried to adjust it and look at him at the same time. Her expression was worried.

He laughed. The sound of it surprised both of them. He said, "You look like a dog I used to have that tried to scratch himself when he was walking."

"I was wondering when you'd get around to calling me a bitch. Well, to hell with this." She took off the sandal and the other one, too. Barefoot, she scarcely came to his breastbone. "Are you in real trouble?"

He breathed deeply. It was an old trick to settle himself when a batter had rattled him. "It wasn't just you. Hell, it probably wasn't you at all. Or anyone else. My P.O.'s had it in for me ever since I went to work for Maynard Ance."

"He *is* kind of scummy."

"Next to my brother he's the most honest guy I know. He provides a service for money and goes out to collect it when it doesn't come."

"So does a loan shark."

"Another honest profession."

She fluffed out her bangs, an unconscious, youthful gesture Doc liked. "So can I offer you a lift, or are you still determined to board a bus doing thirty?"

"Forty-five, at least. I'm still checking my toes for tread marks." He offered her his elbow. She took it, swinging her sandals by their straps in her other hand.

The interior of the Trans Am was black and smelled of leather and some kind of sachet from a tiny brown-and-cream jug hanging from the gearshift lever. She tossed her shoes into the backseat, turned the key, and said, "Where to?"

"Can we just drive around?"

"St. Clair's pretty today. We'll take Jefferson up to Lake Shore Drive."

She changed gears smoothly and never missed a traffic light. Doc suspected Joyce was a better driver barefoot than he was with shoes on.

Lake St. Clair, filling a cavity hollowed out by glaciers and transfused by the Detroit River bordering the United States and Canada at the only point where that foreign nation lay to the south of its neighbor, performed as a color-coded barometer of the city's criminal temperament throughout the seasons: blood red in autumn (arson), shroud gray in winter (suicide), heartless blue in spring (rape), blazing white in summer (riot, gang violence, domestic murder). Today was one of its ambivalent days, its surface soft violet under polished blue sky with corpulent white clouds waddling across. Bright sails doodled around on the water like dragonflies dipping and swooping at a pond, oblivious of the hungry fish watching from beneath. The Independence Motel, scene of Wilson McCoy's death and undoubtedly of others less notable, was blocks and a world behind the purring Trans Am, along with the ribbon streamers of yellow Corvettes, red Camaros, orange Firebirds, and other fuel-injected, fully-bored, flames-on-the-fenders engines on wheels already assembling for the daily after-school cruise up and down Jefferson. Next to the five-sided enclosure of a baseball stadium with its own concept of time and rules of conduct, a moving car was the only place of true isolation. Provided it wasn't equipped with a cellular phone. He was relieved to see this one wasn't.

Joyce punched a tape into the deck—Anita Baker singing "Watch Your Step"—and dialed the volume down to a murmur. "What are you going to do about your parole officer?"

"I gave him a reference. Problem is the reference is on vacation."

"Won't he give you the time?"

"Maybe. The other problem is more serious. My reference may not give me a good reference."

She drove for a few bars without speaking. Then: "I'd say you're in deep shit, Miller."

"That wouldn't be so bad if I were in all the way," he said. "All the time I was inside I couldn't think about anything but getting out. Now that I'm out I spend all my time worrying about going back inside."

"What you need is a seventh inning stretch."

"What I need is a good curve."

"Such as?"

"An edge. An angle. A pitch I can go to when my fastball loses steam."

"There's just no end to these horsehide analogies, is there?"

But he wasn't listening. Most of the time it was a shell game: Will he be expecting the change-up, or should you gamble and try to burn one past him twice in succession? Have you established an unconscious pattern by not concentrating, or have you been pissing all over the lot so he doesn't know if you're going to throw the next one in the dirt or scream it at his head? What do the scouts say? Is he a fisherman or a scientist? Will he reach outside the box or does he play the averages, and how much does he know about you? When he goes into his stance, does he peek to see where the catcher is moving his mitt? Do you brush him back if he does, or do you buck the signal, risk catching the catcher flat-footed and putting the guy on base with a wild pitch? Or do you just say to hell with it, close your eyes, fire, and leave the rest to fate? Variables. Odds. Quantum physics. Human frailty. Wind direction. The outfield. Chance.

Sometimes—certainly not often and not quite seldom, maybe twice in a season—it came to you in a kind of voice. It wasn't that simple, nothing was in the game, probably it was just the result of an applied momentum of assured knowledge based on scouting reports, films, scorecards, and statistics combining to create fission, but it flowed through you like a warm gel and you knew it was right. They were passing the big white marble mansions of Grosse Pointe at the time, and Doc worked it out later that that was where the thought had come from, that although the houses were bigger than in Birmingham and the money older, you can only trim the grass so close and polish the brasswork on the porches so bright.

He came out of his slouch. "What's coming up?"

"Fisher."

"Take it." He gave her an address in Birmingham.

"Ritzy neighborhood. Who we going to see?"

"A woman I know. A widow."

Chapter 26

❖❖❖❖❖❖❖❖

Alcina Lilley answered her own door. Her straight hair was pinned up, catching the light in blue aureoles, and the pale lipstick that was her only nod to cosmetic science was in place. She wore a belted blue tunic with shoulder pads, open to the collarbone, beige slacks, and blue pumps that glistened wetly. Her eyes dilated when she saw Doc standing on the porch. The smile was a beat late.

"Kevin! You should have called. I'm just going out."

"Can it wait?" When she glanced down at the gold watch pinned to her lapel he added, "It's about your nephew."

"My—" Puzzlement and then understanding, and a spasmodic glance backward. "He isn't here. He's gone back home. I can't think—"

"Is Starkweather Hall really your nephew?"

Her face, disciplined by many public appearances, was no kaleidoscope, but Doc was watching closely and detected the various sea changes: Shock. Panic. Anger. Denial.

Thought.

"No."

"Is he your son?"

"Yes."

He felt himself nodding. "I couldn't think of any other reason you'd stick your neck out that far. Is he in there?"

"We can't talk here," she said. "Talk is what you want, isn't it? Or you'd have brought the police. Is that your car? Who's in it?"

"A friend." He'd almost forgotten about Joyce waiting at the curb.

"Send her away. I'll call a cab. We'll go to Beatrice Blackwood's apartment."

She closed the door. He went back to the car. "You can go home now. Thanks for the ride."

"You're forgetting what I do for a living," Joyce said. She had one arm laced around the crossbar of the steering wheel. "I'm supposed to just drive off and leave you there with Mahomet's widow?"

"Maybe a reporter wouldn't, but a friend might."

"Suppose the friend is jealous."

"Miss Stefanik, are you declaring your undying love for me?"

"I prefer *Ms.* Stefanik." She used her free hand to start the engine. "I expect another interview when this is over. Not for the magazine. For the news pages."

"That's a lot to expect for just giving me a lift."

She unlaced her arm from the wheel and beckoned him with a finger. When he bent down, she slapped him. The noise in his head was like a bat cracking.

"When I do fall in love, it won't be with a beanpole like you." The Trans Am pounced forward with a yelp of rubber. He backed up quickly to avoid having his toes run over. Anita Baker's voice trailed behind the car like spent fuel.

The cab, a Redtop, beat Mrs. Lilley to the curb. Doc, who held the door for her, noticed that she had changed to black flats to go with a black patent-leather purse. He had a paranoid flash that maybe it was the only purse she owned that would conceal a gun. Finally he decided the blue pumps were just too flashy for Beatrice Blackwood's neighborhood.

"She know we're coming?" he asked when they were under way.

"I called her. She doesn't know why."

"What'd you tell *him*?"

"Nothing. He's sleeping. He sleeps most of the time. There's not much else to do when you can't go out."

And she said nothing for the rest of the trip.

In front of the tired brownstone he had another flash. The gun theory was naïve. If she'd had time to call Beatrice Blackwood as well as the cab company, she'd had time to call others. On how many evenings had Doc seen blocks exactly like this one on the TV news, complete with covered and stretchered oblongs being carried through doors to waiting morgue wagons? In the city of a million disappearances, he'd thought to tell no one where he was going.

This time when he stood before the door on the fourth floor he heard no music, only the groans and gulps and inexplicable thuds of an old building giving in to corruption. Truman the bodyguard, who had apparently been briefed by his mistress, opened the door wide at Doc's knock, but little light came out around his bulk encased in its customary dark suit. His great face with its patches of scar tissue was as dark as skin came but lacked sheen, absorbing illumination and giving back nothing, a black hole with eyes.

There was no visible change when he recognized Alcina Lilley, but he pivoted aside like the second door that he was. Doc followed the woman inside.

Beatrice was seated on the blue leather sofa facing the entrance. The incongruous pageboy wig was in place and she was wearing a loose flowered housedressy thing that had probably cost as much as a formal gown and soft suede rose-colored slippers on her feet. She had traded the aluminum hospital patch over her left eye for one encrusted in jewels that glittered rainbows behind her glasses and looked like a ladies' affectation from *la belle époch*. Lying facedown on the arm of the sofa was the large-print *Copper Sun* Doc had seen her reading the day he picked her up at the hospital. He couldn't believe she was still reading the same book when so many pages had been turned in his own life.

"Alcina, how do you manage?" she asked, raising her hand to lay the fingers in Mrs. Lilley's palm. "This morning Beatrice was looking at her face with her good eye and she said, 'Girl, if you bought a dress that fit this poorly you'd take it back.' "

"Hello, Beatrice. You remember Kevin Miller."

The hand, ungloved for once, fluttered in his. He noticed she had large knuckles. "Beatrice never forgets a handsome young man. Sit down, both of you. What can Truman get you?"

"Beatrice. He knows."

Nothing changed on the old woman's face. The multicolored fussiness in which she drenched herself, Doc decided, was a diversion; if Truman was a black hole she was its dense core. "Go out," she told the bodyguard.

He left. Just like that, no hesitation or argument. A moment later the old elevator clunked and wheezed, descending. Beatrice got up with little of the effort she'd shown on other occasions, went into the kitchen, and came back out carrying a fifth of Hiram Walker's gin and three water glasses, the glasses pinched between three fingers of one hand. She set them down on a glazed rosewood-and-teak table and poured from the bottle.

"I'm not drinking," Doc said.

"You will be." She put down the bottle and sat down with her glass. "Alcina says you know. What do you know?"

"I know she's Starkweather Hall's mother because she told me, but I'd guessed that anyway. I saw him at her house the day I took her home from your party. That was the day the news broke about the police officer he killed. I didn't know it was Hall until I saw his picture on TV that night."

"Who'd you tell?"

"Nobody." When Beatrice's brows lifted: "I'm on parole. I try to avoid the law, and anyway I wasn't sure; I'd only seen him for a second and I couldn't figure out why Mahomet's widow would shield a cop-killer. Also I got real busy." He picked up his glass and sipped. Gin was his least favorite beverage, especially warm gin. But he welcomed the warmth that climbed his ribs afterward. "I'm not too swift when I'm not on the mound," he said, looking at Mrs. Lilley now. "That's how I wound up in prison. It wasn't until a little while ago I figured out why you took me to that fund-raising rally with all those photographers and TV cameras there. Anyone escorting the guest of honor had to draw a lot of attention. An ex-convict former Tiger pitcher would draw even more. I got so busy giving interviews I forgot all about Hall, or at least put him on the back burner. The mayor shaking my hand was a nice bonus. Or was it an accident? Was Young involved?"

Mrs. Lilley said nothing. Beatrice lit a cigarette. "What happened to make you think that was planned?"

"Nothing specific. I just had to look at it with a clear head that wasn't turned by all the publicity." He didn't mention his parole trouble. He was saving it. "Why else invite a broken-down ballplayer—and a white one at that—to a formal banquet to honor a dead civil rights leader? But I was too tangled up in myself to think of it that way. Only someone who's been famous long enough to know what a trap it is would know how to use it as one."

"Was it so bad?" Mrs. Lilley was seated in a pedestal chair with her knees together and her hands folded in her lap, the way he imagined she had sat countless times on platforms waiting her turn to speak. "I saw some of those interviews. You looked like you were enjoying yourself."

"What's your part in this?" His eyes were on Beatrice.

"I raised Gordon."

"Who's Gordon?"

She consulted the length of ash on the end of her cigarette, then returned it to her lips without using the ashtray. "I guess you don't know everything. Gordon Lilley, that's his name. I never could bring myself to call him Starkweather Hall. He said it was his revolutionary alias, like Joseph Dzhugashvili calling himself Stalin and Malcolm Little calling himself X. Gordon always was a great reader. I sometimes wonder, if we'd had video games when he was growing up, whether he might have turned out different. Rogues and bandits fascinated him. He read the covers off a book about Robin Hood I gave him when he was nine."

"I was pregnant when Gerald was killed," Mrs. Lilley said. "He never knew, and of course it was a secret from practically everyone that he had a wife. He suspected a good many of the donations he got from women had to do with the fact that he was good-looking and had a pleasant voice; if they found out he was spoken for they might not have been so generous. That's what he told me, anyway. I was just a girl. I believed him. I had to. Where would I go?

"I have no illusions," she went on. "He wasn't the kind to turn his back on temptation no matter what they say about him now. But he was discreet. I've always been grateful for that."

"Does Hall know Mahomet's his father? Is that why he joined the M-and-M's?"

Beatrice and Mrs. Lilley exchanged glances. Something else was exchanged as well. The old madam leaned forward and laid a gray column in the ashtray. "Mahomet wasn't the father," she said. "Gordon's father was Wilson McCoy."

All the windows in the apartment were open. A car passed by on the street sounding as if it were fueled entirely by high-test rap. The beat throbbed for blocks.

Mrs. Lilley said, "It was in the house where Wilson lived with his mother, where Gerald was killed later when the police raided the place the night of that first riot, the one they called the Kercheval incident. Wilson invited me to come hear Gerald speak. I'd never been to any of the rallies. Gerald said I could get hurt if something broke out. I know now he just didn't want me to see him with women hanging all over him. I was excited. I put on my only nice dress and splashed on perfume. I had an Afro in those days, a big one. I thought I looked like Angela Davis."

She picked up her glass and took a healthy swallow. "Gerald wasn't there, of course. No one was except Wilson. Even his mother was out, shopping for ribs and collards for her little boy. He said I was early and wouldn't I come in and sit on the couch and wait for the others." She laughed shortly, a dry rustling sound. "I don't know how Wilson got his women, but if it was by rape he wasn't as lazy as I thought he was. He was puny and he had the first sunken chest I ever saw; I remember thinking he must've been in some kind of accident. I almost fought him off, you believe it? A sixteen-year-old girl who didn't have anything like the height she'd grow into. But he had a lot of energy, and he was crazy. When he got down to it, it didn't take much time at all.

237

"He wouldn't even drive me home afterwards. I walked, crying all the way. Alcina in her big hair and torn dress with her nose running."

"She was living at my place then," Beatrice said. "I cleaned her up and made her smoke a joint, even though she was pretty quiet by then, which is worse than being hysterical if you let it go on. She wanted to tell Gerald but I said no, don't do that. Wilson used to be a Panther, he had a lot of guns. Gerald was small but he could take care of himself and it was possible he'd catch Wilson unarmed; but you could put Wilson in the hospital for six months and he'd get out and come at you from behind. He'd wait a year if he had to, until you forgot all about it. Wilson never forgot."

Mrs. Lilley said, "I still hadn't said anything a month later when Gerald was killed. That was the same night they arrested Wilson for the murder of those Mafia men. I fainted when I heard about Gerald. That's when I found out I was carrying Gordon."

"You could have aborted."

Beatrice laid the remainder of her cigarette to rest and sat back with her glass. The jeweled eye patch sparkled. "I tried hard to convince her it was best. I had a doctor on call because my girls weren't always as careful as I tried to make them be—a good one with a clean modern clinic he paid protection on, not one of those back-alley butchers you heard about—but she wanted the baby. She couldn't say why, but I knew. She didn't have any people, and when Gerald died she was all alone. Friends can only do so much, be so much. Blood—well, would you believe it, I've never been able to hate my father, even after the son of a bitch tried to drown me? You can't reason with that. But Alcina was a child herself. I raised them both. To this day Gordon thinks of her more as an older sister. Maybe that's why he went to her instead of me when he got in trouble. He was afraid I'd chew him out for killing that Sergeant Melvin."

"So when you put flowers on McCoy's casket," Doc said to Mrs. Lilley, "you were, what, thanking him for Gordon?"

She smiled in a way Alcina Lilley never smiled in public. "Mahomet's widow is too well-mannered *not* to bring flowers with her to a funeral. But I wanted to make sure the bastard was dead."

He remembered his glass and had another drink. The junipers had lost their bite. "Hall joined the Marshals because his father was involved?"

"He never shared his reasons with me or Beatrice. I told him who his father was as soon as he was old enough to understand. I don't think he believed me then. He wanted so much to be the son of Mahomet. I guess being an M-and-M was the next best thing. He did as much as Wilson ever did to organize the group. More, probably. I said Wilson was lazy. He got them into the drug business in the first place because it was the easiest way to raise money. By the end he'd lost interest in everything else. His mind was just about gone by then. He didn't have much to begin with."

"Did he know Hall was his son?"

"It wouldn't have meant anything to him if he did. Wilson wasn't the kind to accept the consequences of his actions."

"That boy was just bad," Beatrice agreed.

Mrs. Lilley set her glass down on the table and rose. But she wasn't going anywhere. She looked down at Doc and he had the feeling he was watching her behind a lectern.

"I'm sorry I underestimated you," she said. "That's the only apology you'll hear from me. I'm nobody's candidate for Mother of this or any other Year, but if my son came to me after killing the pope I'd still take him in and do anything I could to keep him safe. Are you going to tell the police?"

He ducked it. "I'm a parolee with information on the where-abouts of a cop killer. Every minute I don't say anything is another screw in my cell door. What would you do?"

"Melvin was dirty. He was dealing for real, not just to make arrests. Gordon got on his blind side over a negotiation. Melvin was threatening to kill him. It was self-defense. He didn't even know Melvin was an officer until he heard it on the news."

"It's true," said Beatrice. "That dealer whose body they found stuffed in a culvert on Antietam last month? Everyone knew he was Melvin's. He had a reputation as a crazy, whack you if you looked at him wrong. You don't wait for someone like that to make the first move. That Marshal Dillon stuff will just get you killed up here."

Doc said, "Even if it's true, the police have this thing about nobody touching a cop." He was watching Mrs. Lilley. "What would you do if I didn't tell them? He can't stay in your house the rest of his life."

"That's just what it will be if you tell them. The rest of his life."

"Sit down, Alcina. You're so used to making speeches you forgot how to listen. Young man, Beatrice hasn't been retired so long she can't smell a proposition coming. You better slice it up before it spoils."

Mrs. Lilley sat down. Doc drained his glass. The stuff was starting to taste like water.

"I know a detective sergeant," he said. "His name is Battle. The Starkweather Hall case has been his from the start."

"I've met him," Mrs. Lilley said.

"I think he's pretty straight. At least he's not the kind of cop that shoots when he should be thinking. We play baseball Saturdays. I could arrange a meeting and Hall could turn himself in."

"No."

"A voluntary surrender would look good at the trial. It would just be Battle, no backup."

"No policeman would agree to that."

"He wouldn't have to know it was about Hall. We have a personal relationship. As far as he was concerned he'd just be meeting someone he plays ball with. It would be in a public place with plenty of witnesses, in case you're worried it will turn into an execution. I know a restaurant."

He thought he could see Beatrice's corrected eye gathering light behind the patch. "What's in it for you, the reward?"

"It's a lot of money," he said.

Alcina Lilley made a noise that withered his entrails. But he maintained control of his expression under the old madam's scrutiny. Batters had tried to stare him down in the past and encountered only their own reflections in the blank lenses of his eyeglasses.

"Why talk to us?" she asked. "You could have sent your policeman friend to Alcina's house and still collected the reward."

"Something might have gone wrong. The terms don't say dead or alive."

Mrs. Lilley was looking at him in a way different from her friend. "I was right. I underestimated you. You're the most conscienceless thing I've ever seen. At least the men who dumped over schoolbuses full of black children in the sixties were acting out of conviction."

"Calling each other names isn't progress." He stood and started for the door. The gin lay in a toxic pool on the floor of his stomach.

Alcina Lilley spoke his name. When he turned she was holding tight to Beatrice's hand. "I'll call you after I talk with Gordon."

That night Billie summoned him to the telephone. As he lifted the receiver he thought it might be Mrs. Lilley. The first thing he heard was a garbled announcement over a P.A. system in the background.

"Our plane leaves in twenty minutes," said Charlie Battle without greeting. "This better be good."

Chapter 27

◆◆◆◆◆◆◆◆◆

Charlie Battle, looking more casual than Doc had ever seen him on a weekday, in clean canary yellow sweats, Nikes, and a blue Windbreaker, walked into the bare room without knocking and kicked an empty carton out of his way. Most of the color in the room came from the orange wall-to-wall carpet. The walls were dead white and the slipping sunlight made sharp trapezoids on the floor in front of windows without curtains.

"Nice big room," he said, looking around. "That's one butt-ugly rug."

Doc plugged in the coffee maker in the little kitchenette and came out to shake the sergeant's hand. "I can't afford a new one just yet. I'm looking for a color to paint the walls that will distract attention. What do you think?"

"Make 'em purple. What's upstairs?"

"Bedroom and bath. There's a bed with a nightstand and a dresser. I'm getting everything else from Rent-A-Center until I can swing the down payment on a living room set."

"Who's this?" Battle pulled a framed picture out of a carton full of Doc's goods. It showed two rows of young men in baggy

cotton baseball uniforms with an empty grandstand behind
them. A little off to the right stood a white-haired man with a
long sour farmer's face and ears that stuck out like wind wings.

"The Louisville Lagoons. I pitched for them the summer
I graduated high school. That's me kneeling second from
the left."

"Semi-pro?"

"Very semi. Sometimes we played for chicken dinners."

"Who's the codger?"

"Charlie Steiner, the manager. He was the only southpaw on
the Toledo Mudhens pitching staff in 1916. He'd've been with
the Ty Cobb Tigers except they bounced him for drunkenness a
week before they were going to call him up."

"That why you picked Detroit?"

"My father picked Detroit. He had a job waiting."

Battle returned the picture to the carton. "My wife and I
almost separated two years ago. We saw a counselor. I promised
to pay more attention to my family and less to the job. We're on
standby for another flight to Denver day after tomorrow. If I'm
not there she and Junior are leaving without me. What's so hot
you couldn't discuss it on the phone?"

"I think I can deliver Starkweather Hall."

He showed no reaction. "Ance?"

"He's not involved. Yet."

"How many guesses do I get?"

"I'd rather not go into the how just yet. My information is he's
ready to turn himself in, but only with me present and only to
you. If you don't come alone it's off."

"That's all? Why not a first-round draft choice and an out-
fielder to be named later?"

"Excuse me, Sergeant. I wasn't aware you were just about to
arrest him on your own."

"Let's just say when a cop-killer starts dictating terms I don't pop for champagne."

"My information is Sergeant Melvin wasn't much of a cop. He was a dealer and a killer besides."

"I heard that."

Doc assimilated. "You did?"

"If you like money and it's a choice between being pensioned off in twenty years—if you don't get whacked first and the mayor's bridge partners don't empty out the fund—and using what you learn about the junk trade when you're undercover to turn a profit, there's just no contest. Narcotics officers are pricks to start with or they wouldn't put in for a shitty detail like that. It's no trick to turn a prick, excuse the poetry. So Internal Affairs keeps a separate jacket on everyone in the squad. When you're as big a prick as Ernest Melvin it slops over onto a lot of desks. That doesn't mean we're paying a bounty to the man who offed him."

"The way I heard it he threatened Hall's life."

"I'm dying to hear all about it. From Hall."

The coffee was percolating. "Coffee, Sergeant?"

"Got any beer?"

"Refrigerator's not plugged in. Sorry."

"Coffee then."

Battle followed him to the kitchenette and leaned in the doorway watching him fill two mugs. "What's your end?"

"That reward still good?"

"I guess."

"Sugar? I don't have any cream."

"Black's fine." The sergeant accepted a mug. "You surprise me. I didn't think you were a money kind of a guy."

Doc stirred sugar into his mug and unplugged the coffee maker. "I don't know anybody like that. The best third baseman

I ever knew, maybe the best of all time, told me he never picked up his glove without thinking about how much he'd make next season if he threw just two guys out in that game."

"That must be why they call it the hot corner."

"Well, this one's mine, except I only have to throw one guy out."

"Anything else?"

He leaned back against a cupboard. "My parole officer's every bit the asshole you said he was and with interest. He's busting my balls over my attitude, says he's considering filing an unsatisfactory conduct report with the board. That would revoke my parole."

"Sure. The board's just a rubber stamp. Nobody ever checks up on P.O.'s and they got more power than the governor. A grand jury was getting set to indict one of them a couple of years back on charges he had three of his cases pulling heists for him when he went into the hospital for a triple bypass. He never got off the table. Took fifteen years to compile enough complaints against him to put him in the dock. Looking for a recommendation?"

"You offered to help out with Kubitski if I turned something on Starkweather Hall. I wanted to make sure the offer hadn't expired."

"Theoretically it shouldn't matter, or the reward either. Harboring a fugitive in a homicide could dump you back in Jackson until you're too old to bend over and pick up a baseball. Much less throw one."

"But then you wouldn't get Hall."

"Oh, we'll get Hall."

A TV murmured on the other side of the duplex.

"I'll put in a good word," Battle said then, "for what it's worth. Assuming everything's everything."

"Actually I was counting on a little more than that. I want you to call off the dogs."

Battle's hand paused briefly in the act of raising his mug to his lips. He raised it the rest of the way and swallowed, the muscles of his throat making two distinct movements. "What dogs." It wasn't quite a question.

"Even assholes do things for reasons." Doc hadn't touched his coffee, just held the mug in both hands as if to warm them. The indoor-outdoor thermometer mounted on the wall of the kitchenette read sixty both places. "It takes more than a couple of cocky interviews and a legitimate job your parole officer doesn't happen to approve of to get him to go for your throat, unless someone puts him up to it. What made you think I knew enough to make it worth applying pressure?"

"Nothing. But I ran out of leads. How'd I tip my hand?"

"Going on vacation just when I needed you most as a character reference was overdoing it a little. You already had the screws to me. You didn't need the extra twist."

"It isn't an exact science," Battle said. "I'll call Kubitski as soon as Hall's in custody. When will that be?"

"I've got one more arrangement to make. Tomorrow maybe. I'll call you. You want to make your flight the next day."

"Oh, that. I'm not going anywhere. Can't get the personal time while this investigation's on. I was just seeing a friend off at Metro when I called you tonight. I didn't think the special effects would hurt."

"You've got a friend?"

Battle leaned in through the doorway and set his mug on the drainboard. It was still almost full. "It's my job," he said. "If you're looking for personal consideration I'm fresh out. Where we doing this?"

"I'll let you know."

"Hey, we're on the same side now."

"You don't always throw the pitch the catcher's expecting. Some batters look to see where he moves his mitt."

"Life isn't a baseball game, Lefty."

"Sergeant?"

He lifted his brows.

"Fuck you."

After a beat the sergeant decided to smile and stuck out his hand.

Doc shook his head. "Not just now."

"Okay."

When Battle left, Doc poured the contents of both mugs and the carafe into the sink, washed them, and went out to call Maynard Ance from a pay telephone on the corner. Twenty minutes later a cab let him off in front of the bail bondsman's home.

Ance opened the door wearing a striped bathrobe and carpet slippers on his bare feet. His hair was still damp from the shower Doc's call had pulled him out of but as far as Doc could tell the black dye hadn't run. "Where's Cynthia?"

"Playing racquetball or some horse's-ass sport like that down at the Detroit Athletic Club. It's Ladies' Night. What's the scoop on Starkweather Hall?"

"What makes you think it's about him?"

"We were together in the office three fucking hours ago. You didn't call me to discuss the Pistons' play-off chances. Let's go downstairs. I had the place swept for bugs last week."

"Find any?"

"One of those old C-72's the FBI used under Hoover. I bought the house at a tax auction. Before that a bookie owned it." He was walking as he spoke. Doc noticed he had a bald spot the size of a coaster on the back of his head.

The basement smelled of cigarette smoke. A butt smoldered atop a heap of them in an ashtray on the arm of the big recliner. Ance lit a fresh L & M off the butt and sprawled in the chair. Doc selected a stool, sat down, got up, moved it to a spot where he wasn't looking up the bail bondsman's robe, and sat down again. There were flakes of ash on Ance's chest, the same color as the sparse hairs sprouting from the soft pink flesh. "I thought you were trying to quit."

"Shit. You ever see an eighty-year-old man didn't look like he wished he was dead?" He inhaled. No smoke came back. "Where is he?"

"I don't know," Doc lied. "I know where he'll be tomorrow, if you go along."

"Son of a bitch. I thought maybe you had some kind of lead, but shit. Where'd you get it, those pukes you play ball with?"

"Who else?"

"Yeah. You talk to him?"

"No reason. The deal's with Charlie Battle. We're using the Acropolis. For that you cut in for half the reward."

"Who gets the rest, you?"

"No, that goes to Hall's defense."

"Oh, right. Heh-heh."

Works every time, Doc thought. *Give them the truth and they think you're joking.* That's what the town had come to. Just wanting to get out from under wasn't enough, you had to turn a profit while you were at it. Anything less and people got suspicious.

"What time we doing this?" Ance asked.

"I haven't heard back from Hall's people to tell me it's a go. I should know by morning. Should I call you here?"

"No, I'll be in the office early."

Doc fell silent. Ance smoked and appeared to be thinking. Watching him was like viewing film of a leaky steam pipe played backward, the vapor disappearing into the aperture and staying there. A few puffs and the cigarette had burned back almost to his lips. He punched it out. "I'm glad I canned Taber and kept you. He thought initiative was a picture with Warren Beatty and Dustin Hoffman. You could be a bail man, you know it? Why not? I can't do this shit forever. Cindy's been pestering me to take her around the world, I tell her great, who's going to sit on the scroats and jumpers while we're busy humping camels in Cairo? With you minding the store I wouldn't have to sweat it. I bet I don't even call you more than once a day."

Doc gaped. "Are you offering me a partnership?"

"Well, junior. I've got to front for the license on account of you've got a record. We'll call my half of the reward your buy-in. Wait. Don't answer yet. Open that drawer. Not that one, shit, that's full of nails. The one next to it. What do you see?"

The drawer under the edge of the workbench was filled with cans of Planters mixed nuts in rows. Doc reported this.

"Well, open one."

"Which one?"

"Jesus Christ, go eeny, meeny, miney, mo. What'd I say about initiative?"

He chose one and peeled off the plastic lid. At first he thought it was full of rolled-up newspaper clippings. "Looks like a roll of fifty-dollar bills."

"Take it. Now you're paid up through next month. Your luck stinks today, kid. If you picked one of the ones stuffed with hundreds you wouldn't have to come back to me for the rest of the year."

He counted the bills and pocketed them. Now he had enough to furnish the apartment without renting or even buying on time. "Thanks, but what's the idea?"

"I got more in the bank, but I don't trust 'em since the savings and loan thing. Also banks report to the IRS. The idea is the bail business pays better than anything else legal. Our customers don't haggle, the price is set by the courts. I charge ten percent and get collateral for the rest. That's fair. I know bail men who demand a statement of worth and attach everything the client owns. That's bloodsucking but the law says it's okay. There's nothing to regulate what we charge, like there is with finance companies. Ever buy a new car and pay cash? You don't get highs like that from drugs. Best of all"—he swung the recliner upright and grasped Doc's knee—"you can go on playing long after your arm's shot."

Doc extricated himself and got off the stool. "I'll think about it. I'm not sure I want to tie myself down just yet with a business."

"Makes a difference when you do it with a golden rope." But Ance looked surprised and a little disappointed.

Doc told him again he'd call him in the morning and let himself out.

He slept that night at his brother's. He was a long time drifting off, the events of the day skidding through his head on an adrenaline slick like the details of a tough game, and later he couldn't pinpoint the spot where thinking ended and dreaming started.

Miller. Miller! Boy, you listening? Get your head out of your ass!

He looked at the long parchment features of Charlie Steiner: cap square over his large luminous eyes, a lump of tobacco jammed so far back in his right cheek it raised a knot under his ear, pale spotty skin hanging in pleats from his neck. His Louisville Lagoons uniform was too big around the waist as always, the trousers in tucks, belt snugged so tight the end swung loose like an extension of his manhood.

You ever ask yourself why them fellers in the Show are always standing around scratching their eggs on national tee-vee, boy? It's 'cause they didn't have time to do it on their way there. You don't get to the Show on just two good pitches and a shitload of wish-I-wuzzes. It takes harder work than you ever done in your whole masturbating young life.

Doc said, Charlie, is it really you? I heard you died.

Not hardly, boy. Didn't I say I'd be on your butt like a boil till you got where you're going?

But I got there, Charlie. I got to the Show.

Like hell. You just dreamed it. Fellers in the Show don't sleep in their nephews' beds between sheets their brothers paid for. Pay attention, now. In my day the pitcher just closed his eyes and let fly and the batter just closed his eyes and swung and both of 'em hoped the other's luck was worse than his. These days you need brains. Brains to read the signals. Brains to know when to go to first when there's a runner on board. Brains to know whether that boy in the box jumps all over the first pitch or waits for the one that's low and inside. And brains—he leaned forward, close enough for Doc to detect the spoiled-fruit smell of tobacco on his breath—*to know when to just close your eyes and let fly. Brains like that take time to grow. I'll be right here until they do.*

Wait a minute, Doc said. You are too dead. I went to a memorial service. Your widow was there and your daughter and two grandsons. A utility infielder who knew you on the Toledo team read a poem about running it out. He was in a wheelchair. Your picture was there in a wreath. They said you were found lying on the floor of the shower with the water running.

He was afraid then he'd insulted the old man, who straightened to his full height, hitched up his trousers in that way he had even though he kept them cinched tight enough to cut off circulation, turned, and left. Only he didn't walk away, but just kind of faded into the pattern on the wallpaper in Sean's room. That was when Doc realized he was awake, lying with his head propped on the pillow and his eyes open.

He was still thinking about it when the clock radio on the nightstand clicked on. It had been a gift from his sister-in-law after he'd overslept one morning and reported late for work at the John Deere dealership. He recognized the mock-cheerful voice of the morning man at Talk Radio 1270.

". . . Okay, you've got the number and you know my name. Call me up with your thoughts on the death of cop-killing druglord Starkweather Hall at three-ten this ayem in of-all-places Birmingham. Justifiable death, or did the police execute him? Talk to me, I'm all ears."

There are those who would look at the naked statistics of Loyola MacGryff's life and draw the conclusion that it has been tragic.

Her brother Paul was run over at age seven by a streetcar and lost both his legs. Later, while recovering at home, he developed a blood clot that went to his heart and killed him before the ambulance could get him to the hospital.

Her husband Horace was beaten to death by strike-breakers during the labor unrest of the 1930s. He was given a pauper's burial because there wasn't enough money in the Depression fund for a funeral.

She has been robbed twice at gunpoint. Burglars have struck her home three times, cleaning her out once.

A grandson, Horace MacGryff III, has been missing in action in Vietnam since 1972. His grandmother was paged at Tiger Stadium during the American League Eastern Division play-offs to receive the news. She returned to her seat to watch the final two innings.

A freak accident at Tigers spring training camp six years ago has resulted in thousands of dollars of reconstructive surgery to Mrs. MacGryff's jaw, part of which was underwritten by the ball club, but requests for more money have brought no response from attorneys employed by Tigers owner Tom Monaghan.

Despite speech difficulties and an inability to chew on the right side of her mouth, Mrs. MacGryff has resisted family urgings to take her case to court. Says she, "I'd sooner sue King Jesus."

A great-granddaughter, Coral Louise Scyznyck, overdosed on crack cocaine at a high school dance in 1989. In the police car on the way to the hospital, Mrs. MacGryff persuaded the officers to tune in to the bottom half of a twi-night doubleheader between Detroit and Kansas City. The girl remains in a coma today.

But even though this white-haired native Detroiter has spent almost as many hours in emergency rooms and cemeteries as she has in her preferred upper deck, she would not agree that her life has been hounded by ill fortune.

She met Hughie Jennings, overheard Mickey Cochrane chewing out Goose Goslin for trying to field a grounder to first without assistance, had her picture taken with Mayo Smith, egged on Billy Martin during an altercation with an umpire, and sent an expensive necktie to Sparky Anderson on the occasion of his 60th birthday. No Tigers manager in this century has remained unaware of Mrs. MacGryff for long.

Tomorrow, in recognition of eighty-four years of unwavering support, Loyola MacGryff—housewife, retiree, great-grandmother—has been invited by the Detroit Tigers to throw out the opening ball of the 1990 season at the corner of Michigan and Trumbull.

The diminutive senior pooh-poohs comments by friends and family that the front office hopes by this token to forestall a lawsuit for medical damages.

"This makes up for that rude ticket clerk who wouldn't honor my raincheck in 1958."

PART FIVE
Slider

❖❖❖❖❖❖❖❖

Chapter 28

❖❖❖❖❖❖❖

I'll speak to him, Truman."

Doc hadn't been surprised to encounter Beatrice Blackwood's bodyguard at the door of Alcina Lilley's house, nor to be
denied entrance by him. Deaths, funerals, and releases from
hospitals brought out that aging Twelfth Street crowd in protec-
tive herds. The elderly madam was wearing what looked like the
same tailored suit she had worn to Wilson McCoy's send-off. It
was definitely the same flowered hat. She wasn't wearing the eye
patch and he could see the difference in the pupils. The one that
had been operated on lacked the milky opacity of its mate,
glittering like one of the jewels that had covered it.

She let him into the entryway, a shallow room furnished with
carved wooden benches that hadn't been sat on in this century
and what might have been an original Rivera in a simple frame
on the wall facing the door. Truman had withdrawn silently
through a door at the back.

"Alcina isn't seeing anyone," Beatrice said. "You least of all."

"I didn't tell anyone he was here."

"I know. You couldn't have collected the reward if you did."

"What happened?"

"Alcina went to run some errands after she left my place yesterday. She didn't get home until late. Gordon wasn't here."

"Did he leave voluntarily?"

"There wasn't any note, but he wasn't the kind to write one. Nobody broke in and nothing was disturbed. The neighbors didn't see anything. They're quick to call the law here, not like in my neighborhood. He left his things, what there was of them. He was traveling light when he came."

"They said on the news that two plainclothes detectives on their way somewhere else caught him breaking into a car parked in a driveway on Brownell. He pulled a gun and one of them shot him. That's not far from here."

"Gordon wouldn't have gone quietly," she said. "But I don't believe the car story. Alcina could have gotten him a car if that's what he wanted."

"Could he have found out about our arrangement and panicked?"

"Not from Alcina or me. Truman didn't know anything. I have to get back to her now." She waited for him to leave.

He didn't move. "Who else knew he was here?"

"Truman."

At first he thought she was answering his question, but when Truman re-entered the room he knew the bodyguard had been hovering within earshot. Taking it as a dismissal, Doc turned and opened the front door. Looking back: "I wasn't after the reward. I had an agreement with Sergeant Battle to split it between Maynard Ance for the use of his restaurant and Mrs. Lilley to be applied to Hall's legal expenses. You can ask Battle. All I wanted was a break on my parole."

Beatrice said nothing. She and Truman might have been wildly mismatched carvings chosen to go with the painting on the wall. Doc went out. The door chunked into its frame behind him like an axe biting into a stump.

He had the driver drop him at the corner of Neal's street and tipped him a dollar. It was a few minutes after seven on a moist Saturday morning; perfect globes of dew on the grass in the ballfield refracted the early sunlight into primary colors like the jewels in Beatrice Blackwood's abandoned eye patch. Two days earlier, Doc had clipped the grass within two ruthless inches, and with a proper pitcher's mound and a home plate and bases acquired from Dunham's downtown, the lot couldn't be mistaken for anything but a baseball diamond. Neal had surprised him that day with a lime spreader borrowed from work. Now the basepaths and foul lines stood out crisp and white like fresh chalk on slate.

Nobody was up yet at the house. Even Billie had been out late Friday night cooking for an event at the school and was sleeping in. Doc used his key, went upstairs, changed into his ballplaying clothes, and went back out with his glove and the ball and a six-foot plank he kept in the garage. He had asked for a green one with plenty of spring at Builders Square, but the clerk had explained they didn't carry green lumber and sold him a wolmanized plank instead. It had proven more than satisfactory on its first tryout.

He prised up home plate and drove the narrow end of the plank into the soft earth beneath, pounding it with a rock that had belonged to the foundation of one of the houses that had stood there. Just as he made the last blow a window squeaked open on the second floor of a house across the street and a phlegmy male voice shouted at him to knock it off.

Doc didn't spend much time admiring the result. It looked like a headstone erected over the grave of his freedom. He'd marked out a strike zone on the board with chalk, hit it square in the middle with his first three pitches, then missed the plank entirely with the next four and had to chase the ball before it rolled into the street. When he hit, the ball came back off the resilient wood with a crack like a bat connecting, returning to him with identical or superior velocity, providing him with practice in both pitching and fielding. After the first dozen or so pitches he ceased to miss the plank, although he hit outside the strike zone with some regularity, usually on purpose, especially when he threw his slider. The return was more predictable than if the board had been an actual batter with his varying swings, and so he fielded better than he would have in a real game; but that wasn't the point, nor if he chose to admit it to himself was the pitching. The rhythm—kick, deal, catch, kick, deal, catch— was mindless, a kind of sensory-deprivation tank of the spirit in which he went through a series of movements as natural as breathing, acting and reacting in a vacuum of pure physical activity, aware of neither the raw stinging of his palm nor the cracking of the tendons in his arm, the whack of the board and the thud of the glove heard only dimly through layers of sentient callus. The sheer mechanistic repetition of the chain of motions wore down the bumps and whorls that retained thought like puddles in a rutted riverbed so that when he stopped—*if* he stopped, for there was a seductive rapturous self-fueling perpetuity to the thing—the intelligence would come rushing in all of a unit in a reverse climax of shattering clarity. Using, respectively, B & O boxcars, the wall of the barn behind the house in Louisville, a Lagooner named Archie Oliphant, and Tiger catcher Lance Parrish, Doc had resorted to this method four times in his life when he needed direction, and it hadn't failed him yet. Most recently it had helped him decide to face the authorities on the manslaughter charge when he was out on bail and considering flight to Canada.

This time was no exception.

He didn't know how long he'd been throwing when he stopped. He'd left his wristwatch at the house. The light had broadened and hardened and the last of the dew was rising from the grass in gray vapor like spools of thread uncoiling. He was mopping his forehead with his sleeve, sorting out the impressions now filling his skull, when he saw Charlie Battle coming his way across the lot.

"I don't remember you throwing that hard when you were with Detroit," he called. "Training for a comeback?"

The sergeant was wearing cutoff jeans and a summer-weight yellow sport shirt that showed his physique through perforations in the material. His legs were lean and hairless. Muscles jumped in the thighs and calves as he walked.

"Just breaking a sweat," Doc said. "Is it that late? Where's your glove?"

"I'm not playing today. They want me to come down and fork over my paperwork on the Starkweather Hall case. I'm on my way in. Had a hunch I'd find you here."

"That the summer dress code at Thirteen Hundred?"

"Fuck 'em. I was going out for a run when I got the call." He stopped in front of Doc. "I left a message at Kubitski's office. I'll follow it up Monday. Your parole's off the hook. It never was on, really. Tough talk, that's the job."

"Bullshit, Sergeant. But thanks."

"The Hall I've been chasing was too smart to throw down on two cops at once. What spooked him, the deal?"

"He never knew about it. He hiked before anyone could tell him."

"Jesus. I guess when a lucky son of a bitch loses his luck it goes all at once."

"Did those detectives belong to your squad?"

"No, they were narcs. Good ones, too. First he knew they were on the other side was when they identified themselves. Could be that's why he didn't think it through."

"He knew them?"

"The drug world's small. Everybody knows everybody."

"Internal Affairs got separate jackets on them too?"

Battle stuck his hands in his pockets. "They aren't all Sergeant Melvin. That's an extreme case." He shook his head. "I don't know how dirty they are. Hell, maybe they're clean. It happens, even on that detail. You're barking down the wrong hole there. The shooting team cleared them an hour ago."

"Lengthy investigation."

"It's only lengthy when something smells. This one was textbook. Any idea what Hall was doing in a place like Birmingham?" He was studying Doc's face.

"Maybe he was house-hunting."

"Or he'd been hiding there right along and just broke cover. This is Detroit. When you're hot and you don't have wheels, you boost them as quick as you can. You don't walk clear past Eight Mile Road looking. I don't suppose you'd care to tell me who had him socked away?"

Doc gave him the blank owl-eyed stare. "You going to shake my parole in my face if I don't?"

"No," he said after a beat. "Doesn't matter. There are too many more Starkweather Halls out there to waste time poking at this one's corpse. Sorry I had to kick you around. I don't enjoy doing that to a friend."

"It's the job." Doc had been flipping the ball back and forth between his glove and his bare hand. Now he took off the glove and stuck the hand out.

Battle gripped it. When they broke contact he glanced down at his palm and rubbed it against its mate. "Hey, you know your hand is bloody?"

Doc said, "Yeah, I know." He had rubbed it against his bleeding left.

After Battle left, Doc went back to the house for a shower and a change of clothes and a late breakfast of cereal and coffee. Neal was putting in his half-day at work and Sean was in the living room watching the Ninja Turtles. Billie, wearing the baggy shorts and old blouse she tied in front to work in her flower garden, refilled Doc's cup. "That Joyce called again this morning. I didn't know what to tell her."

"I'll call her."

"Are you two dating?" His sister-in-law's tones were incapable of innuendo.

"We must be. I told her my whole story the first time we went out."

"I hope she's not just using you."

"Everybody uses everybody," he said.

Sean came in with his glove. His sweatshirt and jeans had grown soft from wearing and washing. The pants were starting to bag in the seat. "Doc, let's go."

His uncle showed him his raw palm. "Can you pitch a couple of innings? Just until it stops bleeding."

"Kevin!" Billie was pale.

"Wow!"

"Just building callus," Doc said. "I got used to too many rest days in Jackson. It's not as bad as it looks."

"Looks like a big old piece of hamburger," Sean said.

"If that's what throwing a ball around does to you, I'm not sure I want Sean to pitch."

"Aw, Mom!"

"Don't worry. I'll spell him the minute the ball starts to turn pink."

"It's not funny, Kevin." She was holding the coffee pot like some kind of talisman of domesticity.

Doc got up and pushed in his chair. "You had him all to yourself eight years. All I'm asking is to borrow him Saturdays. I'll bring him back in one piece."

"All I know is no video game ever made him bleed."

You have to be alive first. Aloud he said, "We'll be back by suppertime."

Charlie Battle Junior was there when they got to the field. He'd brought his own ball and was playing catch with himself, looping the ball up over the neck of the corner streetlamp and trapping it in his glove when it came down. Doc had replaced home plate and taken the practice plank back with him to the house.

"Sorry your dad's working," he told the youth, who snapped the ball his way. Doc caught it over his head.

"I'm used to it. What's happenin', Sean?"

Sean slapped Junior's open palm. "I'm pitching today."

"No shit? Must be the chromosomes."

Jeff Dolan pulled up to the curb at the wheel of a silver Mercedes and got out, tugging on his Tigers cap. The big Irishman looked bigger than ever in a faded maize-and-blue University of Michigan T-shirt and sweatpants that hung dangerously low on his hips, the elastic waistband shot. Doc asked him why rich accountants always dressed so badly come the weekend.

"How we get to be rich, Koufax," he said, booming a little like his shanty ancestors. "We let you poor folk blow all your dough on snazzy jogging clothes. What the hell!"

The last comment was hurled over his shoulder. Needles Lewis, leaning out the open window of his old Dodge club cab, grimaced at the blow he'd delivered to the rear bumper of the Mercedes. "Hey, man, I'm sorry," he shouted over the percussion from the pickup's radio. "I been meaning to fix them brakes."

Creed leaped out of the truck box and bent to examine the car's bumper, holding his dreadlocks back from his face with both hands. Dolan was there already. He rubbed a scrape in the vinyl with his thumb.

"Fix that right up with a Magic Marker," said Yarnell, who had been riding up front with Needles. He was carrying the equipment.

Dolan straightened, shaking his head gravely. "Six hundred-dollar job if it's a penny. It means yanking the bumper and recovering it."

Needles, who had climbed out and slammed the door, reached back through the open window, took out a satin jacket, and groped in one of the slash pockets. He counted the bills he found there and stuck them at Dolan. "Fifty short. I'll owe you the rest."

"Forget it. The lease is up in another month. Let's play ball." As he walked past Doc, the Irishman muttered: "Drug Enforcement marks all its bills."

"Who's watching the wardrobe?" Doc gave Needles the five-finger handshake.

Needles looked puzzled, then uncorked his barn-door grin. "Old Sylvanus. He never leaves the store."

Doc said he guessed he'd heard about Starkweather Hall. Needles shrugged and started walking toward the diamond.

"Were you friends?" Doc asked.

"Friendly. Old Starkweather was too serious for friends. I would of thought he was too old for that Billy the Kid shit."

"He was twenty-three."

"I guess being old ain't being smart."

Walking with the kid in the wild checkerboard haircut, Doc felt his spirits lifting like the dew from the grass. He hadn't realized how much he enjoyed the young drug dealer's company.

Sean pitched better than Doc had feared he might, although it was clear he'd never make a living from it. When Needles and Yarnell and Charlie Junior all blasted home runs back to back, his uncle, who had been catching for him, knew the boy's arm was tiring. Doc handed the mitt to Needles and took the mound. Sean drooped, then lit up all over when Doc told him to spell Creed at first base. Doc's hand burned when he grasped the ball, but he imagined he could feel it repairing itself, rebuilding the damaged tissue thicker and more resilient. That evening he would soak it in salts to advance the process. In the old days he could shove a needle a third of its length into his palm before it drew blood. He told people that if his arm went he could always support himself making sails.

Baseball was like that, too; healing soul-deep abrasions through activity and repetition, stretching a fresh better skin over the old, deadening the pain and making him stronger for the next trial. It was a salt-bath for the heart.

Neal arrived while his brother was warming up, still wearing the pocket T-shirt and old patched Levi's he had worn to work, and took his official stance behind the plate. His big face was burned a deep cherry color from working outdoors on the heavy equipment. With his huge arms and slight stoop from too much lifting—there was a breed of mechanic that scorned the chain-fall for raising any engine smaller than 200 horsepower—he was starting to look like their father had at his age, thought Doc as he prepared to face his first batter.

It was an odd version of the game the seven played. Everyone except Doc, who knew his own shortcomings at the plate, took his turn playing on both sides, and all opposed Doc at least once. He could see that some enthusiastic recruiting would have to be done in order to form proper teams if he wasn't going to burn himself out his first season on the outside. By which time, he supposed, the City of Dearborn would probably decide it wanted the two adjacent lots and send them all to the showers. He wondered if Charlie Battle had forgotten his promise to look into that.

Despite the lack of rest and the condition of his hand, Doc had a personal one-hitter going into his third inning, with two walks, four strikeouts, and a high fly from Sean—he got good wood on it, pleasing Doc, who had given him a little edge but not much—that dropped into Creed's glove in left field, when Jeff Dolan stepped into the box, snorting like a breed bull and pounding the plate with his bat. It was he who had gotten the hit off Doc with a vicious two-bag drive between first and second in the second inning. Doc figured he was taking it out on that dent in his bumper.

After two balls and a foul that nearly tore the cover off the ball, Doc called time out. Needles trotted out to the mound.

"He likes 'em down and outside," Needles said, wiping his sleeve across his forehead. "I say brush him back."

Doc studied the stitching on the ball. "That's not what I wanted to talk about."

"My fly open?"

"Why'd you bust in on that Mahomet dinner that day?"

"What, you couldn't wait till the game was over to ask that?" When he saw Doc was waiting he said, "Shit, man, I don't know. A bunch of us was shootin' hoops downtown and somebody says why don't we bust the banquet, teach 'em to invite the M-and-M's next time. Hell, we didn't have nothing better to do."

"Whose idea was it?"

"I don't remember. Wait. Shit, it was that Antonio guy."

"Antonio who?"

"Lewis. No relation." Grinning, he added, "Leastwise, not that my daddy ever told me. We deal off him sometimes."

"Is he a Marshal?"

"No, he's indy."

"He wasn't on that list of names I bailed out for Ance."

"He didn't go. Ain't that a laugh? We got busted and the guy whose idea it was stood behind. Well, some dudes does and some dudes talks. Think he set us up?"

"I don't know. I had to ask. It was fucking up my concentration."

"Let's go, girls," called Neal from in back of the batter's box. "We lose the light in six hours."

"Throw strikes." Needles patted Doc on the butt and started back.

Doc bent to scoop up the resin bag and froze. A dusty gold Chevy Nova, fifteen years old with a cracked vinyl top and angry rust creeping up its side like a rash, had turned the corner behind home plate and was coming along the left foul line, all four of its windows down. These were the details he remembered later, but what caught his attention was the way it moved, not as if it were rolling on tires in contact with the earth but floating, the way a vehicle topping a distant hill on a blazing hot day seemed to float on a visible wave of heat. He could never be sure later but that he was already moving when the black rectangle came over the sill of the window in back like a charred stump of tongue lolling out of a gaping mouth. The clattering sounded a long way off when his arms closed around Needles from behind and the two of them went down in a tangle of limbs.

He landed on his elbow beneath their combined weight in a white blaze of pure pain. Beyond it, sounding farther away even than the shots, he heard shouting and tires shrieking and the wail of an engine turning up and then tailing off into the red distance throbbing at the outer edge of the first shock.

"Needles?" He tried to push himself up with his throwing

arm, collapsed under a breaker of fresh pain, and struggled on to his knees, gripping his left arm with his right hand and straddling Needles, who lay on his side. "Needles?"

The checkerboard head turned his way. The face scrunched up against the sun. Doc shifted a little, creating shade. "That you, Doc? I can't make you out too good."

"It's me. You okay?" The ribbed green tank top Needles had on was stained dark with sweat. In three places, maybe more, it was darker yet.

"You see it?"

Doc nodded, then said, "Yeah, I saw it."

Needles grinned, or it might have been a wince. His eyes had the luminous look of an old man's. They reminded Doc of old Charlie Steiner's eyes in his dream. "I didn't see nothing."

"Doc."

He glanced up in irritation at the sound of the new voice. Jeff Dolan stood over them, still holding the bat. But Dolan wasn't looking at either of them. Doc followed his gaze to what he thought was someone's discarded shirt lying near first base, and felt a flash of resentment that it should have been left in the field of play. It was a moment before he realized it wasn't an empty shirt, and another, accompanied by the sight of his brother running in that direction, before he remembered who was playing first base.

Chapter 29

◈◈◈◈◈◈◈◈

The graveside ceremony was no better than the one in the chapel. The minister, a mild thirty with a creaseless face and one of those heads of tightly curled hair that looked inflated with a bicycle pump, didn't know Sean or the family and read the oratory and prayer directly from the book. The mourners sat in folding wooden chairs in front of the gray casket on its hydraulic rollers under a sky swept clear of clouds. Funerals on nice days had always depressed Doc, even when he didn't know the deceased and happened to pass by the cemetery with its burial tent rippling in a warm breeze. The casket was shorter than he'd expected. It had never occurred to him how much smaller the dead seemed than they had in life.

Creed and Yarnell weren't present. The Second Baptist Church, which had overseen most of the predominately black funerals in town for 150 years and all of the Marshals', had scheduled the Epithelial Lewis services for the same time as Sean's. The guests here included Jeff Dolan, enormous in a black suit with an almost nonexistent gray pinstripe, Charlie Battle in blue serge, Charlie Junior, a number of Neal's friends from the dealership looking like dressed-up mechanics, the inevitable faces Doc couldn't place, and the family, among them Doc and Neal's father in his wheelchair wearing a white shirt buttoned to the throat, turquoise bola tie, and new slacks, and two aunts or cousins whom Doc only saw at funerals. The party had left behind three local television news crews at the chapel. Innocent children killed in drive-by shootings were a staple on the Six and Eleven O'Clock reports.

Someone, perhaps the minister, had brought along the yellow floral display mounted on an easel with a card signed by Alcina Lilley and Beatrice Blackwood. Doc hadn't bothered to look around for them. They had seen Starkweather Hall buried under that name the day before and Doc had sent flowers.

In the chapel before the ceremony, he had sought out Battle, accepted his handshake distractedly, and asked him the names of the two undercover narcotics officers who had shot and killed Hall. The sergeant had looked at him as if he thought his mind had collapsed under the strain of grief.

"That's confidential. These guys go by their own names on the street. We don't even give them to the media off the record."

"It's important. You owe me one," Doc added.

"What do you want with them?"

"First give them to me."

"I can't. It's their lives. Hall wasn't the only dealer they put out of business. The only reason *I* know their names is this case was mine." And he had moved off to pay his respects to Neal and Billie.

Doc hadn't approached the casket before or after the service. He knew the boy was wearing the gray suit his mother had bought him to wear to church for Easter, and that he would be lying there with his hair combed by someone else as if waiting to pose for a school picture.

When the procession was about to start, Doc escorted Joyce Stefanik to her car. She wore what was probably her only one-piece dress, a blue cotton shift with a single decorative pearl button at the throat. "Get in with me and I'll drive to the cemetery," she said in the parking lot. "I can miss one deadline."

He opened the door of the Trans Am. "One graveside's like all the others. I don't think this sky pilot's going to become inspired on his way to the cemetery."

"Are you going to be all right?" She touched the cast on his left arm, which rested in a black sling around his neck. The plaster went almost to his shoulder to prevent him from trying to use the shattered elbow.

"Billie probably won't try to break the other one in the car," he said.

In fact she had attacked him physically at Detroit Receiving Hospital when he was recovering from surgery to pin together the fragments of his arm. One second she was silent, exhausted emotionally, wearing the face of a woman a generation older than her thirty-four years; the next she was lunging across the side rail of the bed, screaming and clawing for his face. Neal had gotten his arms around her and dragged her back before she could make contact with her nails. Later she'd apologized, but the words were vacant. She had called him a child-killer in a voice loud enough to carry two floors.

Joyce glanced around, then reached up and brought Doc's head down and kissed him quickly. She left her hand on the back of his neck. "Call me later?"

"I might have a story for you when I do."

"Story?"

"Only hitch is if everything works out okay you won't be able to use it."

"Doc, what are you doing?"

"I'll call you." He kissed her again and left to get into the limousine with Neal and Billie.

The 1975 Nova used in the shooting had been reported stolen from the driveway of a house on Baines. It was found abandoned on Riopelle in the warehouse district. The police had questioned and released two members of the Pony Down gang, aged eighteen and seventeen, who had exchanged loud words and occasional gunfire with the M-and-M's in the past. Both had alibis for the time of the shooting and their prints matched none of those found in the car. The incident was being investigated as a battle over turf.

Maynard Ance left a cab waiting by the cemetery and joined the graveside service in progress. He wore one of his heavy-duty suits and a black knitted tie that looked new. Doc, seated in the front row between Neal and the old man in the wheelchair, turned to acknowledge him. The bail bondsman stood sweating in the sun with his hands folded in front of him. There was no room for him under the tent.

Afterward, Doc found even the minister's handshake listless and uninspired. He thanked him anyway and went back to greet Ance while the other mourners filed past to commiserate with the rest of the family. Billie sat at the end of the front row in a black dress and felt hat with a brief veil. The shadows formed by the patterned lace scored fresh lines in her features.

"Sorry as hell I'm late." Ance grasped Doc's hand. "My third wife picks today to sic the cops on me for back payments. Cost me a hundred apiece to make sure they missed me."

"Thanks for coming."

"Kids, shit, it ain't hard enough to survive all that running into traffic and climbing on things and crap. Your brother need anything? Cash?"

"There was a college fund."

"Christ. I never saw them bury an eight-year-old."

Someone was crying in the direction of the grave. Doc didn't think it was Billie. She hadn't cried or said ten words in his hearing since the hospital. "I've been thinking about that partnership offer," he said.

"Forget it. This ain't the time."

"I'm turning it down."

"You're not thinking right. There's no hurry. I don't figure to kick off in the next month or so."

"I made the decision before—well, before," Doc said. "I didn't get the chance to tell you. I'm no bail man. My skin isn't thick enough. I'd break us both in six months."

"Hey, I wasn't born like this. You got to give it time."

"That's my biggest fault, giving things time. A lot of things would be different now if I didn't just sit back and watch."

"You didn't just sit back on the Hall deal. It wasn't your fault it went sour."

"By then it was too late. For a lot of people."

"Well, we'll talk," Ance said. "Take a week off. I won't need you in the office for a while."

"That's the other thing I wanted to talk to you about before. I'm quitting."

"Fuck that. Now I know you're fucked up. Maybe I can get along without a partner, but I sure as hell need a driver. Fucking cabs are killing me. I'll raise you a bill a week."

Doc reached in his pocket and handed him a roll of fifties bound with a rubber band.

Ance took it. "What's this?"

"That's what's left of the advance you gave me. Most of it's there. I can't keep it if I'm not going to be working for you."

"Fuck it, I said. Take it back."

Doc smiled and gripped the bail bondsman's shoulder. "So long, boss. Thanks for a lot of things."

"Doc."

He'd turned to join the others. He looked back.

"How's the arm?"

"Hurts like hell. They gave me some pills."

"You going to be able to pitch again?"

"I don't know."

"Well, what the hell." Ance was stone-faced. "Grown man looks like a horse's ass in a cap anyway."

Doc got back in time to say good-bye to the cousins, or maybe they were aunts. Battle and his son were at the end of the line behind Jeff Dolan.

Neal said, "Coming to the house later?"

Doc glanced at his sister-in-law, holding hands with one of the aunts/cousins. "Should I?"

"Sure. Uh, you better not try to talk to her."

"I'm sorry, Neal." It sounded more inadequate than ever.

"She knows it wasn't your fault. Hell, I was there too. You want to, you know, blame someone. Shit." He ducked his head.

Doc turned quickly to shake Dolan's hand. In a low voice: "Did you get anything?"

"Here?" The big Irishman looked around.

"If you've got it with you."

"The only reason I'm doing this is I never could refuse a request from a man in a hospital bed." Dolan reached inside his coat and handed him a sheaf of papers. Doc put it in his own breast pocket without looking at it. The suit was the one the state had given him. It was the only one of the two he owned that he didn't mind slitting up one sleeve to make room for his cast. "What is it?"

"Paper trail. That's the only printout. I erased the disc."

"Thanks, Jeff. Ance said you were the best accountant around."

"Just don't tell anyone where you got it." He moved on to

speak to Neal, who had recovered enough to thank him for coming.

Charlie Battle let go of Doc's hand quickly and tried to walk past. Doc touched his chest, stopping him.

"I can't tell you, Doc," Battle said.

"You don't have to say anything. Just nod or shake your head. Was one of them Antonio Lewis?"

The sergeant made no response, verbal or otherwise. He didn't have to. Doc had made a career out of reading batters' faces.

Chapter 30

◆◆◆◆◆◆◆◆

The center of the complex and wonderful political machine that kept Mayor Coleman A. Young in office was not so much mechanical as confectionery, and reminded Doc of the "red hot" candies he had enjoyed as a boy with their alternating layers of wintergreen and pungent cinnamon that chilled and burned his tongue by turns.

The outer layer, and the most obviously cosmetic one, was black. It consisted of the United Negro College Fund types with whom Young liked to surround himself in public, personable young men in conservative suits like the mayor's and the trademark black-rimmed glasses whose polished lenses flashed semaphores at press conferences and testimonial dinners. The faces changed periodically as their owners discovered that holding the chief's coat and laughing at his off-color jokes didn't automatically lead to a private office in the City-County Building, but the breed remained pure. The next layer was white and included Young's personal business advisers and representatives who circulated throughout the monied suburbs surrounding the city and returned with their briefcases bulging with working capital. The most powerful of these, Kenneth Weiner, had fallen from grace as well as from his post as a civilian deputy chief of police—a porkbarrel job given to him as a reward for his successes as CEO of Detroit Technologies, the mayor's private investment company and hitherto the best-kept secret in the fishbowl of corporate America. Black for the next layer, an entire squad of the Detroit Police Department who answered to Young alone and whose duties included the mayor's safety, investigation into the private lives of his political opponents, and transportation for his sister.

The last layer before the man himself was inarguably white. Press Secretary Bob Berg—blond, late thirties, goatee and moustache as fair as his skin, and that fair enough to wash right out in the glare of the TV strobe lights under which he lived— briefed Young before press conferences, read statements to the media on those not infrequent occasions when the mayor chose not to present himself for grilling and the inevitable display of temper, and stood sentry on the rainbow bridge to Asgard when the last of the less intransigent barriers had been breached. When Young elected not to be available, this mild, humorless man attired as often as not in his casual and distinctly non-urban tweed sportcoat with patch lapels was as close as anyone, senator or shop steward, ever came.

At that it was a long trip, and after four days of listening to recorded music over the telephone and reading magazines in beige waiting rooms equipped with matching receptionists downtown, Doc considered that the mayor's press secretary was as hard to get an interview with as most mayors. On the morning of the fifth day, while studying the brushstrokes in an abstract painting in the reception room outside the office of an assistant drain commissioner or something to whom Doc had been directed by an even more obscure official whose name and title he'd forgotten, he heard his name called and turned to face Bob Berg.

The blonde man was taller than he appeared on television and a little less pale. He offered neither handshake nor greeting. "What's your business with the mayor, Mr. Miller?"

"It's personal."

"I have his confidence."

With his good hand Doc slid a thick envelope from his inside breast pocket and held it out. It was creased and a little limp from carrying.

It's an American trait to accept automatically anything that is proffered. Berg didn't possess the trait. "What is it, please?"

"Don't worry, it isn't a letter bomb." Doc smiled.

"Now I know what it isn't."

"It's a newspaper article."

"What is the subject?"

"He'll know that when he reads it."

"If it's about him perhaps he already has. In which paper did it appear?"

"It hasn't. Yet. I thought he might like to take a look at it before it does."

Berg's face was as blank as the envelope. Doc was prepared to admit that the man had that nothing-back stare down better than Doc himself. After an interval during which the air-conditioning system whirred without distraction, Berg took the envelope. "Is there a number where you can be reached?"

The telephone hadn't been installed yet in the new apartment and he was unwilling to direct calls to Neal's home. He gave Joyce Stefanik's number. "Leave a message."

"If you haven't heard from me by the end of next week you've been denied an appointment." The press secretary turned and left through the glass door to the corridor.

Doc stayed home that Saturday to direct the deliverymen who brought his furniture. He hadn't been to the ballfield since the shooting. The last time he'd gone past, the entire lot was encircled by a yellow POLICE—DO NOT PASS tape stapled to surveyors' stakes. No arrests had been made in the case after the two young Pony Down members were released.

The only reason he'd gone there at all had been to move the last of his possessions out of Neal and Billie's house. In his old room, surrounded by Sean's Masters of the Universe posters and the toy soldiers on the wallpaper, he felt the boy's absence as tangibly as the presence of another person in the room. When he pulled open a drawer to take out his shirts, a stack of video games on top of the chest fell over with a clatter. Restacking them, among the alien invaders, dinosaurs, and swordsmen and sorcerers, he found a cassette still in plastic shrink-wrap. The box bore a picture of Babe Ruth swinging at the plate and the title *Home Run! The Sultan of Swat in the 1927 World Series.* He didn't know if Sean had bought the game for him as a gift or if he meant to play it himself. He put it in the box with his things.

Downstairs, holding the box awkwardly under his good arm, he waited while Billie opened the door for him. Before she closed it behind him she asked him to take care of himself. They were the first words she'd spoken to him since the funeral.

On Monday he took a bus to an employment agency and filled out an application. Under SITUATION WANTED he wrote "Athletic coach." The clerk he handed it to, a small black woman wearing a red wig that reminded Doc of Beatrice Blackwood's black pageboy, looked it over and asked him if he had a teaching certificate.

"No."

"We'll see what we can do." She laid the sheet in a drawer and closed it on his aspirations.

He'd seen Kubitski to report that he'd left Maynard Ance's employ. The parole officer sucked on his pipe, adjusted his fan, and said he expected to hear that Doc had landed a steady job by next month's appointment. He made no mention of their last meeting. It was obvious Charlie Battle had been in touch with him. Doc was apathetic. If everything worked out he would never need to see Kubitski again or smell his rotten-apple tobacco.

When he got back from the employment agency he found Joyce's Trans Am parked in front of the duplex. She came out from the back wearing a white tennis outfit that showed off her tanned arms and legs. After they kissed he said, "Message?"

"I slid it under your door. Should we celebrate?"

"When I get back. If there's anything to celebrate."

The office to which the message directed him was in the 300 Tower of the Renaissance Center, Mayor Young's first brainchild and a paean to the parsimony of late-twentieth-century architecture, standing like a display of disposable plastic drinking cups against the ornate dignity of the Albert Kahn designs from Prohibition that still dominated downtown in spite of the current administration's best efforts to eradicate the city's history. Doc felt a stomach chill when he entered the pastel lobby, as if the conditioned air that evaporated the sweat on the back of his neck had gone on to form icicles in his intestines; the central structure of the combination mall and office complex was the Westin Hotel, where Doc had hosted the party that had led to his imprisonment. Knowing what he did of the mayor's political methodology, he doubted that the choice of meeting places was a coincidence.

It was a thirty-fourth-floor office and somewhat modest for that address, with a small deserted reception room done in gray tweed and decorated with framed Certificates of Community

Service awarded to one Andrew S. Beloit. Doc had just started knocking on the door bearing Beloit's name when a familiar voice on the other side called out, "Come on in, Doc."

The inner office had more tweed, white leather panels, and recessed lighting. The entire back wall was tinted glass and looked straight uptown past the assembled skyscrapers and the Fisher and General Motors buildings to where the city lay down and stretched its limbs, merging with the suburbs so smoothly that it was impossible to tell where the leviathan left off and the pilot fish began. Doc could see the crumbling warehouses near the river between which the square, bug-eyed combat vehicles of the Purple Gang and the Little Jewish Navy and the Oakland Sugar House Mob and all the other rumrunners broadsided one another with Thompsons for the Canadian routes during the dry years, and farther up he could see the greensward of over-grown lots where buildings had stood on Kercheval and Twelfth Street before they were burned down in the riots. He saw long straight stretches of pavement where Mustangs and Cobras and Thunderbirds laid rubber when gasoline and motorists' lives were cheap, crowded now with cars half their size and shaped like suppositories, and every third one Japanese. It was like standing on a high girder in the open air. He grasped the edge of the door, certain that the floor was tilting out from under his feet. He knew then beyond doubt why the mayor had chosen this location. It was impossible to come upon that vista unprepared and maintain one's emotional footing.

"Sit down, Doc."

Coleman A. Young was seated with his back to the window behind a desk with nothing on its glass top but a telephone and the mayor's elbows. He was wearing a tan silk double-breasted suit and a brown-and-blue-striped tie on a blue shirt. He seemed to be contemplating a thorny equation on a pocket calculator in his hands, his glasses perched on the end of his nose less than an inch from the device.

Trying to look as if he were walking across a level surface, Doc found his way to a padded chair facing the desk. On the wall above his head hung a diploma in a frame informing him that Andrew Saville Beloit had graduated from the Detroit Institute of Technology with a degree in electrical engineering in 1974. Beloit kept what Doc assumed were his blonde wife and tow-headed daughter in a plastic cube on a leaf to Young's left.

When nothing had been said after a minute, Doc thought the mayor was listening to CNN on the nineteen-inch color TV set on the shelf next to the photographs.

"Damn!" Young threw the thing he'd been fiddling with onto the desk. It wasn't a calculator at all, but a baseball diamond under transparent plastic with steel BB's skating across its surface. The object of the game seemed to be to place all the BB's in holes corresponding to player positions. "If my eyes wasn't any better than this when I was in the Air Corps I could speak Japanese today."

"I thought maybe you were upset about that earthquake in Chile."

Young glanced toward the set. "That? That's company."

More likely, Doc thought, it was a mask to confuse anyone who might be listening in. At any given time there were several investigations going on into the mayor's public and private affairs.

"I didn't know you were that interested in baseball. I mean beyond wanting to build a new stadium for the Tigers."

But the conversation wasn't going to head that way. The man behind the desk opened a drawer and tossed a fair thickness of typewritten pages on Doc's side. It was creased down the middle, and Doc knew without reading that it was the draft of the newspaper article he had given Bob Berg.

"This is all hearsay and innuendo." It came out "inooendo"; it was a Colemanism to pronounce any word longer than two syllables as if he had just learned it that morning. "Where's your evidence?"

Doc took the sheaf of computer-printed information Jeff Dolan had given him out of his pocket and placed it on top of the portable baseball game. Young poked up his glasses, thumbed through the pages, and thrust them back at him. "Summarize it."

"It's a breakdown of all the investment activity involving Detroit Technologies over the past two years," Doc said. "That's your firm. Putting aside extraneous transactions, the company maintains limited partnerships in several local businesses. One of those businesses holds controlling interest in various area investment properties. One of those properties is a men's clothing store on Gratiot. The store is a front for a drug operation run by the Marshals of Mahomet. Your Honor, you own a crack house."

Young had lifted the telephone receiver and was punching buttons. Doc listened to the conversation for a moment, then let his attention drift to the WJR traffic helicopter wobbling over the cityscape outside the window.

The receiver banged down. "Now I don't own a clothing store. You can have your friend rewrite the article to say that as soon as the mayor found out what his business advisers had acquired without his knowledge or consent, he got rid of it. Miss Stefanik has a nice style, by the way."

Doc was surprised and a little worried until he remembered that he'd given Joyce's telephone number to Bob Berg. Tracing it would have been no trick for Young, unlisted or not. Doc said, "I'm just getting started. I guess you and Alcina Lilley are pretty good friends."

"Now, just what in the hell is *that* supposed to mean?" Young was working himself up to one of his famous tirades.

"Just what I said, you're friends. Close enough for her to have confided in you that Starkweather Hall was her son."

No reaction.

"After I saw Hall at her house, she tried to distract me by making me famous. Having you shake my hand in front of a camera was extra insurance. I don't know what excuse she made; I don't really care. My guess is you weren't aware she was harboring Hall. You break a lot of rules but aiding and abetting the escape of a suspect in a police killing isn't one of them."

"I'm not aware of it now."

Doc let it go. "Just in case a puff piece like the Mahomet dinner and the attention you gave me there didn't make the front page, the Marshals tried to crash the affair and got themselves arrested. That's hard news and the press would have to go some to keep from giving it plenty of play.

"For a while I thought you or Mrs. Lilley might have had something to do with that, but I'd rather believe someone set it up on his own initiative, thinking he was doing someone a favor. Needles Lewis, one of the M-and-M's arrested that day, told me the suggestion to disrupt the dinner came from a drug dealer named Antonio Lewis, no relation to Needles. I figure this Lewis, or someone he works for, knew about the situation and decided to help out."

He paused. The mayor had picked up the baseball game and resumed trying to place the BB's in their holes, but it was clear he wasn't concentrating. Here in private, Doc considered that the robust front Young put up under the spotlight covered a deteriorating constitution; his face looked bloated, his eyes puffy and dull behind the glasses. The tight skin of his forehead glistened wetly in the air-conditioned office and he was developing liver spots on the backs of his hands. Five elections, a paternity suit, and a parade of grand juries had opened cracks beneath the seemingly impenetrable surface.

"You know I was involved in a shooting in my brother's neighborhood recently," Doc went on. "At first I thought Needles Lewis or the other M-and-M's who played ball with me every Saturday on that corner were the target, but while I was in the hospital waiting to have my arm set I did a lot of thinking. For one thing the shooting came too close to another I was indirectly involved in, the one that killed Starkweather Hall. I asked some questions of my own, and last week I found out one of the undercover detectives who happened to see Hall trying to steal that car in Birmingham and shot him was Antonio Lewis."

Young put down the game. "I don't know any Antonio Lewis."

"I believe you. Whoever does is someone who knows about the relationship between Alcina Lilley and Starkweather Hall and knew about the plan to keep me so busy with interviews and things I wouldn't be able to think straight, and who put the two together. He has some connection with the police, because he put Lewis up to prodding the Marshals into trying to break up the dinner and he knew or at least suspected when a deal was in the works to turn Hall in. That's why he sent Lewis and another undercover to take Hall out of his mother's house, kill him, and rig it to look like a legitimate shoot-out between a wanted fugitive and the police."

"Why kill him?"

"From Antonio Lewis' standpoint that was an easy decision. I think he was as dirty as Ernest Melvin, the undercover Hall killed. Hall never even knew Melvin was a cop. Hall had to know and trust at least one of the men who came to get him at his mother's or there'd have been a struggle that would have alerted Mrs. Lilley's neighbors. Maybe they told him they were smuggling him out of town. So Lewis was dealing, and he couldn't afford to let Hall stand trial in case that came out. His boss had other reasons. He was shielding you, or thought he was. Well, it's all in the article."

"Everything but who."

Doc shifted in his seat. His arm was hurting again. "That's up to you. Chances are I wouldn't recognize his name if I heard it. Kenneth Weiner has the police ties and if he's guilty of half the things he's charged with maybe I wouldn't put murder past him, but he's in jail and his defense is taking all his time. I saw enough of guys like him in Jackson to know that where there's one Weiner there's likely to be at least one more. It might help you identify him if I told you he's probably the man responsible for acquiring the clothing store." Or woman, he added silently; but what he had observed during the past week of the mayor's system of checks and balances told him that it was aggressively masculine.

Young was quiet for a moment, and even picked up the baseball game and appeared to be absorbed in it. And in that moment Doc was certain the mayor knew whom they had been discussing.

"You got to be six kinds of a son of a bitch to run this town," Young said, "and I've never been accused of being unequal to the task. *One* kind of a son of a bitch I'm not and never will be is the kind of a son of a bitch that lets himself be blackmailed."

Doc said, "I'm no blackmailer. The only thing I've got in the way of evidence is that paper trail linking Detroit Technologies to the M-and-M's, and you just destroyed that with one telephone call. The rest is speculation. If I published that article, assuming any reputable newspaper or magazine would accept it, you'd sue, and you'd collect. That's the only copy. This, too." He laid the computer printout on top of the typewritten pages and slid them across the desk. "Do what you like with them."

Young took them and held them under the edge of the desk.

There was a whirring noise and then he placed his empty hands on the glass top. Doc wondered idly what an electrical engineer needed with a paper shredder.

Months later, Doc came across a news item almost lost in the wake of Kenneth Weiner's conviction and Police Chief William Hart's indictment on multiple counts of embezzlement from the secret police fund, relating to the resignation of one Woodrow Courtland from the civilian police commission for personal reasons left unstated. Courtland in private life was an investment counselor. Shortly thereafter, an FBI sting operation resulting in the arrest of eleven current and former Detroit police officers for providing protection to known drug offenders netted Antonio Lewis of the Narcotics Squad and his lieutenant, Thomas Horatio Talbot. With that, Doc knew the names of everyone involved.

"So in return for being a concerned voter who comes in to make the mayor aware of a troubling situation," Young said, "you get—what?"

"Not much. After Hall was killed Antonio Lewis or his boss tried to tie down the last loose end by shooting me and making it look like just another drive-by. All I got out of it was a broken arm. Needles Lewis was killed. Also an eight-year-old boy whose only crime was having a baseball player for an uncle. Nothing can make up for that."

"That being said, what do you want?"

"Two things. An unconditional release from my prison sentence. No more visits to my parole officer."

"Impossible. Only the governor can grant a pardon."

Doc refrained from pointing out that Coleman A. Young elected the governors in that state. Diplomatically he said, "Your recommendation would carry a lot of weight."

"What's the second thing?"

"The deed from the City of Dearborn to those adjacent lots where the shooting occurred. I'll get you the plat numbers later."

"I know where they are. You're costing me a lot of markers I might need some other time. What you planning to do with the property, put up a God damn monument like they did for that plane that went down on I-94?"

"Just a small one. A sign. THE SEAN MILLER MEMORIAL YOUNG PEOPLE'S BALLPARK. If there's any trouble with zoning I'd like your help on that too."

"Why not name it after Epithelial Lewis? He was killed too."

"It's too late for the Needleses in this town. The Seans still have a chance."

The thin white moustache turned up. "Going to clean up the whole city with one of those whiskbrooms the umpires use to sweep home plate?"

"Just my corner of it."

"Well, at least you got 'Young' in the name." The mayor rested his chins on his chest for a full minute. Then his shoulders started to shake with silent laughter. He leaned forward and stretched his hand across the desk. "Deal. This is my contract."

"This is mine." Doc laid one more paper in the available hand.

He had consulted Maynard Ance, the former lawyer, on the wording, which was simple and mentioned only the last two points they had discussed, including the part about zoning; "in appreciation for services rendered the Detroit community and Mayor Coleman A. Young."

Young read it twice, then produced a gold fountain pen, signed the bottom of the sheet with a flourish, and slid it across to Doc. Again he stuck out his hand. "Now?"

Doc grasped it. It was as strong as before, but it should have been warmer. It should have been hot.

Detroit Free Press, Tuesday, April 10, 1990:

WOMAN, 87, SLAIN IN BREAK-IN

The body of 87-year-old Loyola MacGryff was discovered by a family member yesterday morning lying on the living room floor of her house on Trumbull. Police said she had been beaten to death.

The house had been broken into and the suspected motive was robbery.

Mrs. MacGryff, a lifelong Detroit Tigers fan, was to throw out the ceremonial first ball to open the baseball season at Tiger Stadium yesterday. Tigers owner Tom Monaghan performed the ceremony when she failed to appear.

A feature story about Mrs. MacGryff's nearly nine decades of dedication to the Tigers appeared in last Sunday's *Detroit* magazine.

Police said they have no suspects in the slaying.